ADVANCE PRAISE FOR

Bestiary

"Fierce and funny, full of magic and grit, *Bestiary* is the most searching exploration of love and belonging I've read in a long time. Family, immigrant, queer, magic realist—none of these tags can quite capture the energy of this startling novel, which is all of those things, yet somehow more. K-Ming Chang has created something truly remarkable."

—TASH AW, author of *We, the Survivors*

"Told by many voices, *Bestiary* is a queer, transnational fairy tale whose irresistible heroine is a Taiwanese American baby dyke. Written in a prose style as inventive and astonishing as the story it tells, to read it is to enter a world where the female body possesses enormous power, where the borders between generations are porous and shifting. A worthy heir to Maxine Hong Kingston, Lois-Ann Yamanaka, and Jamaica Kincaid, K-Ming Chang is a woman warrior for the 21st century—part oracle, part witness, all heart."

—JENNIFER TSENG, author of *Mayumi and the Sea of Happiness*

"K-Ming Chang is ferociously talented, one of my favorite new writers. She understands the language of desire and secrecy. Here is a book so wise; so gripping; so mythical and dangerous; so infused with surreal beauty, it burns to be read, and read again."

—JUSTIN TORRES, author of *We the Animals*

"In *Bestiary*, K-Ming Chang upturns earth and language in equal measure. Every page is percussive, hypnotizing, and maddeningly smart. I am stunned by the imaginative reach of this debut, the remarkable prose. Chang isn't just a new voice in the landscape; she is building a new landscape entirely."

—T KIRA MADDEN, author of *Long Live the Tribe of Fatherless Girls*

"I didn't read this novel so much as become immersed in it, a jungle filled with surprises, countless moments of desire and pain and light."

—CHARLES YU, author of *Interior Chinatown*

"Crafted at the scale of epic poetry . . . These are fables I wish I'd had growing up."

—ELAINE CASTILLO, author of *America Is Not the Heart*

"This searing, lush novel can't be justly summarized—you must read it yourself, for K-Ming Chang is a fearless, singular talent."

—SHAWNA YANG RYAN, author of *Green Island*

"[A] vivid, fabulist debut."

—*Publishers Weekly*

"Every line of this sensuous, magical-realist marvel . . . is utterly alive."

—*The Oprah Magazine*

"A visceral book that promises a major new literary voice."

—*Kirkus Reviews* (starred review)

Bestiary

Bestiary

A NOVEL

—

K-Ming Chang

HAMISH HAMILTON
an imprint of Penguin Canada,
a division of Penguin Random House Canada Limited

Canada · USA · UK · Ireland · Australia · New Zealand · India ·
South Africa · China

Published in Hamish Hamilton paperback by Penguin Canada, 2020
Simultaneously published in the United States by One World, an imprint
of Random House, a division of Penguin Random House LLC, New York
and in Great Britain by Harvill Secker, an imprint of Vintage Books,
a division of Penguin Random House Ltd., London

www.penguinrandomhouse.ca

*Publisher's note: This book is a work of fiction. Names, characters, places
and incidents either are the product of the author's imagination or are
used fictitiously, and any resemblance to actual persons living
or dead, events, or locales is entirely coincidental.*

LIBRARY AND ARCHIVES CANADA CATALOGUING IN PUBLICATION

Title: Bestiary / K-Ming Chang.
Names: Chang, Kristin, author.
Identifiers: Canadiana (print) 20200169068 | Canadiana (ebook) 20200169076 |
ISBN 9780735238824 (softcover) | ISBN 9780735238831 (HTML)
Classification: LCC PS3603.H3637 B47 2020 | DDC 813/.6—dc23

Book design: Andrea Lau
Cover design: Michael Morris
Frontispiece illustration: shuoshu/Getty Images
Cover images: Private Collection © Cristina Rodriguez/Bridgeman Images,
soleil420/Getty Images, GB_Art/Getty Images (girl); Private Collection De Agostini Picture
Library/Bridgeman Images, Julia August/Getty Images (goose); Anna Lukin/Getty
Images, tigerstrawberry/Getty Images (bones); Yuliya Derbisheva/
Getty Images, Khaneeros/Getty Images (envelopes)

Printed and bound in the United States of America

10 9 8 7 6 5 4 3 2 1

Penguin
Random House
HAMISH HAMILTON CANADA

For MaMa

"The name of the river is what it says."
—*Li-Young Lee*

"There is a lot of detailed doubt here."
—*Maxine Hong Kingston*

Bestiary

MOTHER

Journey to the West (I)

Or: A Story of Warning for My Only Daughter
Moral: Don't Bury Anything.

Ba doesn't know where he buried the gold. Ma chases him around and beats him with her soup ladle. You've never been to a funeral, but this is what it looks like: four of us in the backyard, digging where our shadows have died. A shovel for Ba, a soup ladle for Ma, a spoon for me and Jie to share. We dig with what we don't want—piss buckets, a stolen plunger, the hands we pray with. We even use the spatulas gifted to us by the church ladies, after their days-long debate about whether Orientals even used spatulas. It was decided that we didn't but that we should. Hence our collection of spatulas, different sizes and metals and colors. Ma mistook them for flyswatters. She used them to spank us, selecting a spatula based on the severity of our crime. Be glad I use only my two hands on you.

I see the way you wear your hands without worry, but someday they'll bury something. Someday this story will open like a switchblade. Your hands will plot their own holes, and when they do, I won't come and rescue you.

You've never been to this year, so let me live it for you: 1980 lasts as long as it rains. It rains the Arkansas way, riddling the ground like gunfire. Years after this story, you're born in an opposite city, a place where the only reliable rain is your piss. You ask why your grandfather once buried his gold and forgot about it, and I say his skull is full of snakes instead of brains. He's all sold out of memories. One time, he pees all over the yard and we follow his piss-streams through the soil. Pray they convene at the gold's gravesite. The gold in his bladder will guide us toward its buried kin. But his piss-river runs straight into the house and floods it with fermented sunlight.

—

When the church wives come to give us dishes of sugar cubes and a jar of piss-dark honey, my ma tells them that Orientals don't sweeten tea. Don't sweeten anything. We prefer salt and sour and bitter, the active ingredients in blood and semen and bile. Flavors from the body.

Ba says he'll find the gold soon. Ma beats him again, this time with a pair of high heels (also a gift from the church wives). Ba says the birds will tell him where he buried it all. Ma throws a flowerpot at his head (seeds via the church wives). Ba dances the shovel too deep and hits water. Except it isn't water, it's a sewage line, and the landlord tells us to pay for the damage. The rest of the month, we wade the river of everyone's shit, still convinced Ba can remember, still convinced memory is contagious. If we stand close enough to him, we'll catch what he lost.

The gold was what Ba brought from the mainland to the island. That's how soldiers bribed the sea that wanted to steal their bodies. He paid his passage with one gold bar the width of his pinky and swallowed the rest, the gold bleached silver by the acidity of his belly.

In wartime, land is measured by the bones it can bury. A house is worth only the bomb that banishes it. Gold can be spent in any country, any year, any afterlife. The sun shits it out every morning. Even Ma misreads the slogans on the back of American coins: IN GOLD WE TRUST. That's why she thinks we're compatible with this country. She still believes we can buy its trust.

After twenty years of gambling on the island, Ba lost all the gold and tried to win it back and back and back again. When they met, Ma already had three children and one dead husband who returned weekly in the form of milk-bright rain. The local men said she was ruined from the waist down but still eligible from the waist up. She wore a heavy skirt that tarped her like a nun. Ma donated her three daughters to her parents and birthed two new ones with Ba.

I'm the second of the new ones. We're the two she kept, brought here, and beat.

When Ma married him, he was twenty years older. Take the number of years you've lived outside of my body and plant them like seeds, growing twice as many: that's the thicket of years between your grandmother and grandfather. Except Ma doesn't measure her life in years but in languages: Tayal and Yilan Creole in the indigo fields where she was born blue-assed and fish-eyed, Japanese during the war, Mandarin in the Nationalist-eaten city. Each language was worn outside her body, clasped around her throat like a collar. Once, Ba asked her to teach him to write the Tayal alphabet she learned from the missionaries. But she said his hands were not meant to write: They were welded for war, good only for gripping guns and his own dick. Jie thought this was funny, but I didn't laugh. I have those hands. When you were born, I saw too much of your grandfather in you: rhyming hairlines and fish-hook fingers, the kind that snag on my hair, my shadow, the sky. You made a moon-sized fist at every man, even your own brother, who tried to bury you in a pot of soil and grow you back as a tree. You think burial is about finalizing what's died. But burial is beginning: To grow anything, you must first dig a grave for its seed. Be ready to name what's born.

Decades ago in Yilan, Ba shat out his last bar of gold, along with a sash of seawater and silt. He buried it here, in this yard we never owned and that you were born far from. Ma liked Arkansas because it sounded like *Ark,* as in Noah's. All of Ma's words are from the Bible. Most are single-syllable: *Job, Ark, Lot, Wife, Smite.*

The only way we'll find the gold is if we shoot Ba's skull open, extract the memory of where he buried it. Ma tried it once. She pointed the shotgun at Ba's head and stomped the floorboards while saying *Bang,* believing the memory would evacuate from his head. Instead, Ba wet himself and Jie had to mop the floor with a dress. Apparently Ba needs a war to motivate him. Ba won't unbury anything unless there's a boat to be bought and married. We have a week to hire a war to come to our house. Or else, Ma says, the gold will stay buried and we'll have fed all we own to the trees that grow moss like pubic hair.

Jie suggests we hang Ba by his feet, upside down, so that all his memories flee upstream and pool in his skull. We'd have to unscrew his head somehow. I tell her it doesn't work that way, but Jie's been taking anatomy lessons at the high school ten miles away, meaning she knows how to diagram a body, meaning she's drawn me a penis with veins and everything, shown me a hole or two it could go in. She pulls down her pants so I can see. I ask her to show me where all my holes lead to, and she says if I dig into the dark between my legs, I'll find a baby waiting to be plucked like a turnip. (Don't worry, I didn't scavenge for you. You were conceived the carnivore way.)

Ma shaves soft wood from our birch tree and skunk-sprays the strips with perfume to make incense, burning it in bunches. The smoke keeps mosquitos from marrying all our blood.

We pray to god and Guanyin, in that order. Pray for Ba's gold to fall as rain or grow a hundred limbs and shudder out of the soil like metallic shrubbery.

We consider other strategies: If we borrow a bulldozer, we can flip the whole yard like a penny. But we need our money for that, and our money is buried like a body.

—

By the creek, Jie teaches me to read out of the Bible. We sit under a grove of trees belled with apples. The branches applaud in the wind and drop what they hold, concussing us with fist-hard fruit. Last week, rain rutted a hole in our roof and everything flooded, so we're drying the Bible on a tree branch, its pages flapping like moths. I can pronounce only easy words, no proper names, no verbs. Jie says fluency is forgetting. Says I've got to un-name my mouth and crack my tongue like a whip. When I pronounce the word *tongue* with two syllables, Jie pushes me facedown into the mud.

When I get up from the riverbank, I swallow the mud of my tongue. Jie says she once saw two girl ghosts kissing in the creek. I mishear her and think she means they were cleaning the creek. *Why?* I say. Jie says, *Because a god made them want but didn't give them a word for it.* I think Ma is made that way too, unable to name her need.

Jie and I climb the trees and pretend to be monkeys, swinging to steal the neighbor's apricots like we're Sun Wukong thieving a peach of immortality from the garden of gods. He was punished for this, but we can't remember what the punishment was, so we swallow our apricots whole and without mercy. We shit the pits out, and they rattle the pipes of our toilet when we flush. Ma can't stand us dirty when we come in from the yard, but she's the kind who calls the sky a stain, who tries to bleach a bruise.

Two months ago the church people got a toilet installed for us. When we first used it, we squatted on top with our feet on the seat. It was Jie who told us we were doing it wrong: Our asses were supposed to go inside the halo. Don't laugh— there was a time you didn't know how to do this either, when I told you that the toilet is an ear that the sea hears through, and even now I sometimes see you with your head inside the bowl, conversing with another country.

—

A boy at the Old Colonial Diner teaches Jie how to make a metal detector out of a radio, a broomstick, cardboard, copper wire. I won't tell you all the details, in case you try to build one yourself. In return for the lesson, Jie lets him finger her in the back of the diner. Jie washes dishes at the sink while he stands behind, three of his fingers spidering around inside her. His nails snag on her pubic hair and she hisses, twists the faucet hotter, scalds off her calluses.

We use the metal detector in the yard behind the house to search for the gold. Jie holds the broomstick and I hold the radio. The copper wire wraps around both ends of the broomstick and the radio is taped to one end, the hair-clump of extra wire dragging on the ground like a tail. Jie switches the radio to AM and the morning news sounds like someone getting strangled, all static, a sound like the sea muffled inside our mouths.

We discipline the dirt. Rake into rows and follow along. I warm the radio on my skin while it announces the weather: the sky cussing rain at us in the afternoon, more rain tomorrow morning. Jie skims the soil with the broomstick, sweeping its splintered end in half-circles, shushing me even though I'm not talking. When we're near metal, the radio will whine with another voice, a song in gold's frequency. I hear nothing until the static sours into something higher and raspier, almost Ma's voice. Jie says, *Dig here.* We're on a square of land where shadows don't seem to survive. We dig with our bare hands, but we're only a fist deep when we find an old lawnmower blade. The radio sings in three more spots, but the quicker we dig, the sooner we surrender to our suspicions: that the gold's gone. In its place: five spent bullets, a dog whistle, a saw blade, some pennies, a bike chain, a whisk, a blank dog tag. The bullets glisten like dog eyes and my toes remember when they were shot, their ache outdated and residing in my spine.

Jie finds and adds two more bullets to our metal shitpile. We've never seen the gold ourselves, and neither of us says it, but we know there is nothing here. The radio's still tuned in to the soil's soprano, the static louder where we've dug up nothing but the dark. Jie throws down the broomstick, stomps on it with both feet. It breaks easy as bone. *I hope there's really nothing to find,* Jie says, though I disagree. I think it's better to have something to lose, even if the gold's now archived with the bones and the bullets. But Jie says the gold is better off buried, womb-safe, our lives spent waiting for its birth. Jie and I rebury everything we find. It feels like we've disturbed a cemetery, rifling through lives that aren't ours to remember. I keep the blank dog tag and promise to carve it a name worth carrying home.

———

We find Ba in the bedroom, bellydown on the mattress, his face so glossed with spit he looks candied. While he's asleep, Jie says, we should detect for metals in his body. Maybe the gold is still buried inside him. Maybe he forgot to shit it out after he got off the boat. I hover the broomstick over his belly and hands and head and hips and feet. I remember the first time he showed us the shrapnel. His back embroidered with bits of bullets, some of them showing, most of them shelled in his skin. We tapped on them in his sleep to test if they hurt, but he never stirred. He was scaled into some hybrid species, armored against Ma.

When I wave the broomstick, scanning him from head to ass and back up again, Ba's whole body sings. Wires smoking, the radio rides every note, high and low, transcribing the bullets under his skin into a song he wakes to. He opens his eyes and the shrapnel magnetizes, lifts him to our hands. I think about bringing the broomstick down on Ba's body, beating him soft as peach meat, parsing through his bird-shy bones to find whatever gold is still bobbing in his belly. But there's nothing inside him we can spend, not unless grief is a currency.

—

Ma's started throwing things out the window, searching for the gold inside our home. We remove all the windowpanes so she can't keep beating them with her fists, bruising the sky behind them. Now the rain doesn't know to keep out. Floods are so sudden we never know if it's coming from inside or outside our bodies, if it's raining or if we're wetting ourselves.

The one thing Ma never throws is the three-legged card table in the kitchen, set up with a single photo of my half-sisters still on the island, plus a handkerchief with a blood-stain aged brunette and a piece of white jade the size of my thumb. I thought it was an altar, but Jie says altars are for the dead, and the sisters are as alive as the flies that feast on our boogers when we sleep. One of them might be married now, or at least pregnant. One is still being raised by my aunts. You've never met your great-aunts because they die faster than I can remember their names: A typhoon tore out the oldest one's legs, so she had to be piggybacked all day, and your youngest great-aunt picked chilies until her hands wore the seeds and singed the skin of everyone she touched.

In the photo on the card table, Ma is pregnant with Jie and holding two babies like they're grenades with the pins pulled out. She's waiting for this picture to be taken so she can throw them far out of frame. There's a third girl in a white dress standing in front of her. The photo's too water-wrinkled to see any of their faces, and the oldest girl is out of focus, a

streak like a tree. Ma never acknowledges the photo or the
table, which makes their presence even more a punishment.
Once, at dinnertime, Jie asks what their names are. Ma locks
her out of the house that night, and in the morning, Jie is
curled like a stray on our doormat, one arm jammed through
the mail slot like she's been trying to fold herself into a paper
daughter.

Ma stands at the not-altar, holding the handkerchief in her
left fist and the jade in her right. There is no god we know
better than her fist. Ma never looks at the photo. She turns to
the kitchen window and watches the mosquitos fatten into
moons, light salting all the lines on her face. She prays to the
sisters whose names I don't know. Her prayers robbed of a
god.

Jie and I were born thieves. Born to orphan our sisters by
birthing our mother into this country. You don't know about
gold, about grieving what you could have owned. Your grandmother's grief has grown its own body. She raises it like another child, one she loves better than me and my sister, one
that can never leave her.

Today she complains she's married to a manhole, a shaft
for memories to fall down, a man who can see only the sky
above him. But Ba's smarter than she knows. The one time we
got robbed, the thieves didn't know to dig. Couldn't find anything worth taking. Only our door was missing. We were sure
they took something else from the house, but we didn't know
what to look for. How to search for an absence.

When Ma stews the apricots we steal, she never asks
where we get them. She knows nothing belongs to us, and
that's why she won't let us sit on chairs until she wraps them
in cheesecloth or scrubs off our skin. We can't put pictures on
the walls, if we had any, or fully unpack—she still thinks we'll

have to give everything back. Jie's mouth is still magnetized to the word *sister,* but outside of her dreams she's stopped asking for names. Jie goes to church and her English has gotten so good she's started reading aloud the billboards outside our house. One of them is the phone number of a divorce lawyer. One is for bail bonds. One is for a casino, which tempts Ba until Ma throws her quilt basket at him, tells him to sit down or she'll snip his balls off and sew them to his earlobes. Jie and I can't stop imagining Ba wearing his balls like earrings, and we laugh until we piss, the stains in our laps symmetrical.

—

We dig beneath so many trees we've given them nicknames: The one with the bent knees. The one that sways like a drunk. The one with a woman's hips. The gold is under none of them. It's the earthquake that finally wounds a way to the gold: I sleep through it, but Jie claims it felt like the whole earth was operating on itself, scraping back its own skin, re-arranging its organs.

On our porch, one of the floorboards splits open and shakes off its scab of moss. Light spits from it and we flock to the crack like moths. Underneath the porch is a finger of gold, bedazzled with flies and reclined on a sheet of butcher paper. Ma dances on the kitchen table for a whole hour, her feet for-going gravity. She stacks the gold on the not-altar, directly to the left of the photo so flat and dull in its frame. The gold is too exposed, like looking directly at someone's bones. We are all looking at it now, the gold and the photo, our eyes alternat-ing between the glow and its shadow, the payment and the cost.

DAUGHTER

Hu Gu Po (I)

California, a generation later

Mothers ago, there was a tiger spirit who wanted to live inside a woman. One night when the moon was as brown as a nipple, the tiger spirit braided itself into a rope of light and lowered itself into a woman's mouth, rappeling down her throat and taking the name of Hu Gu Po. But the price of having a body is hunger. Hu Gu Po could remain a tenant in the woman's body as long as she hunted. When she smelled the sweat-seasoned toes of children, her belly hardened into a beetle of need and scuttled out of her throat, a scout in search of salt. Craving their toes, she climbed into the children's bedrooms at night. With her teeth, she unscrewed the toes of sleeping daughters and sucked the knuckles clean of meat, renaming them peanuts.

Every morning, Hu Gu Po walked through the market and appraised the fish dragged in from the river, their bodies like oiled opals. A fisherman's wife, smelling something that scarred the air with its smoke, turned to Hu Gu Po and asked what she was eating.

Peanuts, Hu Gu Po said, shucking nut-bones with her teeth.

The fisherman's wife asked if Hu Gu Po might be willing to share.

Hu Gu Po laughed. *How much would you pay for one?*

The fisherman's wife named a price.

Slipping the skin off another nut, Hu Gu Po said, *That's not enough for me to make a living.* She laughed, her black braid unraveling to ash, charring the air.

The next morning, every child in the village woke with a toe subtracted from each foot. On each of their pillows was a five-cent coin, rusted dark as a blood spot.

The fisherman's wife had no children, but when she heard what had happened, she remembered the woman in the market cleaving peanut shells with her teeth. When she opened her door, there was a skin pouch lying in her doorway. She slit open the pouch and it spilled dozens of toes, deboned and dusted with salt.

—

My mother lifted the bedsheet over us both when she told me this story, crouching down over my feet, grasping them in her fists, and ferrying them to her mouth. My toes squirmed like minnows in her maw, swimming against the current of her spit. In the dark, I watched the geography of her face rearranging: the mountain range of moles on her forehead, the hook of her lip lowering when she fished up a story. She let go of my feet when I begged her not to eat them, but one night she concluded the story by biting down on my big toe. Her teeth encircled it like a tiara, resting on the skin rather than breaking it, but I could feel her trembling, her jaw reined back by something I couldn't see. In the morning, my toe wore a ringlet of white where the blood didn't return again for months.

Some nights, I woke to my mother's finger foraging around in my ear, nicking out the earwax with her hooked pinky nail. She liked to joke she was digging for gold. She lifted the canoe of her pinky nail, loaded with my grit, and brought it to her mouth. I yanked at her wrist and said, *No, no, no no no.* But she ate it anyway, laughing when I said it was gross. *I used to eat my earwax when I was hungry,* she said. *My ears were always so clean. That's why I can hear everything.* My mother said if I let the earwax live inside me, it would eventually grow beetle legs and scuttle into my brain, nesting there like shrapnel. She said she was saving me by eating my ear canals clean, allowing the sun to tunnel into my skull and keep all my memories lit.

—

In the bedroom I shared with my brother, our mother told us stories about Arkansas/the rain, her sister/my aunt, her ma/my ama, her ba/my agong. How my grandfather buried two gold bars that an earthquake gave back, and how they spent the gold to get to LA. I was born from breakage: My mother left Ama and Agong in LA and moved six hours north, planting my brother and me in soil unsalted by memories. She summarized her life in slashes, everything a choice: Leave/Stay. Mother/Daughter. Love/Live.

She told me the history of her hands: Her first job was

working in a chicken barn with her Jiejie. There were no windows, and the chicks were born with their eyes blank as buttonholes. No need to see, no light to learn by. It was her job to rake up the sawdust every week and add a new layer. Sawdust doesn't settle: It got into her eyes and her ears and her nostrils and her anus. Her shits were sugared with sawdust and she bled to pass them. It even sanded down the walls of her womb, and that's why it hurt to birth me. My mother said the sawdust had nowhere to go but into her body. When she raked the floors, it rose around her like ash. Like being awake for your own cremation. She kicked at the hens until her sister said it would break all the eggs inside them and they'd never lay another one whole.

One time my mother kicked a board out of the barn wall so the sawdust could find its way out. One of the eyeless hens escaped through the slot and fled to the woods, and she lied and said a raccoon tore a board off the barn.

I told my ma it didn't matter how many hens ran away, she said. *I said we could bury all the eggs and the birds would grow back.* Later that summer, my mother and her sister saw the missing hen rising out of the woods, flossing through the trees as it flew, clearing over the roof of the barn. My mother said she always suspected chickens were pretending they couldn't fly, their wings tucked away like weapons. She said the escaped hen must have fucked a red-tailed hawk and founded its own species. She saw the hen-hawks pecking at the feet of trees, fringing the forest behind the house, shaggy and big as dogs. She saw a whole flock of them take down a snake, pin it to the soil. *I thought only gods could create new species,* I said. *Then we must have been gods,* she said. I imagined her hen flying above California, glossed like a plane and pregnant, looking for a place to lay us.

My mother said hens ate their own eggs if they were left alone with them too long. *I used to wake when the sky was still a shut eyelid,* she said. If she out-slept the sun, there were no eggs left to collect. My mother opened her mouth, guided my fingers so deep down her throat I felt the hilt of a feather and plucked it out. She coughed as I cleaned off its scabbard of spit. I asked her what it did. *All voices have wings,* she said, *that's how they travel.* I told her this was a regular chicken feather, flightless, but she said it's easy to assimilate into the air. You just have to believe your bones hollow, no marrow no mother no memory.

———

My mother always wore white socks with throats of lace, and when I asked her why, she said, *My feet are hibernating.* When I asked my brother, he said she probably had fish fins instead of feet, and to find out we snipped a hole through her socks while she was sleeping. We slit her socks along the sole, parting them to show the stone pads of her feet. On her left foot, the three littlest toes were gone. No wound, no scars or sign of stitching, just stumps with rings like a tree. Sleeves of space where three toes might have grown up, been given names. My brother and I ran back to bed and hid the scissors under our mattress. In the morning, our mother was wearing a new pair of socks.

Where did they go? we asked, and our mother refused to answer. I asked if she'd been preyed on by Hu Gu Po and she said not everything was a story. Weeks later, we found an assortment cookie tin behind the other cookie tin that held my birth certificate and her sewing kit, both of them in the pantry where our mother kept inedible things: blankets, batteries, retired knives, a titanium baseball bat. There was a cartoon bear indented into the lid of the tin, and the blue paint had been battered off.

Inside it were hardened rings of ash and in the center, brown stones. At first we thought they were chrysalises of some kind, bark-covered tubes rattling as if something inside were trying to hatch. But there were nails still growing from them, caramelizing in the tin's body heat.

We had found her toes. They hummed as if they owned our hearts, and we thought there was still a chance they could be sewn back on. When we showed her, she said, *I don't want them back*. My brother and I held a ceremony to bury the toes, even writing a eulogy: *Here lie the toes of our mother. May the soil eat them and shit them out as beautiful trees that smell like our feet.*

When our mother found out, she whipped us with a wet sock and asked us to show her the spot, watching us dig them back up. Untrimmed for a week, the toenails had grown six inches long, enamel swords with worms pierced alive on them. She returned the toes to the cookie tin, neutered their nails with a file, and taped the tin shut, saying she would need them later. When I asked her what she needed them for, she said all losses have lifetimes, always longer than we think, and her toes would someday find another source of blood, a new mouth to metabolize them.

DAUGHTER

Girl in Gourd

California, still

I was born with a gourd-shaped head: My mother kneaded it back into a sphere while my bones were still milk. The left side of my head still wears her handprint. My mother joked that if she'd ever dropped me, I would have split open into symmetrical bowls, spilling a head full of black seeds.

Every night, I sat cross-legged on the floor while she sat in a chair above me, holding my head between her knees and squeezing my skull into a shape that could sit in her palm. Her fingers fattened the strands of my hair with horse-oil cream. When her knee-bones ground against my temples and milked tears from me, she lapped them off my face like a cat and said she was almost done. She had to make sure my head was round enough to remember who loved me, sturdy enough to carry the stories she was going to crown me with.

Eventually the gourd juice emptied out of me: I pissed twice as much as my brother, a spray so forceful my mother said I alone could have ended the California drought if only I knew how to aim. I was always sweating, my skin shifting like sheets of sea. My mother had to wring me out twice a day like a towel. Back before we lived in a house, I slept on a mattress at night, between my mother and father, my brother on a fold-out futon in the farthest corner of the room. Every night, a puddle flared around me like a skirt, wetting the whole mattress and waking my mother, who dreamed a typhoon had torn me from her tit. My mother feared my veins were full of salt, that my bones produced water instead of blood. To prove that I bled, she punctured one of my veins with a boiled sewing needle. The blood corkscrewed out, confirming its color on her hands.

I was conceived at night during a rainstorm, which was why I was born with too much water inside me: The rain had collected in my mother's body like a gutter, and I was born from her rupture. After my birth, she begged my father not to touch her on the few nights it rained, afraid of what weather his body would bring.

—

My father, god of water, could make anything grow. Before my brother and I were born, he went to school to major in rain. His favorite things were irrigation systems and trenches and hoses—all the ways water could immigrate. What he knew about thirst was to outsource it. *Irrigation is surgery. Like threading veins through a body,* he said, and demonstrated with his arms how to shovel through anything, how to break up the dirt that's well-versed in thirst. When my mother said, *I want this world waterless,* he laughed and said she was prejudiced against rivers, alive or dry, because she'd nearly been drowned in one. But he wasn't afraid of rivers. He ran them. Back then, he used to tell my mother: *I'll be a god syringing rivers into deserts, injecting lakes into droughtland, seducing salt out of seawater.* Then my brother was born and he dropped out of school, taking a job moving two-by-fours at a construction site. Work that wrung all the water from his body. I came second, a daughter shaped like floodwater, and by then he was coming home late every day, shimmying off his sweat, watering the carpet until it grew past my ankles. I ducked under the kitchen table, fleeing the radius of his rain, trimming the carpet down with a pair of eyebrow scissors.

When he left the room to shower for hours, spending so long in the bathroom I wondered if he'd become water and gone down the drain too, I crawled where he'd rained all over the floor, touching my tongue to his sweat, divining where his body had been based on taste. He'd been at the beach, I told my brother, and he'd kidnapped all the salt from the sea, holding it hostage here.

After work, my father irrigated our apartment building's shared courtyard, scooping trenches too straight to be veins. *When it rains,* he said, *the water won't flood. It'll be outsourced.* I asked him how he knew where the water had to go, and he pointed at a pack of bushes with finger-shaped flowers. *Water follows want,* he said. *If the body is really mostly water,* I asked, *then how come it can burn?* My father said something about parts and sums: how water is a part and the body is the sum, but I didn't want to do the math and ran back inside.

The first time I saw him install a water hose, I asked him what he was holding and he said *a snake* just to scare me. At school, when the teacher told us the snake was temptation and Eve was evil, I thought of my father cradling that green hose, feeding bushes that weren't his, shucking petals off a flower and licking them like stamps to press onto my cheeks. When he turned the hose on, water sprang from its mouth and that was a miracle. I remember him whipping my brother with that hose, its metal mouth striking between my brother's rolled-back eyes. I remember him saying, *I'm sorry, but this is the only way you'll grow.*

—

My mother got a job at a company that manufactured photocopiers. In the mornings, she drove west to a building so tall it sanded the sky smooth. All day, she sat at a desk and answered customer calls with an accent. *The only reason you haven't been fired is because you're a minority,* said the woman from marketing.

When they promoted her to receptionist, my mother had official access to the black-and-white photocopier, where she made copies of handwritten notices to be circulated around the office: Please refrain from using air fresheners. Please refrain from bringing food with nuts or shellfish into the communal kitchen. Please do not flush menstrual products down the toilet. Menstrual, which she spelled *minstrel.*

The day she was fired, she cleared the refrigerator of half-finished Caesar salads and waxen ham sandwiches, took them home in her purse, and ate them for dinner after cooking pots of fishball soup for us. She only ever ate leftovers, lifting the lace of burnt rice out of the cooker, sucking marrow out of the bones I didn't eat clean. *I'm on a diet,* she joked. *A diet called life.*

The day she was fired for photocopying my birth certificate, my mother watched the green laser swipe the glass pane like cleaning a window. The glass was blue-white and cool as ice. Beneath layers of powder, mother's cheek was a swollen gourd. After photocopying both sides of my birth certificate, having seen on TV a story about a records office burning down, all citizenship undone to smoke—my mother pressed the start button again, though she had nothing left of me to copy. She pressed her hot cheek to the glass as the laser beam flitted across it. What printed was a map of her right cheek, its broken veins like tributaries, a bruise beginning to blue from nose to ear. She held the photocopy in both hands, lifted it to the fluorescent light. Folded it. She touched the cheek on her face, then the one on the paper. Couldn't tell which was the evidence and which was the crime.

My mother was always covering up our crimes: Once, when a candied shrimp slipped out of my mouth and stained the carpet, she threw a napkin on it so my father wouldn't see. When I was asleep, she bleached the sauce out of the carpet, though the bleach sucked it out too well and left the spot brighter, too white, a spotlight where my stain had been.

—

While she cooked, my mother told stories she claimed were from the Bible, though I could never find them later in any translation. When my father told my mother to teach us a mainlander story, the one she told was Meng Jiang Nu, the girl born from a gourd.

The story begins with two families on neighboring estates, one known for its fruit and the other for its flowers. Between their yards was a gourd tree, its trunk so wide even the wind could not wrap around it. The tree's roots lived on the Meng family's land, but most of its branches—including the branch with the largest gourd, so gold it blinded birds that flew past—crossed over into the Jiang family's yard.

While the Meng and Jiang families argued every day over the ownership of that gold gourd, it grew to the size of an infant, juice-bloated and so tender it bled in the breeze. When it fell at last, the rind split open to reveal a child, a daughter. They wept at the miracle. The Meng family insisted on naming her Meng Nu, while the Jiang family wanted to name her Jiang Nu. The girl starved for two days as the families argued, before someone said that the girl would die before they ever decided. So they named her Meng Jiang Nu, daughter of both families, daughter of two bloods.

This story is wrong, I told my mother. *If she was really a daughter, neither family would want her.* She couldn't be milked until she was a mother, couldn't be bartered until she was a bride. My mother never finished the story. I never asked if she had wanted me, if I was the kind of daughter who doubled as a battleground, who was fought over. Later, my mother would say, *Remember, it wasn't the girl they were fighting over. It was the gourd.*

Maybe, when the gourd split open, they wept not to celebrate her birth but to grieve their lost gold. They cursed gravity as thievery. I remembered watching families in restaurants fighting to pay a bill, and maybe that was what Meng and Jiang were fighting over: a bill they were too proud to let the other take. To say a daughter is a debt they could afford to pay.

—

On Sundays, our mother woke us up with the end of her broom to clean every room, saran-wrapping the sofa and spitting on the windows to lubricate the light that entered them. To keep my language clean: gargle saltwater twice a week. To keep your teeth from leaving you on wings: tally them every night with your tongue. She rinsed the dishes so bright we had to squint while eating; she sang to a knife in the sink as if auditioning to be its blade. *We can never be clean enough for this country,* she said.

Weekly, my father accused her of loving the apartment better than her husband, of kneeling to clean but never kneeling for him. My mother said that keeping a clean home was a sign of wealth and keeping a husband was a sign of stupidity. When my father raised his hand, my mother always raised something else—a vase, a chopstick, a sofa cushion—not to deflect the blow, but to meet it midair, to return it. When my father took off his belt, we held on to the other end to anchor it, give back its gravity. Sometimes he beat us with it just to hear us beg him to stop. *This is the only thing I can give you,* he said. Not money or a house. Just this, his hands overflowing with us, just this: his mercy.

Some Sundays, after my mother finished scrubbing every seat in the apartment that had fraternized with our asses, my father taught us to make kites with rice paper and disposable chopsticks and twine, our arms acting as spools. He told us to draw eyes onto our kites, or else they'd be blind to the path of their own flight. In the backyard, the kites tugged me onto my toes, the paper wings so thin the stars teethed through them. My father told me stories of flying over a salt lake, his kite slitting the sky's belly, the winds so strong they could hike a child up onto a cloud. My father tethered me by stepping on my feet. While my brother punctured his kites on trees and powerlines, the string lurching out of his hands, I could fly

for hours, even at night, my paper kite a second moon, a man-
made light.

My father stayed up with me and watched. He told me
that kites were once used for war. Once, an approaching army
set up camp just outside the city. The army was banked on all
sides by a fog thick as milk. To trick the enemy, the city
strapped children to paper kites, gave them gourd-flutes to
blow as they flew. The army, walled by fog, heard the children
making music in the sky and assumed they were surrounded.
The men surrendered within an hour. The city was saved by
its smallest members.

My kite's eyes blinked at me from above: It could watch
itself being flown, my father perching me on his shoulder-
bones. *You're flying me,* I said. He gripped both my ankles—
one in each fist—as if the wind would lick me away. *Kites
were once made of skin,* he said. Flown to frighten the enemy.
I misheard him and imagined my skin made of kites, how
anything could wound me, tear me: wind, getting wet, getting
dressed. I wore my shirt backward once and my father called
me careless, tugging me back into the house by the collar. He
asked me what people would think if I went outside with my
head facing the wrong way. In the kitchen, I practiced putting
my shirt on, taking it off and putting it back on until I couldn't
lift my arms above my head, the shirt trembling when I tried
to hoist it, a failed flag of surrender.

——

I wanted to teach my father how to make something too, so I
showed him how to make sock puppets we'd learned in first
grade. You put a sock over your fist and made it speak by

opening your hand, blinking its button eyes. My father said I should cut it a mouth, a real one that could eat. To make anything real required butchery. So I used scissors on one of his white socks, long enough to roll over my forearm, and cut a mouth into it. My mother said he would kill me for doing that, but instead he sat with me in the kitchen and fed my fist everything that would fit in it: a found fishbone, a peach pit that had rolled under the cabinets, his own thumb. I bit down with my fingers and twisted his thumb until he yanked it back. I wasn't sorry, but I blew on his thumb with my sock-mouth. It blued anyway.

When I saw that my sock-mouth was stronger than my born one, I spent weeks speaking through my fist, holding it up to my mother's ear and asking her to call me through it. She held my fist like a seashell to her ear, whispered back to it. Only my wrist heard her words, and in bed I tried to replay them, dialing my hand in the dark between my legs, waiting for her voice to come out of me.

—

Weeks before his visa expired, my father decided to work a few years at a cousin's slot machine factory in Jiangsu, where he'd examine and approve the machines before they were sent to Macau. My father had learned most of his English playing Texas Hold 'Em with college kids at the park after dark: *Hit me. Raise. Stay. Stay.* At night, he renamed all the constellations after card suits, pointing out a spade in the sky, a club, then a heart, telling us stories of his biggest wins. *Money's like the moon,* he said. *By morning they're both gone.*

The night my father left for the airport, we ate a whole

fried fish, a broth so thin it evaporated on our tongues before we could swallow, vegetables boiled translucent, ghostly. We ate with our elbows on the table and didn't speak. We let our knives narrate. My mother caught crickets in the backyard and panfried them with sesame oil. Bent over the table, my father packed his stomach like a suitcase, folding pieces of pork in half before sealing them into his mouth. The fish was for good luck. He'd carry the luck in his body and shit out its bones in another country. When my mother ran out of dish soap, when she didn't want to pay for water, she spat directly on the dishes. Erased his hunger from every plate.

Packing for the mainland, my father folded his steam-ironed white shirts in symmetrical stacks. He took one of the fake-leather belts he wore and left the other one dangling on a hook in the closet, tame without his hands around it. He packed gifts for all his cousins, Band-Aids with cartoon characters printed on them, boxes of Cheerios, disposable dusters. My brother and I sat on his suitcase so he could jimmy the zipper, and the second before it shut, I saw a white sheet sliding out from between two shirts. It was a piece of paper with drawn-on eyes, a half-finished kite.

When we drove him to the airport, I counted the hours his flight would take, calculated that he would land the hour I woke. I didn't sleep that night, telling myself that as long as I never woke, he would never land: our father forever mid-flight. That night, flying my kite in the rain, I saw the paper shrivel into a fist before falling. From the sky, my father said we'd make a new one, a kite so large we could strap it to our backs and leave the country. I lost the kite that night, stayed out till morning to watch it reappear, as if light could undo any loss. It was years before I realized that kites were only puppetry and could only fake their flight. Real flight involved no leashes or strings. Birds did not come with girls tied to them, girls reeling them down, girls the opposite of the sky.

My father called from the mainland every week with nothing to say. When we picked up, he was twelve hours ahead in the day, answering from our future. We pulled the phone toward our mother, yanking the spiral cord straight. My father's roommate—another cousin whose name we didn't know—sometimes talked to us instead. He complained that my father never spoke, that silence had shrunk his throat to the width of a string. This worried my mother, but comforted me: It meant I could reel him back to me. I knotted the phone cord around my wrist, tugged his voice taut like a kite-string, but I couldn't pull him back into the sky I could see.

———

Meng Jiang Nu grew at the rate of a tree and could be fed only soil, silt, water, insecticide in the form of vinegar. The two families took turns watering her, but she never grew more than an inch per year. By the time she was a girl, her mothers and fathers were dead. She outlived the second generation of the family, then the third, each generation leaving a written set of instructions for the care of the gourd girl: *Keep her buried waist-deep in soil at all times. Turn her face to the sun. Stimulate her roots by stroking them. Water her. Prune her hair twice a week. If you see moss on her skin, beat it off with a broom.* Meng Jiang Nu was planted in a trench dug between the Meng and Jiang courtyards. Her body was hollow, and the neighborhood boys liked to sneak onto the estate. They carved her a pair of earholes and shouted into them, heard their own names echo back. They dared one another to cut her down, bring her home, plant themselves in her body.

In Jiangsu, my mother said, *where my ba was born, there were daughtertrees.* When a daughter was born, every family planted a camphor tree outside their home. Its branches grew parallel to her bones. Sometimes the tree grew scales down its trunk and sprouted a single jellied eye, like a fish, and sometimes the tree had a mouth in the center of the trunk, where birds were born, except these birds had no feathers, just skin, flightless as fists. When the matchmaker walked by your house and saw that the tree had grown to the width of a waist, she knew it was time for your daughter to be married away. The daughtertree was cut down, chiseled into trunks to carry her clothes and bedding. When my mother was born, Agong tried planting a camphor tree outside the military village where they lived, but the soil there was incestuous with the sea and too salty. The tree was salt-sick, its trunk crumbling. Every day, Agong measured its waist with his hands, but it remained the width of his wrists. My mother was relieved: As long as the tree never grew wide enough to be wed, she'd never have to leave home. She asked of every tree she saw: *Don't ever grow a body worth cutting down.*

It was Agong who felled the tree one morning, plucking the trunk from the ground as easily as an arrow shaft, its only two branches braided together like my mother's legs when she was born. After he broke the tree into shrapnel with his bare hands, my mother tried plucking the eyelash-fine splinters from his palms, but the shards submarined through his blood, merging wood with marrow. That's why he was so flammable, why his memories were already smoke. Why he wasn't allowed to touch the stove, newspapers, our hair, this story, anything that could be translated into fire.

—

When my father sent money from the mainland, we folded half of it into the duct-taped shoebox under my grandmother's bed, gave the rest to pay our late rent. My mother's period was three months late. She miscarried in bed while I slept in my father's place, on the moonsoaked side of the mattress. Blood ribboned between us, and I woke with both wrists bound in red. I checked my body for a wound, but it was nowhere on my body. My mother sat up in bed and corked her crotch with a fist. She told me to get a bucket. I ran to the kitchen and emptied a bucket of brine into the sink, scrubbing away its ring of salt with the hem of my shirt. When I brought her the bucket, she squatted over it for the rest of the night, her blood baying into it, making a sound like a trapped dog. The air turned to salt and crystallized around my lips and eyes. I fell back asleep, and when I woke my mother was still crouched on the floor, naked from the waist down, staring down at her blood like a mirror. In the morning, I helped her carry the bucket to the bathroom sink. The blood was only two inches deep, but it was heavy as bone. As if death had a hidden density. We tipped the bucket together. Later, my brother would complain that the sink wasn't draining properly, that something down there was clogged. I would catch my mother spooning beef broth down the sink, feeding the drain like a mouth.

—

In my version, Meng Jiang Nu marries another tree. This other tree is a daughter like her, with branches too soft to be switches, a trunk holed into nests. The tree is marrowed like bone. The story silvers into a mirror: One day, while stretching her roots under the soil, Meng Jiang Nu butts into the roots of another tree without a shadow—a bone-tree—and the two are married through friction. By striking their branches against each other, they invent fire. Unlike Meng Jiang Nu, the bone-tree eventually outgrows her soil, her roots forking into human feet, her fruit ripening into a face. The bone-tree dresses as a boy and becomes a gardener, guarding Meng Jiang Nu with a pair of silver shears.

Late in the empire, the bone-tree is drafted to build the Great Wall. The Wall contains so many corpses—so many men dead of exhaustion—that it can be built through the night. Bone is a source of light. When the bone-tree dies working on the Wall in midwinter, her bones are so cold they shatter into sugar. The next worker in line paves over her body and moves on, builds the next rung of the Wall's spine.

When the bone-tree doesn't come home, Meng Jiang Nu decides to walk north to her wife, all the way to the Wall. She uproots herself and brings two bladder-bottles of water and a flint. By the time she reaches the north, it's already the next winter, her eyes frozen to fruit pits in their sockets: She can only look ahead. She reaches the campfires lining the base of the wall. To keep warm, men sleep inside scooped-out horse carcasses, wearing their entrails as scarves.

Meng Jiang Nu searches a thousand miles of camps, opens the belly flaps of each horse pregnant with a man. In my mother's version of the story, Meng Jiang Nu weeps so hard the Wall collapses, and another generation must donate its bones to rebuild it. Her river unravels the spines of cities and drowns a million men, each body pickled in her salt. The river rinses out her wife's skull. The skull bobs down the river. She fishes it out, brings it to her lips. For the rest of her life, she drinks from it. For the rest of her life, the army hunts her from city to city, this woman whose grief has the strength of gods. Who can kill a whole country by weaponizing the water in her body.

DAUGHTER

Hu Gu Po (II)

A week before I woke with a tail, my mother was outside in the front yard, arguing with the new neighbor about his encroaching eucalyptus tree. Its shadow bruised the side of our house all eggplant-black. Its sap ran fast as a nosebleed and hardened into shards of gold glass on our driveway. This was the first house I'd ever lived in—we'd moved in after my father left for the mainland, sending him the key inside a bubble-wrapped package, along with an assortment of my latest-lost baby teeth. The house had smoke-scarred windows and a balding lawn and squirrels that died in its walls and attracted funerals of flies. Our rent was paid in envelopes of cash my father sent back from the mainland. Every hinge in the house was loose and our doors fell out with the frequency of baby teeth. At night, we nailed our windows shut to keep them from panting open in the dry heat. The only grocery store in the city was so dim inside you had to bring a flashlight. Hundreds of advertisements and posters were taped to

the windows so that no light was let in: The store was barricaded by the faces of missing daughters and posters of local
psychics promising to predict CA lottery numbers. Coupons
fled in flocks from the parking lot, offering discounts on pipa
gao and tuoxie and dried tongue-looking meats that my
brother and I licked and put back in the bin, disappointed
that they didn't make a sound in our mouths.

—

My mother chose this city because it was a drivable distance
to LA and Agong, but still far north enough from Ama that
they spoke only on the phone:

Ma   *yes*   *home*

                                  is Ba

wearing underwear   *today*   *shit*

                    isn't here yet

Today my mother pointed at the chasms in our concrete
driveway, flooding with rare rain from the week before. She
threw her wire hairbrush at the neighbor, and when he didn't
turn from his mailbox, she said: *Look at these! The roots of
your tree are canyoning me!* The neighbor swore at her in Si-
chuanese, a dialect that sounded to me like ducks being
deboned alive. *Don't be so racist,* my brother said. *It's not racist if he's a mainlander,* I said.

My mother's dislike of mainlanders was medical: She
claimed to develop a rash or lose a tooth every time she spoke

to one. She rubbed my thumb against her silver fillings and said, *This is what you get from kissing a mainlander, from marrying one. Remember: This hole in my tooth is the one you were born through.* I said, *But Agong was born a mainlander,* and my mother said, *Agong doesn't even know he's been born.*

Our mother's teeth were brittle with lies. She earned all her cavities not from kissing our father but from working night shifts at a Baskin-Robbins when she was new in LA, back when she ate ice cream every night for dinner. We didn't blame our mother for her lies: We loved them into littler truths. For instance, she was not the last granddaughter of a Tayal chief but descended from lower-ranked warriors, born with a shark's tooth under her tongue. Another one: Our mother once ran from an entire army, climbing a tree so soft-boned that it collapsed, shish-kababing two soldiers and ending martial law on the island forever. The part about the tree is true at least. Her wrist wears a scar like a bracelet, where the bones battled out of her skin. She imagined the soldiers skewered and strung, her injuries dormant inside their bodies.

My mother said, *It's like martial law on this goddamn street,* when the mainlander moved in next door. He was a renter like us, but he paid his rent on time, while my mother spent whole months writing excuse notes: *My husband is working on the mainland and the money was swallowed at sea. My husband is a raccoon and currently unemployed. My husband is a pilot and we plan to set the roof on fire to signal him home.* Our Russian-speaking landlord survived an army too and gave us extensions out of sympathy. She and my mother traded stories as a truce, stories gouged of their truths. About husbands that grew trees to hang their mothers from. About soldiers with striped uniforms, dizzying the enemy to death.

I like Chinese people. I love China, the landlord told us monthly, as if to assure herself we were worth the stories we'd sold her.

Nicknaming our neighbor Duck Uncle, my brother and I made quacking sounds with our armpits whenever he spoke. When my mother threatened to hang raw meat from the branches of the tree to attract raccoons and coyotes and flies to his yard, Duck Uncle retaliated by stealing the knob off our front door, coaxing pigeons into our home, dressing a rake like a woman and staking her in the lawn, impersonating our ghosts. When they fought, they leaned toward each other at the same angle, their shadows braiding on the sidewalk. My mother slowed her words, mocking the make of his mouth. *Don't touch my house,* she said. *It's not even yours,* he said, and she retaliated by filling my brother with cans of Pepsi and Hong Van and paying him a quarter to pee somewhere on Duck Uncle's property, somewhere he'd see. When Duck Uncle accused her of deploying my brother, she told him it was a dog that did it. *Must have been a smart dog,* Duck Uncle said, *because it peed its initials on my door.*

In the morning, my mother felled the tree with a single wire and her will, standing for hours in the sun while she sawed the wire through the trunk. She'd threatened Duck Uncle with a bent screwdriver until he retreated into his house and locked the door. Crossing over into Duck Uncle's front yard, she began flossing down the tree. By the time the landlord came, the tree was broken in the middle like a bone. We were asked to move again, to pay for all damages to plant life. In the end, it was Duck Uncle who spoke to the landlord for hours. Afterward, we were allowed to stay. *What did you say?* I asked him. We stood in his front yard with the tree stump between us, wet and scabbed like a sore. Duck Uncle was the tallest man I'd ever seen, a man whose body doubled as his own building.

I called her a racist and told her that cutting down trees is a cultural thing, he said.

What's a "cultural thing"? I said.

Like a funeral or a wedding, he said. *Like you.*

This was how my mother came to thank Duck Uncle for keeping us in a house we couldn't afford: My mother had seen him bury a key under the bush by his front door, so she knuckled into the soil, uprooting the key like a seed. With her fingers wet, she unlocked his front door and found his room, doorless with a skin-thin curtain. Behind the curtain, Duck Uncle was changing into his work clothes—a suit vest embroidered with his name—and my mother could map the whole city of his body. The wet street of his skin, the forehead greased into sky. Duck Uncle was not surprised to see her in his doorway: It was like looking at himself, like looking into water and seeing your own face stitched there.

After that, we ate for free at Duck Uncle's dim sum restaurant, which had a name so generic we never learned it. The food was so greasy it shot down our throats before we could swallow. My brother and I tried hating him, but Duck Uncle's Sichuan accent was honky and high-pitched and made us laugh until our throats tied themselves into bows. He even promised to teach us to hunt ducks, cutting targets out of shoeboxes and letting us shoot them with his BB gun. My brother had the best aim out of the three of us, threading the pellet through the penciled-in eye. I was too afraid of backfire, so I only pretended to pull the trigger, making the gunshot sound with my mouth. Duck Uncle pretended to believe me, said I'd killed so many. But I'd aimed at nothing, the bullet unspent as our silence, the ducks just make-believe.

—

In a past life, our city was a landfill. In the summers, the air smelled as if it had passed through our bowels, hot and sour and slurred. My brother and I debated if the stink was spoiled plums or our farts or our father expiring from the country. Before I was born, the city bulldozed over buttocks of garbage for the roads to be built. The landfill lived just below us, digesting itself, flexing its belly. The soil was too soft to stand on and every year the houses kneeled deeper in their dung. In the backyard, my brother and I dug down to find what was dying.

Our mother bought us snorkel masks to wear outside, as if sipping air through a smaller opening would shrink the scent. We met after school in the backyard and drew holes in the dirt with our toes. The grass was a ghost of its former green, and most of it had been scalped away by the heat and our feet. In the grass we found trash that smelled recently deceased: soda can tabs, beer bottles with a piss-colored liquid living inside it. My brother said we probably wouldn't find anything else, but I said the point was the hole itself. I'd learned that there were gases trapped in the soil wherever trash was buried, and if we didn't dig holes for the ground to fart out its gas, this whole city would explode: Houses like knocked-out teeth. Blacktop rising as a crow flock.

Tracing three more holes in the dirt, he asked me what color the gas was and I said, *The same as our breath.* That's what made it lethal: Its taste camouflaged with our tongues. When it entered your lungs, it became a blade inside you. From the kitchen window, our mother watched as we plotted the rest of our holes. When we came in, she scrubbed us so raw we couldn't sleep with the sheets on our skin. Still we kept digging, saving the city from its flatulent past.

We dug with our hands and waited until evening when
the smell of the landfill was only as bad as our breath. My
brother kneeled first. He shaped his palms into bowls and
flung fistfuls of soil onto a pile behind him. I kneeled to follow him, but my hands dawdled too long in the dirt. My
brother was elbow-deep now and sleeved in soil, but I couldn't
go farther than a fist down. *Spit on the ground to soften it,* he
said. I mimicked his mouth, spitting a syllable of saliva into
the hole. My brother had learned to spit from my father:
tongue recoiling in the mouth, flinging the spit like a whip.
Our mother always slapped my brother for it. One time he'd
spat in a temple, a coin of spit faceup on the prayer stool, and
everybody had turned to look at it. *Learn to swallow it,* she
said. She trained her throat to swallow twice an hour while
she slept, and she sometimes wore a bandanna as a muzzle.
We'd never seen her drool before, her pillow clean in the
mornings.

After we spat in the soil, digging felt too much like burrowing into each other's mouths. We took a break to play
with the Snake, the water hose christened by our father. Unspooling its length, we pretended it was alive, fat with blood
and a spine. We dared each other to jump over its body, to
touch its toothless mouth. We laced it around our necks and
pretended we were being strangled. My mother told us never
to turn on the Snake because we were in a drought: If we
spent too much water we'd get fined. But we thought if water
came from the sky it should be free. We socketed the Snake's
mouth into the holes and fed them water until they flooded.
The soil boiled into a stew around our ankles. When the water
was deep enough to hide a fist in, we danced in it. Grass spun
like compass needles on the water.

We let the water run until our mother was home. The

Snake's body was wiring water directly from the sea. We mistook our sweat for its salt. Laughing, we beckoned our mother out of the screen door and into the yard, her feet lighting the water like fish. She stepped into one of our holes and whipped forward into the water, landing on her belly. The mud made a fist and dove down her throat. She thrashed like something stolen from the deep and released into the shallows, gasping through the gill-slit of her mouth. We laughed, thinking she was performing as a fish. She wanted us to hook our fingers into her mouth and tug her free of the mud. Her limbs slashed the water, scarring its surface. When the water backlashed against her face, her chest, we realized she was drowning. Flipping her onto her back, we licked her face awake.

She stood up, her lips pared back from her teeth. I thought she would spit at the both of us, breaking her own rule to dirty us. Taking my hand, she looked at the dirt loitering under my nails, the soil packed into the lines of my palm. She said I'd gone too deep: Digging was surgery and I'd forgotten to numb the body. *Never bury anything,* she said, *unless you want the dead to spend it.* She began to tell me a story about the time her father buried gold in their yard in Arkansas, but I told her this was different: We weren't burying anything. We were doing the opposite: birthing. She stared out at the yard, the soup of our labor, the holes gulping water and breeding more of their mouths. I knew what she was reaching for before I could rename it: My brother and I had seen our father make the same movement, the Snake's throat necklaced by his hands.

My mother swung the Snake. I dodged its tin mouth, hot and hissing. She was the only one who could bring the Snake to life, loaning it her blood. The Snake missed my buttocks and rang against my shoulder-bone. My father liked to begin softly until our skins adjusted, and then he flung the Snake around like light, aiming to land on everything. If our father treated pain like a plural, our mother was singular. *Where is she?* my brother and I used to ask when she beached inside herself and didn't speak for hours, shoring somewhere she didn't know us. *In a memory,* I said. In another life, something had warned her away from water, and we had disbelieved her, filling the yard and reminding her lungs of their holes.

When the Snake reared its head and bit my lower back, above the crack of my ass, I went down on my knees. My brother was somewhere in the mud playing dead, pretending to be a belly-up fish.

She whipped the Snake through the air, lassoing it around the sun before lashing my back. Hunching to make a bunker of my bones, I prayed to swap skins with the water I stood in. She called me by her own name, beat herself out of me. I knew the words to arrest her hands: When I called her Ama, the Snake stopped flexing its spine. Its silver mouth had flung off and become the sun somewhere. *Ama,* I said again. My mother dropped the Snake and said, *That isn't me.* I said, *IknowIknowIknow.* Snaking my arms around her waist, I beached my lips on her belly button, kissed her hard as a fist. Named her my prey.

—

After she fed me to the Snake, there was a scab above my butt cheeks where the Snake's silver head nipped me. When I shoved the scab aside with my fingernails, there was a hole beneath, deep as my finger and bloodless as a glove socket. I slid my forefinger in, trying to diagnose what kind of hole it was. I named every hole-species I knew: wells; wombs; wounds; spots in the wall where my brother stuck his pencil through, thinking the walls would scab on their own, and when they didn't, he sealed them with his boogers and let them petrify into stone; lakes; seas, which meant most of the world was a hole, which meant I was native to holes, animal burrows, anuses, atlases. Twirling my finger inside the hole above my ass, I decided that it must be the beginning of a fault-line, a seismic shift of my spine.

I considered telling my mother, but she always said holes were dangerous and led only to disappearance. *They're the number-one leading cause of loss.* But I told her the holes in our yard were parallel to her throat, same depth and degree of darkness. *Consider them a tribute to you,* I said, the day after all the floodwater evaporated from the yard. But she watched them as if they were birth-holes, as if I were the midwife of some disaster. I watched her in the yard, checking them one by one like animal traps. When she began kicking soil back into the holes, I went outside to stop her, grabbing at her ankles.

She wriggled her foot away, sat down hard on the soil, and said: *Before digging a hole, you need to know whose hands you own. Your Ama,* she said, *has the stamina of a river when it comes to discipline.* She said she'd tried to be the mud, what hems the river in, but she couldn't redirect a woman like that.

Remember, she said. *I'm your mother,* she said, *but you made me first. You needed me first, and now I'm shaped like your thirst.* Standing by the kitchen window and looking out at the holes with me, she said I should be prepared for when

Ama comes in the night to eat our toes. *Where will she come from?* I said, and she pointed at the holes. I laughed and said no woman could fit through a hole that size. If Ama ever lumbered out like a tree, I said, we'd fell her together, cleave the woman from the tiger inside her. When I asked her for a practice axe, one I could learn to wield against Hu Gu Po, she refused. *You're my mother,* I said, *and you're supposed to prepare me for any future.*

But who, she said, *can prepare you for the past?*

The Walking Trees: An Oral Story in the Voice of My Mother

What I remember about Arkansas is the weather. Same as the island. We saved all that money to fly, and in the end we arrived at the place we left. It rained, rained our sweat. Our blood turned the color of mirrors and mosquitos mated with our skin. I could name every species of tree, copy the posture of their thirst. It was typhoon season when we left Yilan, and it was like the typhoon had saddled us, rode us here. Our farts took the form of wind and fled here. Arkansas was landlocked, the opposite of the island, but the weather here spoke the same sky. It was so humid, the air was white-haired with steam, and we were the ones being boiled of our knees. And the trees that grew there, they looked just like the trees in Yilan, big-hipped and knuckle-boned and mustached with birds. There's a story where I was born. About trees that could walk. At night, they stood up on their roots and left the earth. They walked through rivers, roped up all the water, and left them dry-mouthed. They walked to the city and kneeled into the cement, planted themselves on the street. They walked to the sea and hollowed them-

selves into canoes, slid away on their bellies. They walked and walked. And in the morning, the trees were never where you left them. They'd be lounging on their sides, or linking arms in a circle, or gone except for one. And my sisters and I, we went searching for the other trees. We went to all the neighbors and asked what they'd seen. But the trees, they went missing. Walked off. There were these holes in the ground where the roots used to be. They went deep, so deep my ba had to paint circles around the holes with pigblood to warn kids away, keep them from falling in. One time an ox walked into one of the treeholes and broke all its legs. Each leg was pointing in a different direction: at me, at the sea, at my sister, at the trees. My ba shot it with his army pistol. In the forehead, here, where my finger is. Here. Oxen aren't like pigs, they don't make a sound when they die. They just fall over. Like trees. My father drove the oxen so hard, they died of being tired. Just fell over in the fields in the middle of plowing a row. And there wasn't even any meat left on their bodies to eat. They were hip-bones and hide, a molar maybe. All we could eat were the eyes. And my sister said, I bet if we plant those eyes, we could grow a whole new ox. *But animals aren't like trees, they don't grow back. I learned that. In Arkansas, we were the only ones of our species. Some men carried a gun, but they weren't soldiers like Ba. They looked at us like we were broken-legged animals to shoot, not because they hated us but because they wanted to save us from the hole we'd fallen into. Every other family had a car or a truck, and they drove to buy food. And we, we walked. We walked miles and miles. We walked to the grocery store and bought our meat in cans and found out later it was cat food. Why do cats get their own kind of food? Why wasn't our hunger specified? It wasn't bad, the cat food. It didn't taste like anything. We stopped being able to taste after we landed. We weren't fluent in the flavors here. Our tongues receded, beached in the back of our throats, whaling, amputated at the name. We walked until our feet were fish-floppy. We walked like those oxen: to death.*

DAUGHTER

Hu Gu Po (III)

My mother was ready for work before the sky chose a color to dress in. Her latest job was at the foot spa, where the blacked-out windows were clotted with dust and the sign outside said: THE TREE DIES FROM THE ROOT—THE HUMAN AGES FROM THE FOOT!!!!! *I hate feet,* she said, buttoning her polo shirt with the logo of a footprint. *They look like skinned fish, dead in my hands. I just want to fillet them open and pick out their bones. When I oil a foot, I pretend I'm preparing to fry it alive.* She practiced her massages on me, submerging me to the ankles in a bucket of tap water, grating at my callused feet. She said every region of the sole corresponded with an organ inside my body: My head was the big toe, my lungs were my bunions, and my heart was in my heel, so I should watch what I stepped on.

Today the hole in my back birthed a sapling: stiff as my brother's morning wood, a kind of kindling. It was a tail, orange with black bangles, fur tangling in a syrup too thick to be blood and too thin to tar. It tasted of smoke. The tail was the length and width of my forearm, but it ached at the core, the way my bones did when they were outgrowing me and nearly breached skin. It was growing, pulsing like a gone-bad tooth. On the mattress we shared, my brother turned around and saw me wringing my tail like a neck, trying to strangle it with both fists. He laughed so hard his last baby tooth flew out and shot down the ceiling fan.

Telling me to stand up, my brother looked at the back of my pants, saying no one would really notice my tail unless they were looking for it, and no one would look at my flat ass even if it was on fire. I told him the tail wasn't the problem so much as the symptom: I was tigering. Hu Gu Po was the new governor of my bones. In the bathroom, I tugged the tail to remove it at the root, but the fur was too oily to grip. The tail must be breeding with my bones, seeding what would breach my skin next, claws or canines. Tomorrow my mother would ride me through the house, a daughter she smuggled into a hunter's body. *I told you not to dig those holes,* she'd say while petting my neck, spaying me with a pair of garden shears. *The only hole that's natural is the one you shit from.*

She told me to fear holes because of what might enter them, but I was more afraid of what would exit. Once, she lectured me for days on the importance of not letting men enter my room. *But there's one living in my room!* I said. My mother said that brothers weren't men until they were married, and my own brother would never get married because he wasn't allowed to love a woman more than his mother. *I heard that,* my brother said. *And I've already decided not to love anyone. That way it's fair for everyone.* The rest of her speech was this: Tampons are American propaganda. The string hangs out of you like a grenade pin. When you pull it out, a period of martial law begins in your body.

—

The next morning I was the same. Gowned inside a girl. My skin still my skin. Maybe I needed to wait to be shaped: My mother always said the moon wasn't whitened in a day. I meant to sew all the yard-holes closed, but they bred behind my back: I couldn't guess what was fucking them.

That night, I heard a humming in my sleep. A voice dislocating the dark. My tail humped the mattress and I made a fist around it, strangled it into silence. The humming sounded like my own, but when I rose, it led me away from myself.

It was early in the night and the sky was bad-breathed, freckled with stars like white bacteria on a tongue. Since growing my tail, my night-seeing had improved: My eyes homed to heat. I could always see the shapes of faces but never mouths. I could see the shapes of bodies but not their distance from me. I kneeled in the soil, skating my ear above one of the holes. It had my teeth. It was breathing bullets of heat. The hole whistled at me like a man. I got up from my knees. Flaring open like skirts, the holes mouthed words that hadn't yet given birth to their meanings. I looked inside the nearest one and slipped my hands into it. After a minute, the hole loosened around my wrist and gagged my fist back out. When the holes were silent again, steam stealing out of their lips, I went back into the house, following my hands like lanterns. They were clean to the wrist, no evidence of what they entered. In the morning, I told my brother about the holes and their breathing. He asked me to show him and we went together into the yard. *They smell so bad,* I said. *Because of the landfill,* my brother said. *Because they're bodies,* I said.

My brother bent to examine each of them, the deepest as long as our legs. In the center of the middle row, one of the holes was squared off and looked more like a window, like the word for mouth: 口

I prayed over it: *dear shangdi please flip my tail like a switch and turn me into a tiger or not I don't care just choose one. Make me my own species with no name for her hunger but hole no name for history but still happening.*

—

My mother never admitted to taking Duck Uncle's money, but this year all our bills were paid on time and he bought a new low-riding car that sharked down the street without stirring air. His restaurants now had three locations, each place with the same imitation-crystal chandeliers and red carpeting and suit-vested waiters and dim sum carts so brightly gilded you had to avert your eyes to order. My mother started waitressing part-time at his nearest location, and she collected tips in the waistband of her gold-trimmed pleather pants.

Between shifts, my mother wrote on the back of receipts, listing probable affairs my father was having: *His boss's new receptionist is a whore from the provinces. The woman who cleans his dorm is a whore from the provinces. The telephone operator is a whore from the provinces. He calls her every day, pretending to ask for a call transfer, and one day he professes his love, toll-free. Her voice turns into a dumb pigeon and collides into glass when it tries to fly into his bedroom. She dies and he marries the bloodstain on his window.*

On the phone with my father, my mother's voice deepened like a bowl, carrying its contents too far down to understand. *We went to the zoo today. Meimei saw a tiger for the first time and peed herself. Gege peed on his snow cone, put it down his pants, and ran through the aviary shouting FRESH PEE-PEE CONE! EAT IT FOR FREE.*

At the zoo with Duck Uncle, I recognized the tiger's ringed tail, exactly like the one I sheathed in my sleep. I slept with my tail on top of the sheets, afraid that if it touched my body it would contaminate me into a beast. I'd wake with my mother's severed foot in my mouth. I told my brother to be careful beside me: I'd hunt him in his sleep. *Protect your feet by duct-taping them to the mattress,* I said. *Count your toes in the morning.* I counted them aloud before he woke, not allowing myself to breathe or look for light in the room until there were ten. Every morning I said my hungers aloud, rehearsing for my future body: *Today I want to eat my mother. I will eat as much of her as fits in my belly, and then I will rebirth her. I will eat her into a new future.*

Duck Uncle packed three Tupperware containers of dim sum, shiu mai with peas crowning the meat, har gow straining out of their skins. We ate it all with our hands, sitting at a picnic table we'd elbowed a white family for, licking our fingers till they glowed. There was a feeding scheduled for the tiger exhibit, so we went back to watch the zookeeper attach the frozen steak to a thirty-foot pole. He extended the pole through the bars, past the empty moat beyond, and out toward the brown field and faux-stone cave. The tiger, napping on its side, didn't even look at the steak-pole waving its meat flag ten feet away.

My brother kicked the bars. The tiger slept. We kept watching even after everyone left to watch the seal feeding at three. We were the last ones to leave the tiger that day, the steak defrosted and growing a rind of rot. It stank, slotting its scent through the bars. We watched anyway, convinced that as long as we stayed, the tiger would wake the full width of its hunger, show us what was done in the wild. The steak would reverse into a cow and walk into the tiger's mouth. Instead, we drove home as evening opened its purple cape. Duck Uncle said, *In China, the tigers are real, not far away like that. You can pay a man to throw in a roped-up goat, and they'll let you watch up close from a bus.* The words *in China* stilled my mother's hands on the wheel, and she sped until the road beneath us was rain. In China, tigers were already extinct. There are no more breeding pairs in the wild.

Duck Uncle's restaurants closed during the recession. On TV, when I heard the word *recession,* I thought it meant the same thing as recess, when you were free of teachers who slid their rulers into your mouth and told you your accent was an inch off. But this recession did not mean free, unless free meant that no one could afford to pay. Duck Uncle's secret ingredient for his black sauce—fermented garlic—was stolen by another chain. He sold the rest of his recipes. By then, Duck Uncle didn't sleep, his neck thin enough to make a fist around it, his teeth indented from sleepwalking into his tree. Even his voice was less like a duck and more like the gun.

Prayer to Disappear a Tail: To Be Repeated Twice Nightly and Once in the Morning (Prior to Counting Every Toe in the Household)

dear shangdi dear papakwaka please let my skin rescind all scars all tails let my teeth be benign as butterflies let my tail be a fuse if I light it the fire deletes me dear papakwaka if you are the mountain that mothered us all like my ama says please let

me not become her   hu gu po please let the world be extinct
of children so I will have nothing to eat but myself dear
papakwaka dear ancestors who took up spears toothpicked
the dutch like fancy finger food who bombed back the qing
dynasty with bags of farts who turned all japanese soldiers
into beads with holes in their bellies please open my tail like
an umbrella build me for protection not for prey keep
buffering from girl from girl from girl from girl to   please
stop stalling   if I have to transform let my new species be
a window a bar of herbal soap   my mother's thumb in my
ear   dear papakwaka   I know this story   is outside
your language but is hu gu po born one limb at a time or all
at once which part of her   am I already o papakwaka
mountain teat   mouth of us all   please don't
strand my body   outside its myth

—

Before he left, we ate at the largest of Duck Uncle's restaurants, an hour away in a mall that sold fake phones and sour
plums. Duck Uncle told us the rules before we went in through
the glazed double doors: *No spitting anything out, even if*
you're choking on it. No swallowing your noodles whole and
then pulling them back out through your nose. No removing
any item of your clothing at the table. No disturbances. The
red carpet made my eyes runny and the plastic chandelier
hung so low we ducked for it. Dozens of dim sum carts spun
in a carousel around the room. My brother and I pointed at
everything that swept by, the table so crowded we ate fast to
keep it from collapsing.

I filled my cheeks with boiled peanuts, then spat them at
my brother's head. *You broke the rules,* my mother said, while

pinching my lips shut with her fingers. Duck Uncle said he'd feed us so well that we'd beg for bigger mouths. I tasted blood but didn't know what dish it was coming from.

At the end of the meal, Duck Uncle said he'd been waiting to surprise us. *I made an investment,* he said. He signaled for the waiter, who nodded and walked back into the kitchen. Four waiters wheeled out a fish tank. The tank was at least as tall as me, the water a dyed-blue that was almost opaque. There was nothing inside the tank except for a floating red ribbon, flickering. *A dragonfish,* my mother said, and when I leaned closer to the glass I saw that it was a fish, that the ribbon spooled and unspooled on its own, an eye sewn on like a bead.

It costs 10,000 dollars, Duck Uncle said, *but I got it for half that.* I'd heard of dragonfish in big hotels on the mainland, where my father had gone. They were smuggled out of rivers. The shinier their scales, the more luck it would deliver its owner. The dragonfish was the length of my arm, whipping from one end of the tank to the other.

After Duck Uncle went bankrupt in the recession, he returned the fish tank. He bagged the dragonfish and took it home, releasing it into his toilet. Said he'd flush it back out to the sea, but we knew the salt would kill it. My brother and I scooped it out of his toilet with a bucket and slid it into our filled kitchen sink, watching it try to lasso itself.

Let's sell it for 10,000 dollars, my brother said. My mother said the fish was a fake. She'd known it wasn't real the moment the light hit it: The scales were painted on, probably with nail polish. She butchered it the night he left, scraping the shell of pigment from its skin, and then we could see its real scales underneath, a color like smog.

The night before Duck Uncle left, we saw my mother straddling the stump of the eucalyptus tree she'd felled in his yard. She said the stars were fish. *But they're not moving,* we said. *Because they want to be caught,* my mother said. She raised her hook-finger to the sky and we waited all night for it to lure something. Near morning, a plane came to unzip the dark. It flew low, tailing light. *It's on fire,* I said, and thought of Duck Uncle inside it. If we slit open the plane's belly like a fish, he would spill out all shiny and scarfed in guts. I thought it was unfair that she was the only one being the bait, so I stuck my tongue out at the sky and wriggled it like a worm, luring all the lost.

DAUGHTER

Hu Gu Po (IV)

The cost of being fatherless: Shut off notices from the water company (hang up, bathe with baking soda). Shut off notices from the electricity company (ignore: the house will starve itself dark). No exterminator (kill the ants with duct tape, termites with vinegar, rats with our hands). No calls from my father for two weeks, then months, then the trees started growing new beards. The fall my father stopped sending money or answering calls, my mother bought us plane tickets to the mainland, said she'd either bring him home or kill him there: She hadn't decided which would punish him more.

We got our passport photos taken in the living room of a Shanghainese man my father once bribed for a faster visa. The man told me to show my ears in the photo, tucking my hair back with one broad thumb. His hands were like my father's: bruised nailbeds, knuckles loose as screws. I felt guilty for summoning my father through some other man's body.

We packed in the dark, my mother cursing my father's cousins, their factory, my father, who must be dead, my father, who must have forgotten us, my father, who hadn't called back, my father, who must have fished himself another family, another woman whose knees he prayed between. My brother begged her to turn on the lights, but she didn't want us to see her face, its increasing resemblance to fear. I pretended we lived underground and had lightbulb-heads and were packing for our first trip to the surface. On the plane, I slept with my head leaning against my mother's and woke with the sun running like a yolk across the window. Buildings toothpicked the sky. It was so humid I could gargle the air and spit it. In our hotel room, my brother and I slept on the floor, my mother on the skin-colored bed. The sheets were so thin they let light into our dreams. Our shadows sharked across the floor. The first night in Jiangsu, I dreamed my mother was kneeling over me, one of her hands balled inside my mouth and the other pressed over my nose, caging my breath in my chest. I woke believing that my tongue had dried into a cricket and leapt out of my mouth, and I crawled to every dust-clotted corner of the room searching for it.

In the morning, we took a taxi to the brim of the city, where my father and his two cousins managed the slot-machine factory. Clouds mopping up the sky's spilled light. We drove down a half-paved street with apartment buildings so tall I thought they'd been built from the sky down. My father was the rain that day. We watched from the taxi as my mother entered each apartment building on the street, repeating my father's name until someone told us he had left. The slot-machine manufacturer had halted production months ago, and most of the workers had been deported from the city

at night, carrying nothing but their teeth. They guessed my
father had gone home to the city where he was born, a city
west of every named body of water.

We took the overnight train to Anhui. My brother and I
wanted to go home, our boogers black after two hours of
walking outside and breathing. We asked why the boys who
begged outside the hotels all had the same parts of their bodies missing: a left hand or both feet or tongues. I mistook this
for kinship, believing that somehow all the boys without feet
found one another by holding up their hurts and pairing their
pains. But my mother told me it was because gangs would
buy children and injure them the same way, assembling them
in teams to go out and earn pity with their new bodies. They
knocked on the windows of taxis until the drivers cursed
them away.

My mother gave them nothing. She shut the door on one
of the boys' fingers, his hand purpling in the hinge. His fin-
gernail fell off and landed in her lap and my mother flicked it
away. I plucked it from the seat crack and tossed it out the
window like a coin I could wish with. My mother slapped my
hand and said not to touch those boys' fingernails because
they were dirty and we didn't know what they'd been touching. I reminded her that she touched feet for a living; toenails
were her terrain. She gripped my pinky and yanked the nail
clean off its bed of skin, so fast I didn't bleed, the pain a bright
bead, rolling back and forth on my tongue until I couldn't
taste anything else. *Don't compare us to them,* she said. When
another of the boys wedged his wrist through the window slit
and offered his palm, my mother spat in it.

—

We found my father in a top-floor apartment, where my mother knocked on the door so long her knuckles split one by one. He answered. It was blue-hot in the apartment, and my father was bare-legged: I'd never before seen his kneecaps, the hair on his thighs.

When he saw my mother, he stepped back. In his right hand, an apple lit up without its skin. My mother gripped our shoulders, herding our bodies in front of hers, shifting us into the light that swung from the ceiling bulb. This was why she'd brought us along: to say *Look what you've left me with.*

My father ate his apple, saying he'd get a new job soon. Said, *The mainland's where the gods are still giving. America has retired on us.* My mother said he was cursed: Every country was another one he couldn't afford. She told him to come home. He told us we shouldn't have come. The apple brightened his teeth. Sweat sequined his upper lip. He told my mother to come into the bedroom and locked her in it, then took turns whipping my brother and me as we balled on the sofa. He used a spoon, the cord of a lamp, his sweat-stiffened shirt. It was as much my mother's punishment as it was ours. My brother's head knocked against mine as we rolled toward and away from each other. His skull sounded hollow, mine full of water. To distract myself, I churned my tongue in my mouth, tasting my blood in real time.

My mother, locked in the bedroom, begged to be let out. Said, *We thought you were dead. We thought you were dead. You were dead.* My mother always said that speaking a prayer out loud would keep it from coming true, that a voice cancels out its listener. By speaking his death, she was keeping him alive. When my father finished, he cried into my neck. His apple, half-eaten, was a bright pulp on the floor. He always said that it hurt him to hurt us, that each of our bruises cast a body-sized shadow behind him. My brother threw up over the rail of the balcony, a comet in his belly. The blood in the vomit was bright as confetti.

———

On the rooftop of my father's building, you could see an amusement park with an imitation Great Wall. It was spine-shaped. My brother paced one side while my father sat me on his lap, saying this was the perfect place to fly a kite. He showed me the railing that had retired to rust, a place where I could tie several kite-strings at once. He asked me to stay with him. I could live with him while my mother and brother went home, back to the country where I was without a name. He told me he was learning to cook, showed me the scars on his forearms where he'd tossed oil out of the pan and onto himself. When I didn't speak, he showed me the edge of the roof and tested me, pointing at faraway things and asking for their names in Mandarin: *Sky. Cloud. Bird. Car. Crosswalk. Airplane. Night. Child.* Then he pointed at himself. *Man,* I said. He cinched his fist around my wrist, and I felt the bones rub like flint, starting a fire under my skin. *No,* he said. *Father.*

He made me repeat it until night. When we returned to his apartment, my father unlocked my mother from the bedroom and tucked us in with her, arranging us on the bed that smelled of him, tugging the sheet over our heads as if shrouding us. I pretended the sheets were made of water and we were treading the bed together, that we were somewhere where sound was a stone, swallowed and sunk.

Back when he was a boy in Texas, my father taught himself to swim in a public pool where white kids thickened the deep end and played Marco Polo, their swim trunks in pri-

mary colors, their striped and patterned towels laid out like
the flags of foreign countries. My father began in the shallow-
est end, where even babies could float without their parents.
Even on his back, the water folded over him like a sheet,
dragged him deep. He gave up on floating, decided he would
learn to swim with his belly skimming the pool floor, like
those bottom-feeding fish that lived on their sides. My father
trained himself to hold his breath in the bath at home, filling
a vegetable tub in the kitchen tap and then mixing it with the
shower's rationed hot water. He planted his head in the water,
felt it finger his mouth open. The first time, he swallowed half
the water and spat out the rest. He practiced until his throat
and nostrils hinged shut. The next time he went to the pool,
he could sit at the bottom of the pool for hours at a time, pretending he was one of those monks that sat under a waterfall,
unlearning pain. The next time, he swam.

He snaked along the floor into the deep end, weaving between legs with his eyes shut. He slithered between calves,
nose-bumped someone's ankle. Up on the surface, someone
said, *My god, there's something down here,* and the pool was
evacuated by the lifeguard, who mistook my father's sub-
merged body for some kind of escaped reptile.

Years ago in California, my father taught us to swim this
way: He plugged the sink with a cucumber, filled it to the
brim, pushed both our heads in. I heard my brother exhale
underwater, his lungs orphaning their air, my tongue swell-
ing into a mouth-plug. When we struggled, he pushed our
heads in deeper, one hand holding my brother's wrists behind his back, his weaker hand holding mine. My brother
buckled first, dropped to his knees, water ribboning out of his
lungs. I buried my breath deeper in my belly. When I finally
came up, my wrists were free. My father stood behind me, my

brother kneeling beside him, wet from the neck up. I kneeled beside my brother. *Longer next time,* my father said. *The longer you can hold it, the farther you'll go.* He twisted a kitchen towel into a rope, wet it in the sink, whipped us until it was dry.

—

The night bruised its kneecap moon. My brother woke up and saw a white kite leaning on the wall beside the bed. My father had left it there for me, so that I'd wake and see it before light: the kite he'd packed and brought all the way from California. Maybe he thought it would remind me of when we flew together, or maybe he thought I'd mistake the wingspan of white paper for a ghost and leave sooner. When my brother saw the kite there, he tore it apart. He snapped the frame made of disposable chopsticks. *Stop, please stop,* I said, and ran forward to save what I could, which was nothing. I crouched on the carpeted floor and brushed the kite-confetti into a neat pile at my knees. Above me, my brother's breath was backfiring, unable to leave his lungs.

I asked my brother why, looking up at his shadow-battered face. My brother didn't answer. He just said, *Why did he bring that here?* I wanted to tell him, *Because he missed me and not you. Because he knows that I can fly, too.* But instead, I bent and plucked paper from between the floorboards. I didn't want my father to find the pieces and think it was me.

Go back to bed, I said, but my brother just looked at me. The apartment was still black, but the sky outside was beginning to dull into a dime-colored day.

Our father now stood in the bedroom doorway. He was relaxed, his hands loose at his sides, and I wanted to tell him we could go to the roof. We could saddle the sky with our kites. His eyes focused on the wall behind us. The bald spot where the kite had been. My father looked at me first, then at my brother. My brother, trembling now, backed into his own shadow. I spoke to wedge my words between them: *I broke the kite. It was me.* I reached into my pockets and made a fist around the pieces, brought them out into the light. The paper scattered from my hands, snowing between my fingers.

I told my father I tore the kite up, that I was still upset that he wasn't coming home and couldn't bear to see anything his hands had made. My mother woke, stirring the sheets on the bed. She saw all three of us in the far corner of the room, my father putting his hands on my brother's shoulders, telling him to kneel. *Pick it up,* he said, pointing to the pieces.

My brother bent his knees halfway but stopped. I could see him straining to be straight. He said no. My mother got up from the bed, palms up as if she were coming to pet us. Her mouth pleated quiet. I kept saying *I did it, I did it, it was me,* but my father didn't look at me.

My brother dropped his knees to the ground. I heard their bones. My brother's upper lip was wet; what I thought was his shadow was sweat. My brother bent his head to the floor like in prayer as the room was delivered into daylight. He pressed his tongue to a petal of paper on the ground. I imagined it dissolving like a wafer, but it stayed there, pinned and wet. My brother lifted his head. Stood up and spat. We heard it land: a glob of spit hitting my father's cheek. My mother reached up to touch her own face.

My father fisted my brother's blue shirt and tried to lift him. But my brother jerked away. He was always bird-boned, so light inside my father's hands, planning flight. He ran for the door, through the hallway, then up the stairs to the roof.

I'd later ask why he ran up instead of down, but he told me nothing.

It was dark in the stairway, like turning the night back on, but we all followed after him. We scattered on the square rooftop, big as a parking lot, where wet lines of laundry hung heavy and dank as meat. Someone had burned something recently and the air was full of gossiping smoke. There was a chicken coop in the center of the roof, made of plywood and plastic wrap, and the two hens inside looked dead. My brother was standing at the edge, where the rooftop ended. Where the railing buckled its shadow around his waist.

I was the one who got the closest. My thumb snagged the belt loop at the back of my brother's jeans, but he had already climbed over the railing, the rust sloughing off on his hands. I came close enough to see that. He didn't jump so much as sprint past the sky. He didn't fall through the air so much as become it. Then my father was behind me, lifting me by my hair, saying *Come back from there, come back.* I didn't know if he was talking to my brother or me. My mother had not moved since we got to the roof. She was a statue of salt, solidified by my eyes, but I saw she was speaking something, willing his wings.

The building was at least a hundred stories, and when we first saw it from the window of the taxi, my brother said, *It's like a big boner. A big boner in the sky.* I told him to shut up, it was not, it was beautiful, with rows and rows of windows opening like eyes. *Wouldn't you want to live somewhere like that,* I asked him. *The whole world in your window.* My brother said, *No, I'll never live where he lives.*

Now the building was not tall enough. I needed it to never end, for the ground to be as far back as history. My mother, the one who watched, would tell the story better: She would say my father loved kites so much he became one, that my brother borrowed new bones. We both watched my father follow my brother as if tethered, yanked along, tied ankle-to-ankle by a kite-string. I grabbed at his ankle, but the weight of his want was too much for me.

When my brother was halfway down and my father a breath above him, their bodies began to rise. They plateaued in the air, horizontal like kites, and flapped in the wind before riding it upward and out, blade-arcing through the air. My brother breached a cloud, rising up past the roof where my mother and I stood, our hands on the railing, our mouths round as sirens.

My father snagged a different wind and flailed in place, hovering halfway between the roof and the street. Then he banked left, looping once around the building and rising. The smog smudged his body out of the sky, and for a second my mother and I forgot they were men. We watched them, two kites riding the air. My mother watched kite-fighting when she was little, the way the strings were coated in powdered glass so that they could cut each other. The losing kites were severed from their tethers, returning to the earth as ash.

My father and brother carried the sky on their backs. They tilted toward each other, circling, and from the ground it might have looked like they were fighting or dancing. Kite-strings unraveled from their underbellies, descending like strands of spun silk. The strings dangled in the air, clear as braids of rain. My mother and I held out our hands and grasped them by the leash, angling our wrists to rhyme them with the wind, coaxing them toward the pecked-out sun, steering them where we couldn't follow.

—

My brother landed first. We waited on the roof for hours, our necks gone soft from watching the sky. It was midday when he came down. He hovered above the roof, and then the wind handed him down to us. He landed hard on his belly and scraped his chin. The scabs would later look like the shadow of a beard.

We watched my father glide in and out of sight, his limbs spread as he starfished in the sky. We didn't wait for him to come down. We left him in midair, retreating from the roof, my brother's chin bleeding into his palm. My mother stepped onto the street and flagged a taxi. Through the window, I watched the sky. The building wagged like a finger. I tried to see if my father was still somewhere in the sky above it, but all the bodies I counted were birds.

—

When my father finally came back to California, it wasn't on wings. It was through the window. He'd lost his key somewhere over the Pacific, and none of us heard his fist frightening the door off its hinges. It was almost day when he decided to break the only street-facing window, glass fluttering down in gowns. He left his shoes on the lawn and he swung through the window, landing on the carpet inside. The shards shucked the skin off his feet. He went to our room first, the bedroom walls furring with so many flies I always woke with my mouth full of their eggs. My brother wet our mattress nightly, dreaming he was a gardener hosing down a field of flowers thorned with tongues, all of them licking his penis till it bled.

When my mother heard a man in our room, she swiped the vase off her bedside table and ran to us. Boxed into the doorway of our bedroom, with her bathrobe fanned open like pale wings, she was more of a moth than our mother. He turned to her. She threw the vase at him and it shattered on the far wall, glass salting the carpet. Later, she claimed she hadn't seen his face. She thought he was a predator come to skin us in our sleep. When the vase missed him, it struck her own shadow off the wall. We waited to clean the glass in the daylight, all of us on our knees, weeding for glass. I plucked up a piece and my thumb cut open, dripping an ellipses of blood on the carpet that didn't end for days, not even when my mother slathered mud on it and sucked it bloodless and knotted a string at the base of my thumb.

Our father hierarchized the house: his dishes in the sink stacked on top of ours, his slippers lined up closest to the door, his place at the table facing the window, ours facing the walls. In my sleep, I sucked my thumbs to the bone, and now my father glazed them in gingerroot to sting my mouth awake. *If it hurts, it's helping,* he said. The pool hall where he once played every Saturday was now a park with platter-sized ponds and overfed ducks building their nests in water fountains. Whenever we went, he told me not to touch the ducks. *The mother will smell that the child's been touched by another animal, and then she won't want to feed it anymore.* When I asked why, he said that touch is territory. A hand is owned by what it holds. A hand is a whole country. Before bed, I touched my armpit, my ass-crack, my peanut-toes, my tail. The belly button that was pecked into my skin by a bird. I touched them all twice. Named each part of me a citizen of the night.

—

The first week my father was home, my tail grew a bone of its own. A bruise trellised up my spine. At night, my mother fol-

lowed him into the man-made dark of his room—he taped
butcher paper on all the windows because perverts could be
watching. At night: the sound of her jaw locking up her teeth.
That wasn't the sound I turned my head from: It was the symmetry of my father's silence, the way sex didn't sound like
two bodies added together but the subtraction of one from
the other.

At night, I consulted the cookie tin in the closet, my ears
magnetized to the toes rattling inside. The toes were butting
over territory, acting like they belonged to enemy bodies. I
knocked on the lid with my fist and they fired out, bulleting
through the lid. One of them flew in and out of my mouth,
threading my spit, teasing my teeth to bite it.

Before my father came home, my mother spent her nights
with me. We watched episodes of *Desperate Housewives* on
the sofa that rose like a loaf of bread when it met our body
heat. I dubbed the dialogue in Chinese and my mother spat
five-spice peanuts at all the blondes onscreen. I asked her
which of the wives she'd want to marry and she said Gaby:
She wore cheetah-print, meaning she must be related to Hu
Gu Po. A shared history of hunger.

At night, my dreams collaged the plots of *Desperate
Housewives* and Hu Gu Po: In this one, Gaby and her landscaper make love in the master bedroom while Gaby's husband is away at work. But the landscaper's penis grows a
crown of canine teeth when he's inside her, his palms serrat-
ing into paws. Gaby hemorrhages and dies. The landscaper
tries to swallow his paws, but it's too late. Her husband comes
home and discovers a tiger pacing his master bedroom, trying to nudge the window open with its muzzle. On the floor
is his wife, a lawn mower circling her body, scalping away the
carpet. When I recounted this dream to my mother, she de-

leted every recorded episode. We'd liked Gaby because she was the only wife with our hair. She had the biggest closet, bigger than our bedroom. There was a crack in the TV screen letting the light out of every scene, striping the image on-screen, queering her face into mine. I wanted to surf Gaby's skin with my tongue, stroke her sweat until it lifted from her skin, wings of crystallized salt. Instead, I licked the screen when her face came on, tasted my blood on her teeth.

—

I knew a story: In some dynasty, when a father was sick, a daughter cut a piece of her own thigh to stir-fry and feed back to her father. Some daughters even donated their knees. Gegu: to cure what came before you. My father pinched the meat above my knee and said: *If I was ever sick, would you give me this?* He said he'd need that piece of me. It was the second day he was home and we were in the kitchen. My father spent hours filling the sink and then draining it, scribbling his name on the surface. I told him the water would never remember it. He stepped back, palming his rib cage, pretending to cough out his own fist.

I'm dying, he said, performing a wound in his side, and instead of offering my bare calf, I ran from the kitchen and into the living room, left him to paddle around in his own pretend blood. Between my buttocks, my tail burned like a fuse, heat clawing up to the root, a pain pinned to my lower back. I bent forward, hunching until my palms were pressed to the hardwood and I was on all fours, my tail flicking between my legs. I could hear my father in the kitchen behind me, standing with his back to me, and I got to my feet, watched the back of his neck where his veins were alive as snakes. My mother once told me that snakes were the severed fingers of a god who lived on the moon, a god who snipped off her own fingers and littered them on earth as self-punishment for trying to steal the sun. Every snake, I thought, must be roaming for blood, seeking the hand it was severed from. When I looked at my father, my tail unfurled like a whip and patrolled the air, licking my legs forward. It butted between my knees and sang and begged: *Fasten my maw to his neck, unspool his veins with my teeth. Bury his hands in the yard for pickpocketing my mother from me.*

Instead, I considered how best to cook my knees and cure him. His blood may have been made of snakes, but saving him was still my story. When he turned around and saw me kneading my knees, crouching low enough to tongue my shadow off the floor, he smiled and asked if I was praying. Tired-lines gathered in a stanza above his eyebrows. Sweat sheening his skin like an oil spill. In the back of his mouth, his molars were silver-capped, cupping the light inside them, and I looked away. Remembered how he once untangled my kite-string when it got noosed around a tree: He told me that cutting the line wouldn't save the kite. It would only flee me. So he climbed the tree instead, unsnagging the string from the bark until I could finally tug it back, easing the kite out of the sky's fist.

Running to the bathroom, I sat on the toilet and let my tail dangle into the bowl, its ache receding as the water stroked it. In the mirror above the sink, a shadow striped my face into halves, and my tail curled around my thigh like a hand, choking me above the knee. It wouldn't release my leg until I promised to let it hunt for me, hurt for me.

DAUGHTER

Bestiary

My brother and the other older boys swung their bats at the crows that clotted the sky and clung to the backstop fence. I watched the game every day and walked in circles around the baseball field, measuring the radius of my appetite, daring the sunlight to lash my skin into stripes. My tail would learn like a lightning rod, absorbing the heat of those boys' hands, and then it would detach into a baseball bat. Belong in my hands as a weapon. Today, one of the crows gripped the side of the batting cage with one foot, its left wing pimpled and pink. Neck plucked clean as my pinky. One of the boys pivoted to swing. The crow shivered and groomed itself, the sun mirrored on its one good wing. Standing on the sidelines, I shouted to warn it away from the fence.

But the bat struck too fast and the crow crumpled like a fist, dented the dirt. The boy twirled his bat like a baton and ran a lap around the bases, wiping the blood off on home plate. My tail ticked back and forth across the border of my spine, synced with my pulse, eager to intervene. To bound into the diamond and eat the boys, their severed feet flopping alive in the field, flaccid as fish. The teachers would have to burn the corpses and call my mother, who'd strap me to a pole by my limbs and harvest me for my marrow, distill me to tigerwine. I turned away, willed myself still.

When the sky bruised into night, I turned back and saw the crow splayed on its back in the dirt, flat as its shadow. Someone had erected a fence of feathers around the crow, enforcing a perimeter around the body.

It was Ben, Ben of the blacktop tarring our knees, Ben of the drought-drugged city, Ben of the monkey bars where she swung like a bell, Ben of the bowl-haircut, Ben of the sun that puckered above us like an asshole. It was the girl from Ningxia, the one who'd come halfway through the year and could spit a watermelon seed so far it skipped the sea and planted in another country. She came out of the batting cage wearing a helmet. In her palm, a perched plum. She bit it to bone, spat the pit at my feet. It was a fossil I'd unbury later, dating it back to today: the birth of my thirst. In her other hand, she held a feather like an unsheathed knife. She had what my mother would call radish ankles, thick-boned and dirt-coated, as if she'd been yanked from the soil in the last hour, birthed into the air by her hair. Beneath my skirt, my tail moved like a compass hand and tautened in her direction. I shut my legs so she wouldn't see.

When she took off her baseball helmet, her short hair was glazed to her neck with sweat. Her eyebrows were so straight they hyphenated her forehead, and I wanted to draw a line with my finger to connect them. I did the math: She was 1.5 shades lighter than me and two inches closer to the sun. One of her eyes was single-creased and the other double-creased, what my mother called dragon-phoenix eyes: One eye saw everything farther away than it was, and the other saw everything close-up. I was both far across the field and close enough to be baked by her breath. I wanted to be what she saw of me: many-bodied, standing everywhere like a field, so that at every moment, every step, she arrived at me.

Ben squatted in the sand and her skirt rose sunward. I looked at the cursive of hair on her calves, then at my own blank skin. She speared more feathers around the crow's body. When I asked her what she was trying to do, she said, *Keeping the sun out of its wound.* I told her it was dead already and she said, 再看一遍.

I looked at Ben's shadow, trying to avoid looking directly at her face, at the four moles traversing up her chin to her lower lip. Around her neck, Ben wore a chain with something silver dangling. The pendant ducked down under the neckline of her shirt, and my eyes kept trying to breach that border.

The bird between us was missing feathers, blood moating around it, its heart lying beside its body. I looked for a wound in the crow's breast, a hole from which the heart had popped out like a button, but there was none. The heart in the sand was the size of my thumb and beating itself blue. I didn't know a heart could beat outside of its body, but Ben didn't seem surprised. We watched it pump nothing, its skin crimping, the force of each beat rolling the heart farther away from the body.

Ben kneeled close. I thought she might lick it up from the sand and swallow it. Instead she said, *We have to put it back inside.* I asked her how: There wasn't any hole to nudge it into. She said, *We'll feed it back to her.* Her fingers were already unhinging the beak. Plucking the heart with my thumb and forefinger, I rolled it between my fingers, a berry of blood, sun-spoiled. Ben told me to hurry up, the bird was open, so I wedged the berry-heart between the blades of its beak. We waited for it to wake. The crow jerked in the sand, gagging once before the heart descended into its dark. Ben cupped it in her hands and walked to the sycamore in front of the trailers where we sat for class. But the bird was trying to open its wings like switchblades, lashing at her hands, and she had to let go before we reached the tree. The crow flew backward, tailfirst instead of headfirst: Ben must have been rewinding the sky like a TV screen, playing its flight in reverse.

That was the first day we walked home together. Ben lived on the other limb of the city where there was no landfill, where there were still empty lots and fields for sale. Our city was in a permanent state of puberty, new buildings and schools and parks and landfills peaking like pimples before fading flat again, the streets scarred by their shadows. I didn't tell her I was south of where I was supposed to be. I was supposed to be home and not on the sidewalk where our shadows touched shoulder-bones. Around her neck, the pendant swung loose and she tucked it back inside her shirt. While she walked, I thought about stealing it, jerking the pendant off its string and sucking it till my mouth silvered. I wanted to own something the same temperature as her skin, a talisman of her touch.

Every block I stopped to look at her. She wore the cityscape like a crown, the buildings sprung from her skull. When we got to the end of the block, Ben squatted to the pavement. She coughed and sand trumpeted out of her mouth, spraying the sidewalk gold. When she stood up, I asked if she'd swallowed sand from the baseball diamond. Laughing, she shook her head and said there was a sandstorm inside her belly, and once in a while the sand passed through her bowels and scoured her insides clean as glass.

Ben told me about the weather in which she was fermented: *I was conceived during a sandstorm,* she said. In Ningxia where she was born, sand formed a pelt over the sky and no one could see for months. They wore wet scarves around their mouths and the sand flayed away their front teeth, their eyelashes. I asked her how she'd known who was who, and Ben answered by closing her eyes and reaching out both arms. *We walk like this.* She kneaded my cheek, inventing dimples. Her touch could name me better than language. I wanted to say I understood about the sand in her belly: There was also a hunger in me that was more than a body's.

Do you think we'll get sick, I said, *from touching those feathers?* In the beginning of the year, when the TV repeated warnings of the Asian bird flu, the teachers had shown up to school wearing face masks with whirring fans. *There are so many of you here, we don't want to get sick.* Species could share diseases, they told us, and SARS came from bats and other winged things. When birds and people get too close, they said, one of them gets sick.

Ben said she was immune to the bird flu. Her grandmother had died from it and she had been exposed, which meant I was exposed now too. She said I could run away if I wanted to, but instead I stayed and asked her what the symptoms were.

It began slow, she told me: First you grew feathers out of your armpits. It would be itchy. Then your lips protruded into a beak and you would only be able to eat sand, seeds, and fingernails. The last symptom was flight. It was safer for your

close family members to release you where there was only
sky, no telephone wires to get electrocuted on, no windows to
mistake for mothers.

At a crosswalk, I looked at her before the lights changed.
Ben wore her FOB dot on the upper right arm, a vaccine scar
the size and shape of my thumbprint. The scar opaled her
skin, changing shades depending on the time of day, the season, and where she stood in relation to light. My mother had
one too, on her left arm, and I liked the way it puckered like a
nipple when it was cold. My mother's FOB dot was lake-
shaped, waiting to be entered. I wanted one too, wanted to dig
the scar out of Ben's arm and swallow its pearl.

We stopped on the sidewalk between an acupuncture
clinic and a seafood store with a sign that said it was selling
shrimp that you had to fish yourself from a kiddie pool. Ben
nodded up at an apartment building that had been painted
white and was now yellowing like teeth. She went up the
stairs without looking at me, her hand skimming rust off the
railing. Halfway up, she turned to look down at me. *My grandmother,* she said from above, *is not really dead.* Her grandmother, I'd later learn, was in Ningxia raising camels to scam
tourists, charging a hundred dollars per ride. Her family
sounded as slant-teethed as mine. I thought of all the stories
I could tell her about my own grandmother, my ama who
owned a severed head and could stitch a chicken's head back
on with a sewing machine. Ben would know how to tilt my
words, listen to them at an angle. Her teeth came out only at
night, like the stars, and her smile stung like a fistful of salt
flung at your eyes.

It took me two hours to walk home by myself. The city
described itself differently in the dark, the streets liquefying
beneath me. I got lost and circled my own house twice before

recognizing my mother's head in the kitchen window. My mother asked if I knew there were men in the world. *Yes,* I said, and went to bed before she could describe all my deaths. In the dark, I allowed myself to remember Ben's face, her breath like a moth beating my cheek. I wanted to lick the back of her sun-mothered neck. In the dark, I could touch myself anywhere and pretend my hand was her hand. I could pretend my sounds were coming from outside, originating with the owls.

The next morning, before I tucked my tail into my underwear, I let it rest in my hand like a hilt. It looked different to me, honed, whittled around its bone. Ben came to school early, leaning against the backstop to wait for me. She said hello in a dialect I didn't know and I answered in English. I bent to drink from the water fountain in the dugout, swallowing slow so she'd have to watch me, water collecting in the fountain like a birdbath, my tongue flitting in and out of the stream.

We spent every day with our shoulder blades unsheathed, our T-shirts knotted up to show our belly buttons, our elbows rubbing like flint when we walked down the hallways side by side, skin sparked with tanbark-burns from wrestling on the playground. We licked each other down to wicks. We ditched ESL together. In history class, instead of memorizing the order of the presidents, we played fuck/marry/kill with the Founding Fathers and decided to kill all of them. We squatted in the baseball diamond and read books below our recommended age level. The Madeline books were my favorite because I liked to pretend I was a French orphan who ate bread and butter for breakfast in a cathedral full of fatherless girls, where the only boy owned a guillotine. I told Ben I related to the guillotine the most: I, too, was a direct descendant of gravity, born from women who belonged inside their countries the way blades belonged inside a body. The Madeline girls all wore black bows in their hair, so I tied one in mine, though it was the same color as my hair and therefore invisible.

In the first book, Madeline falls into a river and gets saved by a dog. She adopts the dog and names her Genevieve. My mother looked at the pictures in every book I hid behind the toilet at home, tearing out pages she said I was too young to understand. For example, she said, I was too young to know what a river means, what shape it can slur into. She tore out the page where Genevieve saves Madeline from the water, gripping the girl's neck in her mouth: It was the scene I reenacted with Ben on the playground. She flailed on her back in the gravel, pretending to drown, while I flipped her over and nipped her sweat-plated neck, my teeth tenderizing the bone there. I dragged her to the tanbark shore, panting through my nose, feeling her pulse ripen sweet in my mouth as a pear.

Ben's favorite books were paperback romances she stole from the teacher's purse, but she pronounced *breast* like *beast* and neither of us understood how a nipple could be pink, unless it was raw or diseased: *Like pink eye,* I said. *Pink nipple. It's contagious.* We both swore never to rub our nipples after reading, in case we exhibited symptoms of salmonella. We guessed that the women in these books had not been properly cooked inside their mothers before birth.

Our teacher told us grammar was the god of language, but Ben was her own deity. We only listened to the assistant teacher, Mrs. Kersaint, who was Haitian and taught us songs in French and Creole and let us stripe our arms with chalk instead of copying sentences for a full hour. Mrs. Kersaint wrote our lessons in red marker on the birdshit-stained window instead of on the blackboard. She said we should always face outside, learn in the direction of the trees. Ben and I asked her all of our questions: Why is water both a noun and a verb? How do we know what tense we're in? What counts as a pronoun? In our dialects, all pronouns shared the same sound. A tree and a girl were summoned the same way. In this language, Mrs. Kersaint said, trees are assigned to different countries, bodies to different ways of being buried.

We got in trouble with the other teacher for never using plurals. When I said that Chinese words have no plural forms, she said, *Then how do you know if it's one thing or many?* I said, *One thing is always many.* Ben got in trouble for not capitalizing the names of countries and people. When the teacher asked her why she'd chosen a boy name, she said, *I liked Ben because it's already short for something. This way, none of you can abbreviate me further.* In class, she asked questions like, *How long ago was the sea salted?* I was the only one who answered: *So long ago, Nuwa was the one who did it. Because otherwise the sea would go bad like milk. Salt is what preserves it.* She misremembered idioms: *I've got butterflies in my bladder.* Or: *A bird in the hand is worth more in the soup.*

We misspelled all the words in our essays on purpose, baiting our teachers so we'd get a time-out together. We wrote: *Baba's a good sky and mama's a good kook   We be leave in rein carnation   We were born hear so you cant depart us.* All our essays were returned red: IMPROVE YOUR GRAMMAR. IMPROVE YOUR SPELLING. IMPLORE YOUR GODS. WE'LL SHOW YOU A SENTENCE.

I mimicked the way all of Ben's sentences ended with *-er,*

a purr that made me feel feline, foreign to myself. Her accent was an axe: *mother* abbreviated to *moth, country* to *cunt*. There was a game where the teacher pointed at pictures of objects on a projector screen and asked us for their names— *apple, bus, cat, doctor*—but Ben had her own vocabulary, made mostly of the sounds different bird flocks produced when they passed over the parking lot. The sound they make, Ben told me, depended on the density of the flock and whether or not they were native to the weather here. She could hear any sound once and continue the strand of it, threading the sound through her left ear and pulling it out of her mouth. At noon, she walked up to me and stole my reduced-lunch hot dog bun, ripping it into confetti-sized pieces and feeding it to the crows. They walked up to the bench and pecked at her ankles, opening their beaks as if to name her.

Ben's favorite animal was an anteater, which she pro-nounced *auntie tear*. My favorite animal was a white tiger because I was born in the year of the tiger, and because I as-sumed anything born white must have a better chance at life. I was right: White tigers had a longer life span in captivity. In our school library, which was just an extra shelf in the back corner of the classroom, we memorized whole pages of the National Geographic encyclopedia, mispronouncing the genus of our species. We pronounced the *Ho* in *Homo* not like *home* but like *hostage*.

The Big Cats spread was our favorite: We wanted flash-light eyes that turned on at night. We went to the bathroom and shut off the lights, foraging for our faces in the dark. In the dark, she made a fist around my braid and presented it back to me like a bouquet. When I told her my favorite ani-mal was the tiger, Ben told me that tigers in myths were al-ways men. *What animals are women?* I asked, and she named everything with wings: cranes, phoenixes, geese. I knew from my mother's stories that snakes were also women, shucking off their skins beneath the meat of the moon.

Whenever we ditched, Ben and I compared our breasts in the restroom. There were three tin-walled stalls and a faucet that never stopped drooling. The tile floor had potholes of piss. We stood on the toilets like they were islands we were native to, each of us balanced on one side of the seat rim, steering each other's arms. We lifted our shirts. We believed our nipples would someday open into eyes. Bras were blindfolds that our mothers wore to protect their eye-nipples from constant light. My nipples were darker and hers were hairier: hairs I wanted to make a career out of counting. I thought I could blink my nipples like eyes, squinting or dilating them depending on her distance from me.

My tail turned copper with sweat and knotted against my lower back whenever she came near. I was afraid to show her its length, in case she pulled on it like a lever by accident, transforming me into Hu Gu Po. I'd bite off her breasts, scoop them clean like grapefruits and flush away the skins.

One day in the restroom, I asked her if she knew the story of Hu Gu Po. We stood on the toilet seat, holding the hooks of each other's arms. I wanted to ask if she saw a resemblance between the story and me, but Ben said no, she'd never heard it. *It's about a tiger spirit,* I said, *who wants to be a woman.* But to keep her body, she eats only what she can kill. She shells toes and calls them peanuts. My mother said it was the only story she wanted me to own. My inheritance was hurt. *Sounds like your ancestors had a foot fetish,* Ben said. I laughed and called her a birdshit, shouldering her off the toilet seat until she stumbled in, displacing water in arcs. She climbed out of the toilet bowl, walking out of the stall and shimmying her

legs to dry them. When I called her back into the stall, hop-
ping down from the toilet seat to say sorry, she smiled and
said, *Watch me,* dipping both her hands into the toilet bowl
and flinging fistfuls of gem-hard drops at me. Turning my
face away, I gripped the wall and laughed, wiping my cheeks
with my sleeve. *Surrender,* she said, as the toilet bowl boiled
over with our laughter.

———

On the next show-and-tell day, Ben brought a birdcage to class
and posed it in the center of her desk until our teacher, a
bleached-out woman with freckled legs, told Ben to put it
away. To the back of the classroom, she said. *Don't distract the
other students.* But Ben was the distraction: She sat behind
me, fiddling with her lips as if she couldn't figure out how to
unbutton them. Her hair knotted itself to any object within
reach: the chair, her pencil, my hands. When it was her turn
to show and tell, Ben carried the cage from the back of the
classroom, holding it high over her head as if she were going
to crown herself with it. The cage was rusted and doorless,
but its damage made it dearer to her. She said it had been
owned by her great-grandmother, born a beast-keeper of the
royal zoo, so skilled at taming animals that she could make a
giraffe bow down and lick her eyelids. Since then, every
daughter in the family was born with a key growing in her
mouth like a milk tooth.

Ben's great-grandmother wore keys everywhere on her
body: dangling from her ears, sheathed in her nostrils, darned
to her skirt. In the royal zoo, there were millions of cages with
one bird each, southern seabirds with glass beaks, desert
birds with two sets of eyelids, a thousand breeds of songless

sparrows. One summer, the animals remembered their past lives and began to behave outside of their assigned species. The royal fish tried walking out of their rivers and died writhing in the mud. The dogs teethed off their tails and jumped from roofs, believing themselves winged. The snakes forgot they were cold-blooded and stayed in the shade until their blood iced over. The canaries plucked themselves bald and converted to carnivores. Ben's great-grandmother was accused of poisoning the animals, of surgically swapping their minds. As punishment, each of her limbs was tied to a different horse, tearing her apart when they ran. The soldiers collected her limbs in a sack, but when they tried to toss it into a nearby river, the sack began to shiver. When they opened it, hundreds of birds funneled out, bright as razors, cutting the sky to pieces.

On the baseball diamond at recess, Ben pulled me away into the dugout and showed me the key to the cage door: It was the silver pendant around her neck. Ben stepped closer until the key was against my chest, teething into my left breast. She said she'd been born with the key, a silver milk tooth jutting from her mouth. It tore her mother during birth, snagging on the placenta and causing her mother to hemorrhage. To this day, she said, the hospital still stands inside a flood. When Ben stepped back, the key swinging in the air between us, I thought about slipping my tail out. *I wasn't born with it,* I would say, *but it's my name.*

—

One afternoon, we ran from our older brothers and their foam-pellet guns. They shut off every light in the house, chasing us through the kitchen and into the yard and back into the kitchen, where we rifled the drawers for a knife to threaten them back. Ben's brother had too-large hands with fingers that curled naturally, adapted for pulling triggers and professional nose-picking. The two boys retreated temporarily to my brother's room, saying that when they came back out, we'd better be hidden or already dead. There was nowhere that could fit both our bodies except behind the sofa, where we wouldn't last. I kissed her before our deaths, pretended the dark was not man-made, pretended our brothers' guns shot real bullets, not jelly-tipped shafts I could catch midair. I wanted permanent damage, a war where one side was the other's shadow, one body was the other's blade.

We kissed, my tongue serenading her teeth. She put her palm on the back of my neck and I was sweating a dress. My hands honeymooned on her hips. The key around her neck nudged me just below the collarbone, but I didn't pull away. Between our chests, the key heated until I thought it would weld itself into a new shape, a hinge between our bodies.

Ben's ribs parted against mine, releasing her heart into my hands, a fistful of feathers. My throat a perch for her teeth. Then I heard the sound of our brothers reloading on the other side of the sofa, squinting to separate our bodies from the dark. We kept our eyes closed, her mouth on my shoulder now. Tomorrow there would be a bruise, a dark spot on the ball of my shoulder, and I'd think for a second that my skin was of another species, that I was finally turning into what my tail wanted me to be. But then I'd remember yesterday, which was today, which was her mouth making my shoulder like a wing. Our brothers took aim, still squinting, unable to tell if there was one body or two. We let them. We were silent when the foam bullets bounced off our thighs and bellies.

Ben fell to her side and pretended to bleed out of her

mouth, her tongue twitching in the dark like a severed lizard tail. The inside of my mouth felt sore, spoken for. It was a lie, letting them believe we could die, but we did it because it was fun to watch them be sorry later. They mourned us by throwing their pellets one by one down the garbage disposal while we rolled over onto our bellies and laughed with all the blood in us. We laughed until we pissed ourselves warm and had to line our underwear with paper towels.

I wanted to taste everything native to her. I held her spit in my mouth, wondered if this was what the teacher meant by exchanging bodily fluids. We'd just begun seventh grade sex education, which mostly meant our teacher explained that the adhesive "wings" of a Maxi pad were not literal wings and could not equip us with flight. The teacher told us to develop a platonic relationship with our bodies. On the list of illicit fluids that could be exchanged, bartered: semen, vaginal discharge, blood. But there was nothing about what we'd done. In the animal encyclopedia Ben and I memorized, every hierarchy had a name. Every violence a vocabulary. Somewhere, there was a name for our exchange, in a language that was kept from us.

—

I brought Ben to my backyard where the holes breathed, introducing her to each mouth I'd made with my hands.

I invented a role for each hole. *This one spits watermelon seeds,* I said, pointing at the hole to our right. *This one tells secrets,* I said, pointing to the hole on our left. I still watered the holes once a week with the backyard hose, as if water alone could heal them.

Have you tried feeding them? Ben asked. I said I had, but she said maybe it wasn't the right kind of prey. Maybe they wanted to hunt for themselves. I told her to forget about them the way I had: I'd learned to live around them, to skirt around the borders of their throats without being swallowed. Ben looked at me, a smudge of mud on her nose-bridge, and said, *Every hole corresponds to something missing. We just need to find what's gone.* Whenever there was something she wanted to solve, she fingered the key around her neck, pretended to unlock her mouth with it. She gripped the pendant-key in her teeth and suckled on it, thinking. I slid the key from between her teeth, replaced it with my finger, flinching when I felt her teeth. She looked at me without blinking, her mouth-O symmetrical to the holes. Waiting for her teeth to cleave me, I imagined my finger severed inside her mouth, twirling like a stem. Ben shut her eyes, her breath burning circles on the back of my hand. Her teeth clasped around my knuckle and then released, skimming the skin so lightly it reminded me of the time a wasp landed on my finger and sipped at my sweat. I'd been so afraid of moving, of baiting its sting, that I didn't breathe. Coaxing my finger into a hook, I twisted it slow as a key until she opened for me.

—

The next day, Ben thanked me for showing her the holes in my yard and said there was something she still hadn't shown me yet. It was taco day at school, and we'd both poured the ground beef out of their neon shells and down our pants, laughing as the minced meat sagged our underwear. We ran up to the lunch chaperones and said we'd pooped ourselves, flashing our meat stains. They panicked and escorted us to the bathroom, excused us from our next class, and left us together while they scoured the lost and found for clean pants.

When they left, Ben pushed me into the bathroom stall and told me to sit down and wait. I squatted on the toilet seat until she returned carrying the cage. She tugged me out of the stall by my wrist. In front of the finger-smeared mirror, she lifted the birdcage with both hands.

The mirror above the sink reflected the birdcage between us, fluorescent light flattening our faces. I was too busy watching Ben's face in the mirror to see it: a shape in the center of the birdcage, a shadow without a body. The shadow was standing on the perch in the center, moving in a familiar rhythm, slight and fast and songlike. A bird. When it opened its wings, I turned my head from the mirror to look up at the ceiling, to see what bird was casting its shadow down on the cage. But there was no body, just the bird-shadow, and I could see only its reflection. I looked at the cage directly, then at its image, trying to align them in my mind. But the cage in the mirror carried more.

Ben guessed the shadow-bird was some kind of ghost, left behind by a bird that had died in it. I told her I was always suspicious of shadows: Mine left me at night to grow its own body. I looked at the shadow-bird again in the mirror, trying to imagine a pigeon or a sparrow, but I decided its species was its own. Ben said she'd tried installing birdfeeders and bottle-caps full of water, but the shadow-bird didn't hunger or thirst or grow. It never tried to leave. For the rest of the hour, while our classmates dissolved in the heat outside, we stood side by side. Not facing each other, just watching the shadow-bird in the mirror. Not naming it either. Though in my mind, I had already given it many names: Mouth with wings. Night in a body.

Setting the cage down in the sink, Ben turned on the faucet and the water gathered black at the bottom of the cage. I turned to Ben and looked her in the mouth, said I had something to show her too. It was something I couldn't name either. It was the sum of my body and its predecessors. Ben let the water run out of words. I pulled her by the wrists back into the stall and turned around, sloughing off my pants.

Silent, Ben reached down. Touched the knotted tip of my tail as if it were a bird that would startle. Lifted it to her nose and stroked it once across her face, as if she could tell its species by scent. *What is it?* I asked her. Ben dropped my tail, watched it hang. Teethed her pendant-key.

Tigers are natural predators, Ben said. When I asked how she defined a predator, she said, *Something that eats other things for a living.* But wasn't that everything? Ben said I should look at the food chain, but the only chain I'd memorized was the pendant-string around her neck: I lived inside its radius. *Cats and birds are natural enemies,* Ben said, pointing at me and then herself.

Do you mean we're enemies? Shaking her head, she said we were many species, many bodies. *But what am I becoming?* I said. I wondered if she'd ever feared I'd hurt her, if she knew how I'd once tried hunting my father. If I ate her someday, she had to forgive me. Ben said she couldn't forgive anyone if she didn't have a body.

Can bodies cross into other bodies? Ben said I was always asking the wrong questions. I told her I knew about evolution and finches, knew all the concepts we were taught, but she said my tail wasn't shaped like a line: It was shaped like a life, circling itself, growing backward from tip to root. The sinks outside were overflowing, flooding us to the ankles, water-rings coiling like snakes. Ben said it didn't take generations to change, to adapt to a new predator or environment. Sometimes one body could do it. She talked like a scientist of survival. I told her that there was no evolutionary line between tigers and people, and if there was, it still meant I was moving backward.

There's no such thing as forward or backward, she said, her finger circling in the air. There was no such thing as progress, just accumulation: A long time ago, she told me, when a man died of exhaustion while building the Great Wall, the man behind him just bricked his body into the wall and kept going. That's why it's studded with skulls, she said. Why it's shaped like a spine. It's a burial ground, not a building. I asked her if this story was meant to comfort me.

She told me not to worry. *We're not alive. We're just between deaths right now.* She laughed and reached around for my tail: It thrummed like an antenna, broadcasting her touch all over my body.

If we stayed in here, she said, *and the water kept outgrowing us, what do you think would happen?* I told her we'd drown, but Ben said I was wrong. *We'd grow gills,* she said.

Holding open the stall door, she walked me to the sinks, water receding around us. It listened to her feet when she told it to leave. She turned off the faucet, her cage bobbing in the sink. The pendant-key punctuated the center of her chest. Lifting the cage with both hands, she offered it to me. If she unlocked it, I wondered, would the shadow-bird leave? Would we see it flee?

Ben said she'd let me hold the cage if I let her see my tail whenever she wanted. When I asked her why, she said, *I like what it does to my hand. It behaves like it's befriended some-thing wild.* I said she could steal it from me anytime. In her hands, my tail was potential, a hilt waiting to be drawn from me.

Later—when we were in the classroom closet for our time-out, having flooded the bathroom and cut PE—I whispered to Ben in the dark that I might still eat her someday. Her laughter lit the dark between us, torched it to ash. When I told her to stop laughing, that it could really happen, Ben said I shouldn't be afraid of what the tail wanted me to be. *You're becoming the species that will save you.* But neither of us knew what I needed to be saved from. Neither of us knew what a beast was born to do.

DAUGHTER

Birthdate

Or: Why Fathers Fail as Sources of Water

On my brother's birthday, my father asked if we wanted to go to the zoo. It was the same one Duck Uncle had taken us to. Our mother told us we had to go, even after my brother faked sickness by stewing vomit on the stove: He boiled water and cornstarch and an apple peel for color, then poured the pink glue of it down his shirt, pretending to gag it out of his mouth. But my mother wiped him off with a dishrag and said our father was our father: He carried us the way birds carry the sky. *The sea shoulders the boat,* she said. *He's the water, we're what floats.*

Water can sink a boat too, I said, tracing a hole in the air with my finger. My brother and I finally agreed to go not because we thought our father was the sea, but because our mother begged us, and she was the only body of water we believed in.

After my mother took the bus to work, my father drove us there with the windows down, our cheeks ripened by the

wind. Our eyelashes knitted to the dust that blew in, a powder of sun-dried cowshit and dirt from the fields along the
highway. Some summers, the fields caught fire and grew trees
of smoke and my mother dipped bandanas in the sink to tie
around our mouths, telling us to breathe careful: Our lungs
could be lit up like logs.

I fell asleep with my head rolling in my brother's lap, his
hands petting my hair along its part. He roved his palm over
my face like a stethoscope, but it was his heart I could hear,
accelerating as the car did. When we neared the zoo, I could
hear him counting his own breaths, numbering them backward from a hundred, something he only did when my father
was near.

On our way to the bird enclosure, where the white nets
were stiff as calcified wind and the parrots swore like men,
my father bought me a popsicle that was supposed to resemble a pineapple but was the shape and color of a frozen
booger. When we arrived at the parrots, my father pointed at
a macaw with an orange band around its foot, a girl's flower
hairclip in its beak. *Can you believe how red they are? How
beautiful? People can only be that color if they bleed.*

I ate the popsicle stick-first, teething it to slivers, arming
my tongue with quills. My father paid two dollars for us to
ride in the back of a safari car that drove us along paths as
twisted as arteries, past tanks full of bright fish the size of
punctuation marks, past an enclosure where one of the monkeys slotted his penis through the bars and pissed at a pass-
erby. My father and I laughed ourselves raw when we saw it,
our mouths making symmetrical sounds, and all I could hear
was our resemblance. He sat me on his lap so we wouldn't
have to pay for three seats, but I tried to slide off, fearing he'd
feel the fist of my tail. The spineless popsicle dissolved in my

palms, scrawling sugar down my arms. Wasps came to halo my elbows, stinging the sweetest parts of me. *I want to go home,* my brother said. He was counting his breaths again. The afternoon heat closed around us like a jaw and my father ignored him. When the safari tour ended, dropping us back off at the wrought-iron gate with the faux-wood welcome sign, my father asked if we wanted to go kite-flying. Walking us toward the parking lot, a hand welded to each of our necks, he said he knew the perfect place, the casino by the freeway with a rooftop bar where you could tie your kites to the railing and let them scoop up the air, ladle you a sky.

No, my brother said again, stopping. We were almost to the car: I could see its one-eyed headlights, the left tire with half a dead squirrel still mashed to it, the license plate that began with the first letter of my name. My father stopped too, looked down at me as if I were the one who refused to keep walking, but I said nothing. We were passing between two parked SUVs, heading toward the far side of the lot where our car was, where our mother once stapled the seatbelt to our shirts because she didn't trust us to be safe otherwise.

A sunburnt station wagon passed behind us, windows bruised by the heat, the underwater voices of a family arguing inside. My father made a fist around my brother's T-shirt collar, navy with neck-sweat, and lifted him off the ground. It was the same way he'd held my brother when we were on the mainland, before their bones had borrowed the air and flown. But here, there was no sky that could basket my brother, no string I could use to steer my father. I had no breath left in my body to blow them into kites.

My father made a fist around my brother's T-shirt collar, navy with neck-sweat, and lifted him off the ground. Swung him back and forth, swung him dumb. *Walk,* he said, but my brother shook his head, choking inside his own shirt collar, biting his tongue until beetles of blood crawled out of his mouth. My father put him down, said, *Walk.* I stood behind them both, as if by staying still I could assume the shape of my shadow, flat on the asphalt, flitting beneath the cars and finding the street on my own, go home. My brother looked up, kept his face still as those ancient statues I'd seen only in textbooks, the kind missing their torsos, chipped at every angle, gutted by age into something graceful. Unsettled by the stillness of my brother's face, my father looked down. At the crotch of my brother's cargo shorts: a stain too dark to be sweat, a sweet rancid scent rising from his legs. He'd pissed himself, and on the asphalt I saw the lit trail of it, beginning somewhere at my own feet.

My father's mouth receded around his teeth. He called my brother an animal, a beast that couldn't behave its bladder. Tapping its tip against the back of my knees, my tail orchestrated the air between my legs, a conductor's wand waking the sound in me. My brother stood with his legs apart, straddling his piss-lake, wet everywhere below the waist. A boy newly baptized in his body. As if his water were divine, not the consequence of drinking all the bottles of 7Up my father had snuck into the park by tucking them into his waistband.

When my brother said nothing back, my father gripped his shoulders and pinned his back to the black SUV beside us. My brother pretended to be boneless in his hands, ragdolled against the passenger door. In the heat, the windows of the SUV were warped, darkbright as bug eyes. Scanning each window, I looked for someone inside to call to, for my mother to waft in like a moon. But the rows of cars were endless as a cemetery and I couldn't tell which direction was back toward the zoo.

Heat began in my back teeth, igniting the wick of my tongue. A light lanterned my mouth and I named it rage. I ringed my arms around my father's waist and dangled from him, trying to weaponize the weight of my body. My brother tried to kick back at him, but his foot flung out and kicked the side-view mirror instead, freeing our faces from it. The mirror shattered, turning our faces multifaceted as diamonds, and before its shards hit the asphalt, I saw in it how small I was, how my arms barely circled the width of my father's waist. From another angle, it might have looked like I was trying to dance with him, dip him back in my arms.

I let go of his waist and stood, my spine hammered straight, welded to wound. Beneath my skirt, my tail tautened between my legs, tethering me to the ground. I walked up behind my father, low and crouched, my knees hinged with a strength that was my mother's: practiced at bending and rising, learning all the angles of prayer. My brother's head lolled to the side as my father shook him again, spit whipping out of my brother's mouth, sparkling in the air. Coiling his arms in, he retracted my brother to his chest, and I thought he was either going to hug him or throw him.

I stood behind my father, standing in his shadow while my tail wrapped around his ankle, yanking so quick his leg buckled beneath him. He collapsed on one knee and cried out, the asphalt burning his kneecap bald, gravel gritting into it. My brother, let go, stumbled and leaned against the SUV, looking at my tail as if it might strangle his ankle too: It dangled slack between my legs again, sated. Wringing the sweat from its fur, I tucked it back into my underwear. I stepped back from my father's kneeling body, his shadow truncated at the waist. He moaned a sound too low and gutted for even the car engines to comprehend, his lip metallic where he'd bitten it.

He stood up halfway, cradling his skinned-open knee like a geode: Beneath the broken dullness of his skin, he was rubied with blood, pearled with tendon. Looking up at me through the black blades of his hair, he said my name, his mouth unstitched by it. It wasn't the pain of his knee that kept him from following us: It was my face, my face that was my mother's, my face that made the sun swivel around and witness it, my face backlit and blurred into the sky's blue, resembling what couldn't be touched.

I spoke down to him: *We're going home. You will not follow us.* His face was stunned flat as a run-over penny. We walked and he watched our backs, my brother's shirt sheer with his sweat. My skin was soaked like a dress, a wet weight draped over my bones, so heavy I wanted to kneel down on the pavement.

At the bus stop, we waited for three hundred breaths until it arrived, exhaust unspooling from its rear end. Night came sudden as a sheet thrown over a cage. My brother turned to me and said we had no money. He was looking at me between the legs instead of at my face, as if my tail would descend now and speak for me. I laughed, giddy with what I knew it could do, thinking suddenly of the monkey that had pissed through the gap in its cage, the way a rainbow had refracted through it. The bus doors opened. The driver was Asian and tired and looked down the steps at us. At my brother's collar of thumbprints. He let us on for free.

—

It was raining when we got home, and our mother was standing outside the house, wet hair like guohua, one strand striping her collarbone, the other rain-pasted to the arc of her cheek, the rest coiled around her neck. My brother and I were wet too, having walked from the nearest bus stop. The piss was rinsed from his legs, replaced by rain. *I've been waiting,* she said. She looked behind us for our father, as if he were shielded by our shadows, playing hide-and-seek with our shoulder blades.

At home, she wrapped my brother and me both in her floral comforter, breathing onto our scalps with her mouth while the hair dryer warmed up. She asked what happened, where is he, did he leave you, never looking directly at the bruises cuffing my brother's arms, at the way my knees migrated together, sealing my tail away from the light, her eyes.

When my brother didn't answer, I said that Hu Gu Po had come and taken him from us. I described what she'd looked like: a woman with striped skin, a pelt skirt that moved like oil. My mother stood up, looked at me. Her wet hair clung to her face like a shadow. She asked me what I meant, and I said Hu Gu Po had kept us from being hurt. Turning away from us both, my mother said she was going now to look for him, her hands opening and closing around nothing. I stood and gripped the back of her shirt, tugged on it so hard she bent her knees. She reached behind to unfasten my fist. When she turned back to me, I could see that her eyes were wet as fruit pits, that she was afraid of me. *Okay,* she said. *Hao hao hao hao hao. I'm not going to look for him. But we need that car back.* I said he had probably driven it away.

But you said Hu Gu Po took him.

I said she had, but he would come back. My mother shook her head and lifted her hand. I thought she might slap me, but instead she put it on my shoulder, steered me toward the bathroom. She said she was going to draw a bath so hot it would boil us new again. My brother shivered as he stood, his shoulders knocking against mine, and my mother undressed us both, forgetting to take off our socks. *It's like you're my babies again,* she said. *Raw to everything.* She buttered us with soap fat, cupped her hands to pour water over our heads. We shut our eyes and let her scrub us bright as dimes.

In the morning, she was gone looking for him. On the sidewalk, while I waited for her to return, I watched two crows disrobe a dead squirrel, pecking away its skin and fur to untangle its intestines like a necklace.

How my mother told the story of her search: She took the bus to the zoo, counting cows in the fields by the freeway, mistaking a cemetery for a herd of white-backed calves grazing the green, all of them missing mothers. The car was there, parked where we'd described, and for hours she avoided calling the tow truck, wanting instead to break in, to steal what was already hers, his smell still in the seats, the radio tuned to the only news she listened to, the weather, which Ama liked to say was god's news. He'd taken the keys with him, a way of saying what belonged to him. But it didn't matter where the keys were, where he'd gone to grow back his skin, because my mother was who I belonged to, the only place I'd ever lived, the only person who knew me before I had a name.

While she waited for the tow truck to arrive at the parking lot, she searched the street for a rock at least the size of her hand, but could only find a small one, tapered like her ring finger. She threw it at the window. It pinged off. She picked it up again, aiming at her own face in the window's reflection. When the car was towed back into our driveway, I found a crack in the driver's side window, so small I thought a sparrow must have done it, flown into its own image. She never got the crack fixed, and when we drove in the daytime, the sun siphoned through it, brightened it into a scar. How she knew he was not coming back: There was a bird perched on the windshield one morning, a warbler of some kind, red-breasted as if it had been slit at the throat and was bleeding itself brighter.

My mother beat it away with her hands, but it followed her into the house somehow, and she cornered it where the wall head-butted the ceiling. She cooed at it, then spat at it, then bruised it with the end of a broomstick, but it didn't come down. It hovered there, beating its wings featherless against our walls. So we let it live with us, found its nests wedged behind the toilet or in the back of the oven. We never saw its mate. It pecked open all its eggs and ate the slugs of meat inside, leaving me the blue-veined shells to bury outside.

The night we came back without our father, the tail twined itself around my thigh, clasping like a garter. I pet it to sleep before me. My tail and I were on a honeymoon: We were married now, vowing to defend each other. In his sleep, my brother tucked himself away from me, blowing silver spit-bubbles in the dark. He said my name like the name of a hurricane. Molding a moat of pillows around his body, he told me to keep my tail leashed. *It's already leashed to me,* I said. *It's grown to me.* But he said I didn't know who held the other end of it. Who lived on the other end of it. *A tail is two-way,* he said. *Like a telephone cord. Like something that plugs two things together. You don't know what you're being connected to.* I told him he should be more grateful: Without it, without me, we wouldn't have been able to walk away on our own. Instead of answering, he turned to the wall and wrote something on it with his spit-wet finger, a warning no one could read.

A week later, the phone rang itself red. When I picked up,

silence was on the other end. Heat radiated from the receiver, blistering my cheeks, and I had to hold it away from my face. It must have been a fire calling. But then the silence changed, became familiar, and I could imagine the mouth making it: silver-capped teeth uneven as a mountain range, a fog of cigarette smoke twined through the peaks. He didn't say anything, and I didn't know if he knew it was me, but I hung up after counting to a hundred, let him learn my silence too: Mine was a weapon. Mine was a mercy, too. I gave him a hundred silences to translate into anything: sorry, goodbye, come back, leave, don't, go, stay.

DAUGHTER

Back to Ben

Ben's father bought a lot in another town. He wanted to build his own house, with a porch and a yard and a painted-white doghouse—even though, according to Ben, he was allergic to dogs and once sneezed at a beagle so hard his brains fled out of his nose as a flock of moths. The resulting hollowness of his head caused him to sell their car and furniture and buy an empty lot. No one in class believed Ben until the week she came to school with her father's toolbox, full of nails and screws and other little silver things that looked like ear-bones. We told her that houses weren't built. They existed like trees, grown in from the street.

Ben walked me to the land her father had bought. It was damp and tufted with grass like an old man's scalp. A fence as high as our foreheads split the lot from the sidewalk. Her father was unraveling the fence, rolling it up like a tongue. The land was concave, sunken in the middle, swallowing two trees that stood in the center of it. Ben's father began the foundation by renting a bulldozer and carved a hole so deep we joked he was digging himself back to China.

I walked an hour west on weekends to visit Ben and her family, who moved into a small shed bordering the hole. Ben's father built the shed in two weeks, complete with a bunk bed for Ben and her brother, a dining table made of exposed plywood, and a drain in the corner for showering. Instead of a sink, they owned a bucket. Instead of a kitchen, they stacked a wall of tinned tuna and Spam, a tapestry of meats. Instead of a toilet, there was a spade by the door for us to dig our own holes.

When it stormed, the tin roof chattered like teeth and the walls italicized themselves. Leaks veined the walls and bled rain. When I described it to my mother—bleached walls, a soil floor covered in prayer rugs, plastic-wrapped holes for windows—she said it sounded like a chicken farm, the kind she used to work for in Arkansas.

In a past life, Ben's mother sold one of her ovaries when she was a teenager, after a river molested her city and she needed money to rebuild her house. If Ben and I offered our hands, kneading her mother's neck for an hour first, she'd let us ask her about it. She'd worm out of her skirt to show us: The scar made her loss legible to us, an indented hyphen three inches to the left of her belly button. Ben stroked the blue scar like a bird, as if she could calm it and coax it into her hands. What Ben wanted was to hold our hurts for us. She once told me a bruise was scratch-and-sniff. She scratched the one on my knee and sniffed it and said, *Sweet.*

Inside the shack, Ben and her brother pretended they lived in a bomb shelter: Outside was a war they could win solely by surviving. When we played together, the bunk bed was our only bunker and every cockroach was a landmine. If

I stepped on one, the penalty was death. Ben wore the uniform of a soldier, white pajamas that turned fog-thin with her body heat. I dressed in the uniform of a casualty, a masking-tape X over my heart, a bullet hole penned into my neck. We argued what color it should be: Ben's brother said red, because of blood. Ben said black, because that's the color of the hole itself. I wanted to say neither, but I was already dead.

Ben's birdcage was neutral territory. She placed it on the floor in the center of the shed, and whenever one of us placed our palm on it, we were safe for a maximum of ten seconds. I was the coward that always ran to the cage, placing both palms on its domed top while Ben and her brother waited on either side of me. They counted, and when I dropped my hands from the cage they tackled me at the same time. They stacked on top of me, one sitting on my chest and the other holding down my feet, promising to give me a good death, promising to bury all my bones as neighbors.

Beg us to let you go, Ben said. Her hands corseted my ankles, her thumb stroking the bone.

Let me go, I said, meaning don't.

—

The hole in Ben's lot doubled its depth. I asked Ben if we could fill it up with water and convert it into a swimming pool, maybe even host the Olympics, but Ben said that swimming pools were square and this one was round, an eye socket for the sun. We asked Ben's father why the hole was getting deeper while no house was rising out of it, but he never answered. He drank beer at his drafting table and then pissed into the same bottle. Sometimes he reached down for the

bottle an hour later, forgetting what it was full of. We laughed
when he spat the piss out, the wall a mosaic of stains.

Ben and I stood on the gnawed edges of the hole and
looked down into its cavity, its ribs: Inside the hole were discarded two-by-fours. One time we saw Ben's father stand here
at the edge and pee into the hole, competing with the sky to
see whose rain reached the deepest roots. Circling its perimeter, I told Ben the house didn't seem any closer to done. The
hole was just deepening because her father didn't know what
else to do, and down is the only direction that doesn't require
any imagining. She slapped me, her palm spiked with sweat.

I touched my face with my fingertips, the skin flaring. Ben
stepped back from me and looked at her hand like it was a
hornet, like she was the one stung by it. We stood apart, facing each other. The hole laid behind her like a shadow, and for
a second I wondered if that was the true shape of her.

Ben said I shouldn't talk about other people's fathers
when my own was a myth, a story gone so sour that nobody
wanted to tell it. My tail descended to defend me, swinging
between my legs. I said she didn't know anything about my
father or what I'd done to him. My many mothers and what
I'd do for them. Mothers ago, I was a beast. I stalked whole
countries to eat. I plotted their shores with my teeth. Ben said
I should stop lying. Before she could say anything else, my
tail whipped forward, shifting me onto my toes. I obeyed its
weight and moved toward her, pushing Ben with both my
hands.

Ben stumbled and went backward into the hole, landing
on the pyre of two-by-fours. The breath tore out of her mouth.
I didn't remember calling down to her, but Ben said I did, and
that's how her father heard and brought his ladder, bringing

Ben back up in a mulch sack. He laid her on the soil and slapped her face till her eyes came on again. I watched while my tail retracted, curled and beating at my lower back.

That week, I stood again at the hem of the hole and begged her to push me in. *Do it,* I said. Ben wore a bandage around her ribs to make sure the bones clasped back together in the correct place. I'd watched her father cut it from a bedsheet. I spoke with my back to her, waiting for her hands to decide I was right, that I was a species she didn't recognize. But she never did it. When I turned around, her bandage was undone and whipping the air like a wing. I couldn't look at her face. Behind her, the sky was blue because I'd bruised it. Her voice had salt in it, a rasp I'd never heard before. The word I wanted was *forgiven,* but she never said it.

I'd dreamed once of yanking the key off her neck, giving her my hands to wear instead. A bruise-necklace around her throat. I knew how to make jewelry of my cruelty. Each of my knuckles was named after an aunt I had never known, and Ben touched each one to her cheek. How many of me she had yet to meet.

She knotted herself to the ground, fought her own still-ness. The desire to see me hurt was defeated by the desire to not give me what I wanted. When she didn't push me, it felt more like punishment than forgiveness.

She pulled us both away from the hole and into the shade of the shed. Taking my wrists in her hands, I thought for a second she might twist them into wicks, bring me to my knees. I'd worship whatever pain she gave me. I'd be the saint of injury. But instead, she rubbed her lips against my knuck-les, soaping them with her tongue. When she leaned forward, mending my lips to hers, I thought of tonguing out all her teeth and keeping them alive in my cheek, seeds of her mouth I could spit out and plant later.

Her hand speared down my waistband, wrapped fast around my tail. I tensed, told her to let go. *You once told me you didn't want it,* Ben said, twisting my tail until the bone creaked. She said it looked like things had changed: Now I needed it. *I could take it from you. Right now, if you wanted me to.* I shook my head, afraid if I spoke she'd sprain my tail.

I knew it, Ben said, letting go. She laughed. Withdrawing her hand, she wiped it against her shirt hem. *You don't really want to get rid of it. You love it.* I asked her what was wrong with that: My tail and I were married at the marrow. I knew now how to wield it.

Ben shook her head and said, *Who inside you am I speaking to? Who?* She took a step toward me, standing so close I could see a dried flake of spit on her chin. I licked it without thinking, my tongue flitting across her skin. When she didn't swat me away, I leaned toward her, traced her jawbone with my lips. Slid my mouth up and down the slope of the bone like playing a harmonica, a song humming out of her.

We crab-walked to her bunk bed. No one was home but the light coming in through the window-hole. We took off our shirts and I shut my eyes to the room, my hands on the back her neck. Her tongue towed its heat across my belly. She straddled me, lifting my arms and licking the pits, the black patch of hair where sweat dewed, where I smelled most like myself. We butted mouths, backed up, laughed. I propped myself up on my elbows and kissed along the slant of her rib. Her hands around my breasts like unbroken bread.

The key dangled from her neck and hung above me, lowering into my mouth. I took it on my tongue and suckled it, the key's teeth a copy of my own. When she sat up, the key jerked out of my mouth and caught my upper lip like a fishhook, lancing it open. *A key,* she said, looking down at me. The key swung between us, gilded with spit and lip-blood. *Your tail,* Ben said. *I think it's a key.*

———

Ben and I squatted in my backyard. *All holes,* she said, *just need a key.* I tried to follow her, but my mind was still on her mouth.

Ben crouched over the one in the center, the ⊡. *Where does this one go?* she said, and I said I didn't know. Like all bodies, they didn't lead anywhere except inside themselves. She turned her back to the hole and squatted over it like she was taking a shit, demonstrating what she wanted me to do. She wanted me to feed my tail to the hole, to slide it in like a key. I pulled down my pants and dangled my tail in. The hole healed around my tail, soil shifting as it swallowed me. When the hole opened its mouth again, I fell forward onto my knees.

Stand vigil, Ben said. Hours after the sun was gone, the hole spoke its first word. I listened for its hum. The ⊡ squinted, spat out something white and tongue-slimed. Tugging it loose, I flipped it in my hands. It was skin, wet from being born, poreless and soft. Both sides of it were dyed with words. Inside the house, I turned on the kitchen light and held the hide to my face, deciphering the dark between each word.

A few of the fragments were written in characters, but the only one I recognized was my mother's maiden name. The rest were written in an alphabet. It was my handwriting, my way of stringing letters neat as beads, but the words weren't mine. The skin was moth-holed: My mother said that Ama treated every pen like a needle, piercing holes to make meaning. Ama's first language was not found in books, only in bodies. Tayal was written in the English alphabet, each word a phonetic translation written by missionaries, translated through their hands. The same hands that had beaten children into belief. Those hands were fluent only in punishment. I imagined a missionary transcribing Ama's body, tracing her tongue on paper and burning it so that she spoke smoke.

I read in the kitchen, transcribing into English as much as I could read. When I showed Ben in the morning, she said I should squat over the hole again, but this time it didn't open its mouth for me.

It only works once, I said. *What kind of key only works once?* Ben said. We tried to feed the holes again, this time with water from our palms. We tried prying them open with sticks. We fed them strips of pork jerky. But they chose silence.

At school, I gave Ben my transcriptions on notebook paper. We'd midwifed a language together, delivered it from the dark. When she folded the sheets into her pocket, I told her to be careful, to treat the letter like a daughter. Ben asked me what my ama looked like, and I said I knew her mostly by voice. I reported one of my mother's memories: Once, Ama striped her face with mud and told them about Hu Gu Po, weighing down her daughters' bellies with a swallowed story so that they wouldn't be whipped away by typhoon wind, by wind that flexed the trees like bowstrings.

My mother liked to say she and I were born at the same time, into the same story, and that we were just growing at different rates: I grew like a tree and she grew like a riverfish. She said she'd died and been reborn many times in the span of my life. *Someday,* she said, *you'll go back to the river and give birth to me there, spitting out a jet stream of eggs, all of them me. I'll dew the skin of your fists. I'll hatch when you open your hands.*

GRANDMOTHER

Letter I: In which the river is not responsible

Dear eldest,

Now that you are dead   you can see   why I
never wanted you to live. See how much lighter you
are now?   barren of a body   mother to
nothing? You   darkest of my daughters   in skin
in smoke. I burned you this   ash is yours
rebuild it into anything   you want me to be. This
letter is not   apology   . I am not writing for a
response   a bullet   doesn't ask to be given back.
My second husband the soldier   lives by the law
of loss   kill what you cannot carry   marry what
you cannot bury   writing will wring   lies from the
white   open a gate to our griefs. I have no need to
grieve what I named   . I'm   here shitting my
pants. The zhongyi says   *sphincter   loose as a
sleeve*   says it's because of my age   I suspect

it's your father   the first man   I married for
his soldier's pension   for a future the color   of
tendon   one night I woke to him   between my legs
tongue out   weeding my pubic hair with his
teeth   balding me   said he could see the lice on
me   the size of pearls   stuffed me with what he
plucked   I birthed hairballs the size of your head
rehearsed birth until you   born drilling   my body
into wind

      You   my littleplum   I raised you   braised
in my blood   let me begin   the river is
noodled with snakes   the river is not to blame   I
once saw soldiers throw prisoners into the river
the fish for weeks were shaped like boys   they say
the babies here   born gilled   bladed or
hammerheaded   evolution is the body becoming
its best   weapon. What feeds on your body without
permission is a parasite   children are no
exception. The only cure is to survive   what lives
off you

      The river   steals the sky   a color suggestive of
birds   where the river hinges like my elbow   it
floods   when I say   the snakes rise to the surface
of the river   like scars the snakes have always obeyed
my veins   the evening before you turned four
the rain came   red   my tongue rumoring
snake. I was nineteen   five babies   my
breasts   stones that skipped out of your mouth. You
practiced latching on my finger   firecrackering
my husband the second one   hard against me
prick parting my ass   I told myself be stone   moan
an animal awake somewhere   is smoke   I pour

rainwater into rice   for porridge   four of your
sisters   strapped to me. Two across my chest, two
on my back. I walk sandwiched by their hunger
rain ranting   down our street   you asked to put
on your boots   new ones I cut from my own   you
said you'd never seen a puddle before   a sea you
could span with your mouth   mirror the size of
whatever   I show it. Lake the width of your face
you have mine   nothing of your father   don't ask
me why   I hated you then   your hair grown up
black. You said you'd been watering it   long
you stood in the rain   waited for your spine   to
sky. I held you by the hair   stepped outside   you
dangling boneless   from my hand   my babies I
wear asleep   beaded to me. You   kicking your
feet as if dreaming this   I walked to the nearest
bridge   eight houses away   I counted   in
twos   swinging you   a sack of salt   I threw you
down   my tongue in my mouth   a salted slug
dissolving your name   the river
outraged by last night's rain   ate you   your
white-bellied feet   flippering   so fluent on land
wordless in water   in   in in in in   river
whipping itself   this raw   word   I

     I threw the babies in too. What alive   can tell
me why. I   & unstrapped the cloth   all four of
my babies spearing in after you   I I I   I   even then
they chose you over me   water trotted over
their backs   . Snakes arriving to scalp you   I
watch you open your mouth in the water   brief
flower   the snakes answering from inside you
     Years ago a storm chaperoned   your birth

the soil gave up its trees   for adoption the snakes
singing now   rhyming that year & this morning
my babies buoying   river lifting like a tongue to lick
my back   turn me   around   I do   I
needle my body through the water   stitch you this
new ending   I fish you out one   by one   last
of all you   my eldest   I went in   belting the
river around my waist   on land I lay you   safe
water flocking from your mouth   the river
revised you   a new body   ribs ridging into scales
your skull   a snakehead   legs arrowed into a tail
hands honed into fins

    Snakehead fish can limp   on land their gills
sewing shut   I carried my daughterfish*   home
in my skirt   released you all into a rainbarrel
from the river I take   frogs turtles fish   I scoop
the turtles from their shells   debone the frogs
with my fingertips   feed you minnows   whole
feed the barrel like my own   belly   in the water
you   slough your scales   your fin   fleshes into
a foot   you outgrow your barrel in a week   girl again

    I ask you not to blame the river   you did
anyway   you wanted the river dammed   some part
of you misses that water   umbilical cord of salt   silt
admit it   return to it   your name   the river
loving your wrists   like rope   you   my redgirl
my shithole   my first   to follow little missionary
boys around   hunting sparrows   frying them
on fencewire   candying the bones   I didn't want you

---

*   YOU LUCKED OUT. A TIGER TAIL IS SO MUCH COOLER THAN BEING
    A FISH. I KNOW YOU'RE AFRAID OF IT, BUT I'D MUCH RATHER BE
    FEARED THAN FEASTED ON. —BEN

around those boys I knit you a leash   from reeds
tied you to my calf   you dreamed of slaughtering
both my calves   vealing me   running from me. If
every mother in the world threw her children* in the
sea   how high would the water rise   to hood
me   how much of this coast   do I lose to you daily
    When you died   I asked the crematorium to
wash your body   clean as when it was born
bright as an onion   don't believe any doctor   what
whipped your blood to cream   wasn't sodium sofas
food coloring   it was the river roosting   in you
eroding   your bones into rooms   I've lit. I
admit to putting it there: I   pulled the river
through you like string through a bead   into
the mouth-hole   out the asshole   my life
threaded   through yours

*   小鬼, I WOULD STAY AWAY FROM WATER IF I WERE YOU. —BEN

DAUGHTER

Mazu

———————————————

The snake in Dayi's belly breeds itself into three. A braid of snakes born in the south of her stomach, migrating up through her mouth. Most days they slept in her bowels, wearing her intestines like sweaters. When I shined my flashlight down her throat, I saw a rope-thick shadow shouldering out, tackling her teeth. Dayi said a snake swam down her throat when she was a baby. It grew to adult size inside her, eating everything in her belly and leaving nothing for her blood. I asked her how the snake swam in and she said, *I fell in a river once. When I opened my mouth to shout, it made a home in me.* She said: *Anything open can be owned.* She said: *Never sleep with your mouth open or a man will slide in, just like a snake, and beach in your bowels until you belong to him. The only man you should marry is the moon*, she said, *so you can divorce it every morning.*

—

Dayi was my first aunt, the eldest of my mother's half-sisters. Ama's letter said her first daughter was born to be dead, a ghost in future tense, so I was expecting to pick up a corpse. But when we picked her up at the airport, she was not made of ash. The first thing she said to us was that there'd been no geese. She'd read somewhere that flocks of geese flew into the airplane engines, got minced into pie-meat, and that's how crashes happen. It was the first time she'd ever flown, and she wondered why the windows didn't open. My mother said there were no geese migrating until winter. And I said there was no air up there, only sky, which was not made of air but water. If she opened the window, the plane would flood and everyone would drown. *Just like you almost did,* I almost said, but my tail told me it wasn't time for a confrontation.

In the car, my mother watched Dayi in the rearview mirror. They had rhyming faces: same crow-colored hair that revealed its blue when the light inflected it. Same eyes: sap-soft at room temperature. The left eye and the right eye were siblings, and you could only speak to them one at a time. My mother was lighter than all her sisters, slicking so much horse-oil on her skin that the sun slid right off her.

Dayi was coming to live with us because of her frequent strokes: There was a bird in her brain that laid eggs of blood. My mother offered to take care of her in our house, even though everything my mother took care of went rabid. Her apples grew teeth instead of seeds, and our birch's branches curved down into claws. *We'll take care of her,* my mother said, and it sounded like a threat. There was a vengeance to the way my mother prepped the sofa, punching the pillow into shape, sealing the cracks between cushions with duct tape. *When I was born, I stole a mother from her,* she said. *And it's better to be born dead than with that kind of debt.*

My mother prepared for Dayi's arrival like a pregnancy, locking away sharp or flammable things, compiling a list of English names for her to answer to.

—

We brought Dayi to Costco. I told her it was the only place in the country where you could buy both your cradle and your casket. Your life span was the length of an aisle. Carts so big they looked like animal cages rattling across the concrete floor. I sat cross-legged in the cart and humped the bars until my mother told me to stop acting deranged. I said I was pretending to be a tiger in its cage.

While my mother prodded shrink-wrapped beef, thumbing the meat as if checking for its pulse, Dayi pushed me down an aisle wide enough for an airplane. The ceiling high as a church's. I told Dayi this was a place of worship: sacred were the super-packs of socks on sale, so cheap we wished we had as many feet as a millipede. Holy were the baked hams, fat as infants, waiting to be adopted into our bellies. Dayi and I opened every door in the freezer aisle: peas, pies, poultry. *Americans freeze everything,* I said, and when she asked why, I said it was because their mouths were probably microwaves.

Buy my casket at Costco, Dayi said. *Better yet, don't spend anything. Feed my body to the parking lot pigeons.* The Costco pigeons landed on the pavement in bulk and panthered across the lot, pouncing on our feet. Outside, my mother bought us hot dogs with a coupon and we slicked them with mustard, eating the buns and feeding the meat to the pigeons.

—

Dayi was born without blood. A doctor had to kill a goat and use tubes to siphon goatblood into Dayi's empty veins. But the doctor accidentally pumped too much blood into her, turning her red-hard and bloated as an apple. When Ama bathed her in a bucket, she bobbed ass-up in the water. Every day, Dayi wore something red: a petal she slid under her thumbnail, a handkerchief, a red thread around her wrist, a scar on her belly where her blood was shepherded in. Even her favorite foods were red: pig's blood cake, char siu buns, eels that grew scarlet gills after eating the corpsemeat of the drowned. Whatever she touched could only blush: Green guavas turned the color of biblical apples. Once, when she was a girl, a mutt that bit her on the ass became a bloodhound. When she drank out of the river, it unraveled like a ruddy ribbon all the way down to the sea. The missionaries called her blessed, a girl who could turn water to the color of wine, but Dayi never felt that way. Her molars grew in the color of raw meat, and her bathwater looked like a butcher's sink.

After Dayi touched three of her classmates by accident, the teachers told her to wear gloves to school. They were made of some animal's hide, skin on the inside and fur on the outside.

Dayi was converted by a Chinese missionary who wore two belts at a time—one to keep his pants up, the other to strip off and beat with. He taught the Bible in beatings: If they misspoke a verse, he flayed the brown off their backs.

On Sundays, there were tent-sermons and cheese sandwiches. There were buckets of lemonade and the American missionaries' children, named for the shade they became in the sun: The tallest son was Terracotta, the twins were called Blood, the little blonde girl was Rosewater. Of all the missionary children, Terracotta most resembled his color and went sparrow hunting with Dayi and her cousins, even brought along his own pocket of stones. Dayi and Terracotta shucked off the tail feathers, tore off wings that wore no meat, and grilled the torsos on abandoned sections of chicken wire heated by the sun. Cooked on wire, the sparrows' meat blackened in a grid pattern, but it tasted better that way: They could pretend they were eating something bred in captivity, something caged to collect fat. Dayi and Terracotta could pretend they shared a word for hunger.

Once, he kissed her. They were waist-deep in a river, snakes perming around their ankles. Terracotta taught her to skip stones, but Dayi preferred throwing them in deep, watching the snakes scatter in rings. She liked the way things sank. When he kissed her in the middle of the river, she thought of Jesus walking on water, the river cooling to glass around their bodies. Along the banks, black reeds fringed the water like eyelashes, thick and blinking in the wind. He bent her against the mudbank, buttoned his mouth to her breast. He pinned her by the palms like Jesus, but the holes in her appeared elsewhere. She thought of taking off her gloves, turning him the color of gunshot. She thought: If this is not divinity, then it must be death.

After that night by the river, Dayi checked her belly hourly, tapping it like a melon, not sure what she was listening for. The rest of that summer, Terracotta spent more hours with his father in the churchyard, building birdhouses everyone thought were bird traps. When the priests realized the locals had been stealing eggs and hatchlings from the nests and eating them, they dismantled each house. Terracotta grew two feet in one summer. In another year, he would grow a beard. Cheek-rash began to spread among the local girls, until al-

most every one of Dayi's schoolmates wore the same pattern
of redness on their faces, necks, inner thighs. When Dayi was
midwife to one of Terracotta's bastards, she waited for the
mother to fall asleep before bringing the child to her breast,
pretending it was hers. The baby responded to every sound
but its name, turning its head to birdcall, the telephone, rain.

I was born with a red birthmark draped over my belly like
lacework. Dayi called this karma, said my skin was her punishment for that day by the river. Dayi promised she'd pay to
have it removed when I turned fifteen, no matter how expen-
sive it would be. She said it was a price she'd been waiting to
pay.

—

Dayi was fathered by a ghost. None of us had ever met Ama's
first husband. We knew his punishment but not his crime:
He was in prison for five years before he strangled himself
with a shoelace, knotting it like a bow tie beneath the apple-
core of his throat. My brother said the crime must have been
something violent, like setting someone on fire or smuggling
bombs up his sleeves. But my mother said he was just another accused Communist, that the police threw his body into
a river with the shoelace still noosed around his neck, which
is why no one in this family was allowed to wear anything
with laces. *You'll summon his spirit through your shoes,* my
mother said. She was a self-appointed shoe surgeon, snipping
through our sneaker laces with kitchen shears, taping them
where they'd once been tied. Just in case he came to me in
ghost form, I wore a pair of scissors on a string around my
neck. I wanted to be the one to cut his throat free of its shoelace, the knot he pulled tight while gagging against it, his

tongue exiting his mouth as steam. Dayi called him *my Red father,* and I translated his image literally: a man with a red beard, a pyre made of red logs, a sky scraped red by smoke, a river slit like a vein, Dayi on our sofa the first day we took her home, shelling red-dyed watermelon seeds with her teeth, telling me she once saw a girl die like a melon, a girl who was reported to the police as Red, who ran away into the mountains and drank an entire river until her belly unbuttoned.

—

After school, Ben walked home with me to meet Dayi. When I'd told Ben about Dayi's ability to summon red, she asked me for proof. I said I hadn't seen it yet, but it had to be true. She spent every morning dressing her hands like wounds, wrapping them in gauze before putting on gloves.

Ben and I stood on the sofa, watching Dayi in the kitchen. She was dicing something red into something redder. Then her legs let go of their bones. She fell forward, cracking her forehead on the counter as she came down. Blood sashing across her whole torso. I tried to shout, but my voice calcified in my mouth. Ben and I ran to Dayi's body, holding her head off the floor and pinching her cheeks.

My mother drove her to the emergency room, and Dayi refused to undress. The doctor let her keep her clothes on under the gown, and the nurse cut a slit in her long sleeve to draw her blood. *They better not ask me to shit into anything,* Dayi said. *I shit for no one.* The doctors said it was a stroke. She was transferred to a room where machines charted her brainwaves into mountain ranges. There were bags of fluid feeding the veins in her arms. She was discharged early, given a warning: *No high-stress activities. No sodium.* When the doctor asked if we had a history of heart disease, my mother said no, we have no history, just stories, just a long record of surviving our countries.

Dayi's left side was paralyzed for a week after. She could only walk in circles, turn corners. Her dead thumb slumped forward, and I liked to flick it back and forth with my tongue.

Our word for *stroke* meant *the middle wind.* When the school called, asking why I had missed so many days, I said, *My aunt suffered two winds.*

At home, Dayi still refused to take off her clothes when my mother tried bathing her, so my brother and I dragged her into the backyard, hosing her down with all her clothes on. Her clothes so cheap the color slid right off the cloth. She spat water at us and swore the whole time, said there was no reason for a woman like her to be clean.

—

Dayi told me stories: How Ama carved faces into the fruit to make all her daughters laugh, how one of the neighbor boys accidentally killed one of her chickens with a fastball and Ama made him eat the baseball in front of her. How she worked the oxen till their hip-bones were lace-holed, how she cured colds by stirring dung into tea. How Ama taught my mother how to tie a string around the waist of a dragonfly and leash the other end to her finger, teaching her to see the sky through the fogged glass of its wings. My mother said she didn't remember any of these stories. She began to suspect they weren't really sisters: We'd picked up the wrong woman at the airport and the real Dayi had turned into a goose and flown out of the plane engine. One night, my mother called my fourth aunt to confirm.

Jie, my mother said. *How do we know it's her?* My fourth aunt told her to bring Dayi to water. Anything that resembled a river. *You need to see her inside a memory.*

After dinner, we drove to the birthmark-shaped reservoir behind 7-Eleven. Shit floated on the surface of the reservoir, though we couldn't tell if the turds were human or not. A few uncles tried fishing here, but all they reeled in were condoms bloated like jellyfish, bike chains, plastic bags, lighters. When we drove there after dinner, Dayi stood away from the water, gripping the fence with both hands.

My brother refused to go because he said boys went into the trees around the reservoir and dipped their dicks in and out of each other's mouths. When I asked why, he said, *That's just how they speak.* I imagined their penises as instruments: You blew to make them sing. I looked into the trees but couldn't see any boys holding penises up to their lips like flutes.

Near the shore, a goose pecked each of her babies on the head. When I came nearer to count them, the mother turned to watch me. She ran at my legs, wings flicking out like knives. Dayi let go of the fence, fisted the goose's neck in one hand, and flung it back into the water.

What convinced my mother they were related: Not the way Dayi shied from the shore, held on to the fence like a mother. It was her hand twist-tying the goose's neck. My mother remembered the only thing she'd ever seen Dayi do: Stick a pig in the throat. The throat is where its heart is located. They'd been girls then. Skirts blackened by rain, legs bladed to cut cane. The pig ran into the fields, blood bannering behind it. Strands of blood whipped so high, the sky was red for days and everyone thought it had miscarried the sun.

—

When she lived on the island, Dayi had three miscarriages. After each one, she ate a whole papaya with seeds, prayed to Guanyin, bought all new clothes, cleaned. Her longest pregnancy lasted one summer. The doctor told her to eat only things with seeds or eggs, so she ate only watermelon, the teeth-colored seeds of guavas, the ovaries of fish.

When the city bought her land, Dayi moved to another house, tin-walled. It was so cheap she knew it must be ghost-owned. She was right: A local boy had died there one summer, stabbed in his sleep by his father. His father, drunk that night and craving pork, mistook him for the family pig, though exactly how this was possible—the pig weighed twice as much as the boy, and pigs don't sweat the way sons do—no one really understood. The boy's father later said he knew something was wrong when he stabbed the pig and it made no sound. A pig always died singing its blood. After hearing this story, Dayi stopped cooking pork in that house.

Sometimes she liked to treat this ghost like a son, talking to him at the tail end of night: *Hello, pig-boy. I'm sorry your father wanted to eat you.* She pictured a boy with hooves. She pictured a baby with ears on top of its head. Dayi wanted the pig-boy to stay. Whenever the neighbors retold the story of the murdered son, she always stopped them short of saying his name. As long as she never knew it, she could name him herself. She gave him her maiden name, a homonym for red. It was a relief to love something already dead.

——

My mother said Dayi needed to get a job that would explain her gloves, so Dayi got a gig at the strip mall acupuncture parlor. She showed me her fake license, the laminated card printed with someone else's name. When she took me to work, I sat at the reception counter with my legs crossed, my tongue greening on the guava candies I stole from the reception desk's glass ashtray.

Once, when a customer came in asking about hand jobs, she thought it meant any job you did with your hands. *It's called a strip mall for a reason,* my mother said. *Learn to take off everything but your gloves.*

—

In every version of the story, Mazu is the daughter of a fisherman. When she didn't cry at birth, they named her Mo Niang: unmouthed maiden. Mazu taught herself to swim, held stones in her hands to practice winging through the water with carried weight. She could project herself in dreams, swimming out to save men from the mouths of storms. When she died saving her father and brother from a typhoon, she was rebuilt as a red statue. I asked Dayi if she really was the reincarnation of Mazu. She said no, we were descended from pigs: Oxen could plow and chickens could lay eggs, but hogs were born for slaughter, ferried from birth-hole to mouth-hole to shit-hole. I asked what happened to Mazu after she died, and Dayi said: *America is a kind of afterlife.* Looking at old photos of Dayi back on the island, I almost believed it: She stood on the beach, mouth full of light, braid heavy as an anchor. She was pregnant in almost all of them, her belly casting a shadow no body would fill.

In the last photo we took of her, Dayi held a nail clipper in her mouth. She'd learned not to rely on her hands, to sew with a needle tucked between her two front teeth, tongue authoring the knot. *I can do everything but wipe my own ass,* she said, laughing. *No one's got a tongue long enough for that.*

—

Whenever Dayi fell asleep, my brother and I played our game: Whoever could fit the largest thing in her nostril without waking her was the winner. The first time, we shimmied a bobby pin into her nose before she snorted awake, oinking. After that, my brother called her Pig Aunty.

The biggest thing we could ever fit inside her was the metal rape whistle my mother kept under her mattress. When Dayi breathed out of her nostril, the whistle wailed her awake and my mother came running into the living room with her cleaver raised, asking where the rapist was.

Another time, I fit three of my fattest fingers into one nostril and told my brother I had reached her brain and was feeling it for ripeness. *What's it made of?* he said, and I said, *Birds, a battalion of beaks pecking away my fingertips.* Rescinding my finger from her nostril, I pulled out a nosebleed by accident, kept unreeling the red ribbon of her memory.

—

Ben and I nursed the yard-holes, feeding our fingers into them, searching for another letter, one that would explain what to do with the first. From inside the house, we heard Dayi call for us, and when we ran into the kitchen she was leaning on the counter. Dayi held her belly, but it looked no larger than when she first arrived to our house. We led Dayi to the sofa and propped her with pillows, patting the sweat from her neck and forehead and waiting for our mother to come home.

Dayi moaned and bit a pillow until its seams split. Water puddled in the kitchen where Dayi had been standing at the counter. I wiped the water from the tiles, but the stain seemed to straddle the whole floor. I asked Ben if it was possible to have a phantom pregnancy, and Ben said phantoms don't produce water.

By the time my mother came home, Dayi was an hour into labor and we'd taken off her pants. Ben said we should have taken off all her clothes just to be sure, but I asked her: *What kind of baby is born above the waist?* My mother squatted between Dayi's legs, tugging something out of her: a dark scarf of blood unknotting into a neck. It was a goose, born beak-first, gowned in slime and blood. I pet its back, licked the fudge of blood off my fingers.

When Dayi asked to see the baby, we walked her to the backyard. My mother set the goose down between the holes, let it walk in circles around itself, wings glued down with mucus. Dayi said nothing, crouching. Then she took off her gloves and pet her goose once, head to tail, until it was red, a species no one had named yet.

—

I told Ben I'd dreamt of eating the goose. We were lying on our backs on the baseball diamond, her right hand perched on my belly, restless. Her hand hatched all our plans: When she made a fist and opened it, I knew it meant there was a fledgling idea inside it.

In my backyard that evening, Ben and I untethered the

goose from the fence. In the center of the yard, the □ was open. *Trust me,* Ben said, holding the end of the leash. Ben made a clucking noise with her tongue, coaxing the goose to the center of the yard.

Following Ben and the goose to the □, I watched her kneel beside the hole and grip the goose in both hands, tamping its wings down. She lowered it feet-first into the hole, its wings battling her hands.

I asked her what she was doing and she said, *Birthing it.* I said no, this was sacrifice, this was smothering. Ben said, *All mouths require feeding.* The hole sucked it out of her hands, swallowed it down. Only the leash was uneaten. Ben reeled the rope out of the hole. We stood back, toeing the soil to see if it was tame again. It hiccupped beneath our feet, then burped hot steam in our faces.

That night, I visited the hole to see if it had finished digesting. Shoveling my hands into the hole, I groped for its gag reflex. The second letter lolled out like a tongue, wet with some other country's rain.

I told you it wanted meat, Ben said, as I tugged out the letter. When the □ dilated back to the width of our heads, we reached in and pulled out fistfuls of bird bones crumbling to salt. The skeleton of Dayi's goose-baby. One of the bones we recovered was a rib, the other a wishbone. We each held one end of the forked bone, breaking it between us.

The bone-halves jerked in our fists after we broke them, magnetizing back together. Where they touched, the bones welded themselves, glowing. Above us, crows gathered to knit the night. Ben and I tried to break the bone again, to seduce it from symmetry, but the wishbone flew out of our fists. It hovered above our heads, growing a body around itself. Rot in reverse: The wishbone fattened into fleshcoat and feathers, feet forking from a torso. It rose to join the crows, a goose threading in and out of the flock, going home.

—

After her last stroke, the one that made her forget our names, Dayi decided to go back to the island. She said it was time for her to die on someone else's dime. On her last night, we walked to the reservoir again, tossing the geese everything we could find in the reeds and bushes: bits of hot dog bun, fishbone, pieces of a broken Frisbee. Dayi searched the sky for a red goose, mistaking the sun for hers.

Dayi said that feeding the geese was actually cruelty. *They get too big from being fed by humans, and then they can't migrate,* she said. They could no longer fly south, or maybe they no longer needed to. They were stranded in their bodies.

Before Dayi left, my mother said she was glad: *Dayi's useless. She's practically a piece of furniture.*

Furniture is extremely useful, I said. Still, I wondered if one day Dayi's legs would seam together, her skin leathering, her spine reclined like the sofa. Dayi always joked that she was becoming a goose herself, nested on our cushions, crumbfed. When I asked if feeding her like a goose meant she'd never fly home again, she said this was already home. Here, where my mother replaced all the salt in her dishes with sugar, cooking everything so sweet we spat it back into our bowls when she wasn't looking. Ants infested the kitchen. Dayi and I loved when the ants came. We used pieces of Scotch tape to pick them up in clots. We perforated their lines and counted the seconds it took for more ants to pour into the gaps we'd made. We liked to kill them one at a time, watching

an entire lineage of ants walk over their dead, no one bother-
ing to pick up the body or bring it home. We kept waiting for
the queen to show, but we knew it was winged, somewhere
above our heads and unkillable, her appetite an entire army.

—

For a month after she left, my mother wouldn't throw out the
uneaten jars of baby food we had bought her, all the red flavors: beet and apple, mixed berry, rhubarb. When she died,
we sent paper lotuses to be incinerated along with her body:
My mother folded each palm-sized petal at the dinner table.

At Dayi's cremation on the island, my aunts lifted bone
fragments from a tray with chopsticks and touched them to
the light, discovering that Dayi's bones were filled with red
crystal. They broke all her bones open like geodes. Even her
heart was candied bright as an apple. They sent my mother a
bone splinter in the mail. It shot out of the padded envelope
and bounced twice on our dining table, brazen as a blade. It
was the length of my forefinger, blunt on one end and forked
on the other. In my fist, the bone harmonized with my heat.
Sang me to my knees. My mother said we should sheathe it in
a sandwich bag and pulverize it, but in the end she kept it,
filling a vase with beef blood and planting the bone upright,
watering it every day to grow back Dayi.

GRANDMOTHER

Letter II: In which the clouds are eaten

Dear second daughter,

When you were born you laughed instead of
crying. It impressed me. I liked your honesty. I
humored your helplessness, your misplaced faith
in my body   I lifted you from the river   a fish
in my fist   loosed you into the rainbarrel with
your sisters   you were the last to girl   back
snakes chewed the mud   spat it back out   venom
in the soil spreading to the sugarcane   sour this
year   trees retracting their roots   we begin to eat
the cotton   roll them into balls   our bellies full
of our fists   the neighbors go to hunt the snakes
but they rescind into the water   sink to the bottom
pretending   to be stone
Sometimes I dream   raking the river with my

teeth   staring every fish in the fin   none are you.
You   saltiest of my fishdaughters   I steered you
by the tail   in my rainbarrel   what substitutes
touch: water   hunger   I dreamed the clouds
were calves   I killed to feed you   in the morning
only cotton   swabbing my belly   I envy the river
its boneless   I

    After weeks   your sisters turned back to
daughterbodies   not you   yearly a fish   you
photosynthesize   light into bone   I feed all my
daughters full of cotton   my daughters so empty
they shit streams of fog   one day I'm home   I see
your sisters standing around the barrel where you
glowbone   your sisters so thin   cotton infants in
their bellies   doorknob knees   ghostfins   I see
my eldest with her fist around you   your bone   in
her mouth   your sisters   hunched together taking
turns   biting into you   scales sequinning
their tongues   I beat them till they let go   too late
I forgot   what you looked like as a girl   I saved
what they didn't swallow   some bone   an eye-pit
when your sisters shat out your ribs   I returned them
to the river   beat its surface blue with my hands
the neighbors told me water can't bruise   said I will
never be forgiven   they saw me drop my children
into the river   did I really think they would be
returned to me the same   species   it's true
there was a whale in the river one summer before you
were born   you head-butted my belly blue
wanting to get out of me   to see it   no one knew how
the whale squeezed itself in   but it was there

I swear it was   a whale   I pet its jellyhead   it
mooed at me   you laughed from inside me too
tickling me   on the day your sisters ate you   I
asked the river to give me back   a girl again
instead it spat out a fish-hook   at my feet   said go
hook yourself   another daughter*

---

*   THIS IS HARDCORE. IS IT CANNIBALISM IF YOU EAT YOUR SISTER
WHO'S ANOTHER SPECIES? CAN HUNGER BE INHERITED? I HOPE
YOU'RE NOT PLANNING ON EATING ANYONE SOMEDAY. THOUGH
IS THERE A CHOICE IN WHAT YOU HUNT—WHAT HUNTS YOU?
—BEN

DAUGHTER

Parable of the Pirate

On our last week of school before summer, Ben and I fed her birdcage to the holes. She said the last letter felt incomplete, and we needed to metabolize metal this time. Metal, she told me, could be melted down into water, and the holes were always thirsting. We believed there were three letters, one for each daughter my Ama had left behind. *All losses come in threes,* Ben said, and I thought of my mother's three toes in the cookie tin.

When we lowered the cage into the □, it took an hour for the hole to heal around it. Beneath the dirt, we heard the high whine of bars being wrenched, teethed apart, scoured of rust. I was worried about the shadow-bird suffocating while it was buried so far beneath the sky, but Ben said it was worth killing what was inside. We'd already sacrificed an entire goose. I told her not to remind me: These letters had too many casualties already.

The □ didn't open for four days, and I told Ben to be pa-

tient: Metal was metabolized more slowly than meat. Ben
said I should tell the holes a story: They'd open their ears to
listen, and then we could reach into them and search. But I
said I didn't have any stories, especially if they were about
Ama. She was the voice and I was the ear. *Then tell one of your
ama's stories,* Ben said.

Every other night, my mother used the new landline to
call Agong, but Ama was the one who picked up. Agong's
mind had unmarried all its memories, and sometimes he
called to tell us the Japanese were invading and we should all
find a well to hide in. The nights Ama made him sleep on the
sidewalk, he'd duck under a chili bush and slug into the soil,
awaiting whatever army was morning.

When I was the one who picked up the phone, Ama gave
me marriage advice: *No mainland men,* she said. Agong and
my father were born in neighboring provinces, and look how
they were now: *My husband is gone in the head and your father is gone everywhere else.* She said men were synonymous
with missing. Then she told me to ward off boys by holding a
skinned ginger root between my knees while I slept. I stole
the ginger from my mother's cabinet. It swelled with my
sweat and chafed me hairless, but I ground myself against it
until my crotch burned and it prickled to piss the next day.
My mother said Ama was corrupting me, but the cure worked.
Boys in the neighborhood veered their bikes away from me,
and even my brother said his tongue burned whenever he
spoke to me.

Other times, Ama told me about stealing the neighbor's
chickens, slaughtering and skinning and cooking them so
that there was no evidence of the crime. Ama was the one
who taught me the laws of ownership: *It's yours if you were
the one to birth it,* she said. *Or the one to kill it.*

The story I told the holes was this one:

The first time I got a fever, only months after my father left for the mainland, I wet the bed twice in one night. My mouth was hot and oven-doored, baking my tongue brittle when I tried to speak. After days of staying home with me, of swapping my bedsheets for towels and saran-wrapping my pillow to keep me from clawing out the foam, my mother called Ama. I knew she didn't want to call, but she hadn't been to work in a week and we were running out of grocery bags for me to vomit into. I couldn't hear what she'd said to Ama, but after she hung up and knotted up the plastic bag of my vomit, she swiped the slime off my chin and said, *I have to go to work. Feet don't scour themselves of fungus.*

I knew she wanted me to contradict her, to tell her to stay home with me, but instead I said I wanted to see Ama. My mother stood in the doorway with the bag of vomit flopping in her arms. A leak opened in the corner of the bag and my belly drained out of it, a stew splattering her toes. She stepped through it, came to my bedside. Said I didn't know what I wanted.

But what I wanted was both of them beside me, their arms impersonating a bridge above me, but that would mean I was the river below them, siding with the water that had almost drowned my mother.

Ama took a seven-hour bus, heading north to us with crates of Coca-Cola and a bag of ginger that required two seats. In our kitchen, Ama boiled Coca-Cola with slices of ginger wading inside, a Cantonese cure she learned from the other women at the factory. She held my mouth open and poured in the ginger-cola, wouldn't let go until I swallowed. Her fingers corseting my throat. My mother watched in the doorway, waiting to intervene, but Ama left the next day.

She'd sewn me a charm to put inside my pillowcase, a stuffed gourd of felt and cotton balls. My mother threw it away every morning, but I stole it out of the trash and slept with my mouth around it, a gourd I'd ripen into my daughter.

Ben told me to keep going, that the holes were opening, listening through their throats. But the story was too long for me to speak: My throat would run out like a ribbon. Inside the house, I wrote what I remembered, folded it into squares, and fed it to the □.

———

TRANSLATOR'S NOTE: Ama told me this story during my fever. I didn't remember anything she said until days after she left, when my mother said I should delete all recollections of Ama before they invaded my neighboring memories. But this is a story I don't want to forget. Other things I don't want to forget: The way Ama held my hand when I dreamt I was stranded in a boat, the mattress flooding with my own sweat. When I asked her what the sea was like as a child and she said *here's a story.*

Is it possible that she threw her daughters into a river? Maybe she thought they were on fire. Maybe she thought she was saving them. Is there a way to tell a story without sides?

Parable of the Pirate: Ama's Interlude

[To be read in Ama's voice. Suggestions: Read this aloud underwater, or speak perpendicular to a strong wind, or swallow a fork before speaking. Bleed your voice of its language, then learn a sea's accent.]

—

You tell the story like a white person.* Too much language. I prefer concision,† a story with scissor blades. Useful for what it can sever. Let's say your great-great-grandfather stole his name. Before empires and before men and before my hips began barking at me to sit down, back when blood was sweet, we lived in houses underground. We dug into the mountain soil that was so wet you could wring rivers from it. Our doors were holes. We came home by climbing down ladders. If home is beneath your feet, it means you're always home. We planted our shit in the ground to grow more mountains when we ran out. We didn't aspire upward but downward: The deeper your house, the safer you were from sight, from soldiers, from grief engineered by armies. You think you dig holes in the yard because it's your idea? Digging is the design of your body. Holes are what marrow is made of.

The empire had two categories for us: cooked and raw. If you married a mainlander and let them stew their children inside you, you were cooked. If you lived in the mountains and fucked rivers, you were raw. Grandfather Isaw was yolkraw. He hard-boiled the whites of his eyes by looking directly at the sun and shooting it down. One day, men came up the mountain with pots, ready to boil all the boys in the tribe. Isaw volunteered to boil himself alive and go down the mountain to seek adventure. He fathered a dozen half-raw, half-cooked daughters. He fried you a family. He went to sea on a

*   Ok, what Ama really said here was *foreigner,* but I think we know she really means *white person,* white devil, gwailo, baigui, etc. Substitute your own culturally appropriate term here.

†   See the irony yet?

boat he'd stolen from a fisherman. Cut the man's throat and speared him in the water. The blood summoned a shark, which swam off with the fisherman's balls in its mouth.

He lived as a fisherman until his boat was boarded by a fleet of pirates. My grandfather did not mind being a pirate: He liked it better than fishing, and anything was better than being on land where everyone was trying to cook him. The pirates called him Three-Blades—and yes, of course he carried three blades, all of them different lengths, all of them named after snakes—until he killed his first merchant.

Isaw took that merchant's name because he liked to collect names the way other men collected wives, and because it would help him pass for Chinese. Now all the pirates called him Old Guang. Back on land, my grandmother thought he'd capsized and died, and soon resigned herself to widowhood—she never minded it, really. She didn't love her husband any more than she loved having fungus between her toes. My aunts and uncles didn't miss him either: Old Guang was just a fart that infiltrated the house. Before he was kidnapped, we saw him only once a moon.[*]

The captain of this pirate fleet was a Tanka man[†] named Ah Zheng, younger than my grandfather but taller, slender as a dagger. From afar, his ship looked like a mouth: The wood was sun-dyed white as a jawbone, and along the railing of the ship he'd embedded stakes of ivory that looked like teeth from a distance. The ivory stakes were a form of defense against being boarded. Most of Ah Zheng's people had been slaughtered by the Cantonese, and piracy was vengeance—if

---

[*]   Ama really said *once a month,* but I thought *moon* would sound more old-timey.

[†]   Ama used a slur here—I prefer not to write it.

the Cantonese called him unfit for land life, he would wield the water as a whip. He would capture all their ships, welt their hulls, melt their foreign gold and gild all his teeth in it. All his life, the shore was a father*—he knew he would never be allowed to meet it. Fine by him. He preferred water to women.† He had been conceived and born at sea. Some say he could sing to fish, that they threw themselves into the boat whenever he was hungry. Some say his balls were big enough to shoot out of cannons.

I knew a man like that back on the island. He had a fishpenis and had to live waist-down in water. If he waded onto land, it'd breathe the air and die. All the other fishermen held their breath to blow him. His fishpenis shot eggs down their throats, and they gave birth out of their mouths a month later. You were conceived in a mouth, too. Your mother spoke you in her sleep, during some dream about drowning. Don't believe when she says you've got a father.

The other pirates all said his ship was powered solely by flatulence, that he stood at the prow and farted a wind that blew him anywhere in the world. They say his ship was armed with sharks swimming always beneath him, and that was why he'd never lost a battle. In two weeks he'd won so much loot, his entire fleet began to sink with the weight of all that shine. Now they stored their bounty in seaside cliffs, branding treasure maps into one another's backs. Ah Zheng's feet had never felt land, and the idea of living with his feet locked to the earth—that shit-colored filth—made him physically ill.

The sea, on the other hand, was his glittering garment.

---

*   What is Ama trying to say about my father?

†   More on this soon!

He was so blessed, even the storms bounced off his boat. Ah Zheng resembled an ordinary hog* on land but was handsome on water, especially reflected off a surface—he wore the hat of a Tanka, but underneath, his hair was like water, stroking his shoulders or coiling on its own. He was born with a blowhole on the top of his head that he liked to stick a miniature flag inside, a flag that was just a piece of toilet paper. His eyes were the bitter color of grapes. Always remember to spit out the grape skins or you'll get eyes like that too, all seed. You'll see everything dark as light, everything loved as lost.

All this to say: Old Guang, my beefhearted fishdicked hogspawned grandfather, fell in love with Ah Zheng. At the beginning of his piracy career, Old Guang was seasick, bent at the waist and waddling to the rails. Ah Zheng would clean my grandfather's face with his own silk sleeve. He told my grandfather that acupuncture would cure his seasickness, and invited him back to the captain's cabin. Ah Zheng's acupuncture needles were made of fishbone, invisible to the light. Though Old Guang was afraid of needles, he said nothing.

Ah Zheng was undressing him, and suddenly my grandfather's mouth felt like a sea urchin, spike and salt. When Old Guang was naked, Ah Zheng directed him to lie facedown on the pallet. He sterilized each needle in seawater and strong vinegar, then hovered his hand over my grandfather's left shoulder-bone. Old Guang yelped, and Ah Zheng laughed: *I haven't even put it in yet.*† When Ah Zheng slipped the needle directly into the shoulder-bone, Old Guang moaned. It didn't hurt, but the sensation stayed for days.

---

*   I don't know what an *ordinary hog* looks like, so please feel free to imagine this for me.

†   Is this a "that's what he said" joke? Good one, Ama.

Old Guang and Ah Zheng fucked with urgency. Ah Zheng's beard tasted of sea spray, stinging his whole skin. My grandfather really believed that Ah Zheng was a reincarnation of a god—how else could he be so young and so confidently commanding a fleet larger than the emperor's? How else did he grow such stately long legs, such a deeply cleft ass, a crack all shadows lusted to live inside? Sometimes, their lovemaking was closer to prayer: My grandfather held Ah Zheng's semen* in his mouth for as long as possible, torturing it of taste.

Old Guang was the crew's best navigator. He claimed to have ejaculated all the stars into the sky. Even his crewmates— mostly other kidnapped fishermen—had to admit Old Guang was their best addition. Occasionally, when they did get lost, Old Guang wanted to stay that way: Ah Zheng fucked better when he was lost and needed another body to shore on. The last time they were lost, they loitered beside an island inhabited solely by crabs. Crabs with shells like raw emeralds. Crabs with rainbowed claws. Albino crabs. Crabs so dark they turned the sea to ink. Mirror-shelled crabs. Crabs with a thousand legs that could burrow in stone. The entire island was a beach with holes every two feet. Each hole had its own crab species. With their food running out—they hadn't stolen a ship in weeks— all the pirates tried catching crabs with nets made of their own hair. The crabs were fast, but the pirates managed half a dozen: two hot-pink ones the size of palms, and four thumb-sized crabs the color of tongues. That night, they roasted the crabs on their boats, cracked open their shells with stones.

The next day, the whole crew was too sick to sail. A few of the men even died, and they threw the corpses onto the beach.

---

*   I wish I hadn't just learned the Mandarin word for *semen,* but here we go. And yes, this story is being told in Mandarin. See: linguistic imperialism.

Crabs scuttled out of their burrows and carpeted the bodies. In an hour, only the bones were left. It was karma, Old Guang said. *We ate them, so they demanded to eat of us. The debt is paid.* After that, everyone got better, and they sailed far from the cursed island of crabs. The only person who hadn't gotten sick was Ah Zheng, impervious as ever, blessed by some god that didn't reach the Chinese.*

Nine months later, after the fleet had successfully kidnapped a Dutch ship full of muskets (and after half the crew had blown off their toes learning how to use them), Old Guang felt an ache in his crotch. Even Ah Zheng's acupuncture didn't help. The only relief was jacking off, which all the pirates did nightly, shoulder-to-shoulder on their bed pallets. Ah Zheng was happy to help with this task. One night, after a dinner of stolen Portuguese egg tarts and rice wine, Ah Zheng and Old Guang fell asleep in each other's arms. Near midnight, the ache woke Old Guang like a hammer to his crotch. He was suddenly too large† for his own skin. He ran up to the deck and vomited into the moon-bleached sea. Ah Zheng woke and ran up behind him. *Is it the pain again?*

Ah Zheng didn't know much about pain: He had never lost a tooth or bled or been sore from saddling waves. Some said he was clear-blooded like a fish, and that was why no one could ever tell if he was wounded. But Ah Zheng knew pleasure. So he stood behind Old Guang, close enough to bite his shoulder, and held Old Guang's penis in one hand, moving in a rhythm that mimicked the ship. Old Guang ejaculated into the sea. The relief came like a blade. Ah Zheng tucked Old Guang back into bed, and they slept in the shape of spears until morning.

---

*   See: karma.

†   Enough with the euphemisms. Ew.

In the morning, the whole top deck of the ship was coated in crabs. Crabs of every color and size sequined the ship, filling it a foot deep. The first man to step out on the deck had gotten his big toe pinched off, and his shouts woke the whole ship. When Old Guang climbed up from the captain's cabin, the crabs parted for him. He stepped onto the deck and crabs scrambled away, clearing a path. Old Guang repelled the crabs like magnets, all except one: the biggest of them all, the only crab that was an ordinary orange.

It was the size of an infant, so fat its legs trembled. Old Guang reached out to touch it, and it immediately collapsed and retracted its legs, dead. All the other crabs had collapsed too. The other pirates were frightened: *Did they follow us here? Where were they all hiding?* They kicked each crab back into the sea—thousands of them—too terrified to think of eating the meat. Meanwhile, Old Guang kept the body of the big orange crab, which was already starting to smell of decay. Ah Zheng humored him, but reminded Old Guang that eating the crab could make him sick. Old Guang nodded, but secretly he disagreed. He recognized the crab. In dying, the crab had spoken its name.*

Back on land, his wife and children had gotten an omen of their own: The evening before my grandfather returned home after years of piracy, it rained. The rain was rancid and full of guts, liquefied fish. The next morning, while everything was still damp and smeared, Old Guang arrived at our door, stained to the knees with mud. He didn't speak for weeks, and he had brought nothing with him: no boat, no

---

* Not really sure what this means, but I sense an omen here. Do you? But no woman in my family can be rushed. When someone tells a story, expect ass-to-chair the whole day. She won't even let me use the toilet. I'll wet the page.

brother, no cutlass or evidence of his piracy. Nothing but a silk pouch, dark with blood, and inside it, a spoiled crab. The meatiest crab his wife had ever seen. The only thing he said to her, before resuming another week of silence, was *Cook it for me on a full moon night.* She obeyed. She could do nothing else: Old Guang would not eat or speak or come to bed.

The night his wife cooked the crab, my grandfather finally spoke. He had spent all his days home reweaving his fishnet, cleaving trees for a new boat. Whatever had happened, he was ready to reenter the sea's country. The family watched him shape a fish-hook out of a dog's jawbone, rubbing his thumb again and again in the same place until it began to curve upward. At dinner, his wife arranged the crab in the center of the table. His children ate unsalted rice gruel and a pinch of egg yolk. The crab was for him alone,* wearing a wedding veil of salt, its body cradled in the steamer, glistening with sea-sweat. Old Guang began to pray, and his wife startled at his voice, which now had a sea's accent. Up and down and up, rocking her ears to ecstasy.

He told the story one tooth at a time: Ah Zheng was defeated. The fleet was folded up at the bottom of the sea. They'd met an old warship full of coolies. Ordinarily, they never attacked British ships, which were even better armed than the Portuguese. Even outnumbered, the British had their tricks. So Ah Zheng's men stayed away. But this time, Ah Zheng's fleet had gotten close enough to see the coolies,† the ropes around their necks and feet. Ah Zheng had heard of the many

---

*   Typical internalized Confucian patriarchy. Why do we always have to wait for the man to eat? It's not like they cooked any of what they're eating. They don't even do the killing.

†   *Ku,* meaning *bitter. Li,* meaning *work* or *strength.* Ku-li. Bitter work. Bitter strength. This is for me to remember.

men tricked into contracts or ripped from their sleep, thrown into the bellies of ships and collared. The men who harvested sugar in Cuba or scraped seabird shit from caves in Peru. Cantonese men—the very men that had banned his people from Hong Kong—were now the ones being dragged through the sea on leashes. Ah Zheng believed this was karma. But he also believed in divine intervention,* so he steered his ship straight into the British cargo hold. A hole bloomed open, and the water threaded in, sinking that first ship. The British veered away and fired their guns at Ah Zheng's pirates, felling rows and rows of them. *Oh shit,* Ah Zheng said. *Fuck this.*†

Remember, the coolies were quarantined together in the cargo holds. And most of them could not swim. Remember, too, that Ah Zheng never meant to save the coolies. He meant to drown them, which of course was the only way to save them. Better dead than kuli. Ah Zheng whistled, summoning whales and sharks to head-butt the British fleet. Two of the six coolie ships were sinking quick, and a fourth was injured. Old Guang and Ah Zheng, of course, resolved to die together. All the other pirates chose suicide-by-sea, flinging themselves over the side. Better dead than captured. In the end, there wasn't a lot to see: gusts of gunpowder, cannonballs burrowing into Ah Zheng's fleet, shards of ships embedded in the sea like shrapnel.

Ah Zheng kissed Old Guang a last time, the water already past their hips. It was true: Ah Zheng's blood was fish blood,

---

*   You're probably thinking, *Wait, does that mean Ah Zheng thinks he's divine? A god? Is this story Buddhist or Christian? Karma or god?* Luckily, Ama seasons this story with a variety of faiths. Whomever you believe in will definitely make a cameo at some point.

†   Updated the swearing because extremely specific references to certain deities are no longer relevant in our so-called *globalized world.*

completely clear. Or maybe the wetness was his tears. Either way, the salt of that last kiss scoured my grandfather's tongue, cleared his ears. He knew then. He remembered the crab's name, the crab he still kept below deck. He whistled with three fingers in his mouth, prayed the crab's name in his mind. And it came: It flew out of the water a hundred feet away, its legs webbed into wings. It quadrupled in size, the diameter of an umbrella, and now it was skimming the sky toward Ah Zheng and my grandfather.

They each gripped a wing, and now the crab was lifting them both, tugging them free of the boat's carcass. Old Guang blacked out—from fear or relief, he wasn't sure—and did not remember holding on. And yet, when he woke, he was home. He was lying belly-down on the pier he'd sailed from years ago, before he was a pirate, before he'd sunk and been saved by a crab. Ah Zheng was awake,* standing on the pier, his back to the rain-thawed sky. Now my grandfather knew for sure. Ah Zheng was crying bullet-sized tears. He was rocking the crab in his arms. It was dead again and shrunken back to its original size. No sign of webbed wings. Its legs were leggy again.†

This was the first time Ah Zheng had ever stood on land. It had taken him two hours to get on his feet: The vertigo had overcome him, and his legs could only straighten at a slant. He wasn't used to a floor without feedback, a ground without any groove. But he didn't want to fall too loudly and wake up my grandfather, who had been sleeping as if dreaming, kicking the air and twitching his nose. Now that they were both

---

*   Glad to know that my Ama doesn't subscribe to the "kill your gays" brand of storytelling.

†   I'm not a professional translator, okay? This is the best I can do.

awake and on their feet, Ah Zheng and Old Guang could only stare at the crab, wait for it to confirm itself some kind of god, some kind of patron deity they would now have to spend the rest of their lives repaying. But it remained a rotting crab.

Remember: Ah Zheng was born divorced from all lands, all nations.* He hated the dumbness of trees, the way they never ducked the axe. He hated the shit-smell of soil. Roots disturbed him, those gnarled limbs that thieved water for a living. Ah Zheng was also a hunted man, wanted by the empire for piracy, smuggling, murder, the kidnapping of fishermen. Old Guang was just another of his crimes. Meanwhile, the crab exhaled steam. It was demanding to be brought inland and cooked. Sometimes it hissed with a girl's voice. So they parted—Ah Zheng to the sea, Old Guang to his mountain.

And, of course, by now you know how my mother was born†: Our grandfather ate the crab, steamed with green onions and glittered in oil, and spat a pink mouthful across the table. That wet fist of meat began to mewl and writhe, as if something was tented inside, beating a way out. A fetus: fully formed and orange as the crab's shell. The crab was no god or ghost or demon. It was his daughter, born from a half-cooked man and a pirate, with a name no one could pronounce. The child spoke it herself, a sound halfway between swallow and song.

Be careful what you ejaculate into the sea. A crab could crawl onto your ship and grow your child inside it.‡

---

*   A metaphor for the migrant?

†   See: the beginning.

‡   This part was obviously directed toward my brother, who is sitting by my bed and clearly doesn't realize it's a joke and starts nodding all serious because he's just so weirded out. I mean, who's about to feed their spunk to the sea?

My grandfather, having successfully sired children with his wife and a pirate, retired back to his fishing boat. My grandmother didn't mind having one less person to feed, so he spent the rest of his life scouring the sea, holding the fishing pole between his knees as he doodled maps with both his hands. They were nonsensical maps, maps that were all ocean or all land, that had rivers ending in volcanoes or mountains that punctured the sky and let out all its color. They were maps with no directions, no orientation, no decipherable key.

Sometimes the maps were just arterial collections of lines, rivers balled up like thread, roads without beginning or end. They were maps to get lost with, and when passing boats advised him to turn back, head toward safer waters—when dockhands tried to sell him real maps with real trade routes and real countries—he refused. He was trying to be lost, and he was professionally good at it. As long as he was lost, my grandfather believed that Ah Zheng would have to find him, recapture him from home, place him in the bondage of belonging again with someone.

I choose to believe that Ah Zheng found my grandfather again, delirious with thirst and far from any coast; I still dream about it; I still see him in a fishing boat, small as a hat; then he's suddenly overshadowed by a frigate; Ah Zheng on the deck, waving his shirt like a flag, bare-skinned and salt-striped; the logo of Ah Zheng's new pirate fleet painted in his own blood; a scab-colored crab with a hundred legs; a hundred-legged crab with wings; Ah Zheng scolding Old Guang for leaving their daughter on land, letting her be corrupted by land-hemmed people; but at least there is time enough for a million more children, a million-gendered child;

between them, there is an entire century to father; an entire sea to sire.*

I'm not going to change the sheets for you, not even if you wet yourself. Why do you think you're sweating so much? Because you're sick? It's the sea in you. That stretch of sheet where you've pissed the mattress: a shoreline. The heart's a fish. If you open your mouth, it'll swim out† of you, touch air, die. When I say shut your mouth, I mean survive.

—

When I retold my mother the story, a week after I got better, she said all of Ama's stories were figments of my fever and the only piracy in our family is the bootleg-DVD kind. Our cousins on the island used to send us shrink-wrapped packages full of pirated movies from Hong Kong, and we'd watch them while my mother massaged horse-oil cream into my scalp. She said it'd make me smart. I said, *You think a horse is smarter than me?* My mother said yes, a horse can be set loose anywhere from home and still know its way back. The skin on the back of my neck was always paved with snake scales, drought-crusted and rough. She alternated between slathering the back of my neck and dewing her feet with oil, which she did under a blanket so I wouldn't see her toe-nubs. She said most days she forgets they're supposed to be missing.

---

*   Okay, so these last paragraphs are my addition, not Ama's telling. But it's true, I do dream about Ah Zheng and Old Guang. I prefer this ending, which doesn't end. I think Ama would say I'm sentimental, that I shuttle every scene to the sea, but I'm the editor here. I'm the one who sees salt as a lineage. I'm the one who's saying these two were born in one body. This story is just surgery, sewing together what is already belonging.

†   I cannot confirm the accuracy of this statement.

She said the nubs ache like gums, that she'd rather have teeth for toes. A mare for a mother. I thought she was trying to warn me about Ama, but all she said was *Drinking Ama's boiled soda will rot your teeth faster than anything.* I said nothing, but the memory of sweetness ghosted my mouth.

We watched martial arts movies back-to-back, all of them with similar plots: two brothers, one good and one bad, battle each other for honor on a rooftop. Improvised weapons and a serrated skyline. Guns, sometimes knives. A woman who must choose between the brothers, but in the end she dies (car accident, suicide, or assassination). The two brothers reconcile on the rooftop, but only after one brother's knife stirs up the other's stomach. The movies were so low-budget that each actor had to play multiple men, meaning the murdered brothers came back with different clothes and names and haircuts. It became a game to count how many ways a face was repeated, how many bodies one man could die inside.

The piracy was obvious: We could see the glare of a screen embedded in a black frame, the walls of a theater shadowing both sides. At the climax, a woman in the audience stood up and shouted something at the screen. A row of heads bobbed along the bottom, a shadow skyline. We watched the movie being watched. We could hear a woman whispering in one of the front rows, repeating every line of dialogue like an echo. My mother and I shushed her even though we knew she couldn't hear: She wasn't here. In the middle of the movie, the camcorder lagged and the audio mismatched with the actors' mouths, language spoken in a different time zone from the listener. We saw what was happening before we heard it. The knife cleaved a belly, too easy. The scream was stalled. In this shot, the sky was the same shade as my mother's name.

—

I ran upstairs to get my brother's camcorder and came back down, started filming. When my mother asked what I was doing, I said, *Pirating.* I was the woman choosing between sides, between side-wounds: Ama and my mother, related by blade. I filmed the back of my mother's head jutting into the frame, her commentary when the love interest committed suicide (*I never liked that actress because she has my eyes*), the oil on her hands like sunlight. I wanted to set them on fire, to turn her hands into light-bouquets and capture the smoke onscreen. My mother said, *You'll never be able to sell any of that,* and I said I didn't want to sell her. There was a scene near the end where my mother turned her head to look back at the camera, her face outliving the screen behind her, brighter. She held herself still as if posing for a photo. Behind her, credits ribboning down the black like names of the dead, cueing us to continue. I rewatched the footage later and saw that all the actors were blurred or out of frame, no storyline salvageable. Everything off-focus except my mother's face, the light speaking what I can't subtitle, clarifying for the audience: She's the only one I've been watching.

—

After I fed Ama's parable to the □, its mouth unbuttoned. The hole hummed, spitting pebbles like teeth, and when I pressed my ear to it, I could hear static like a radio, punctuated by the sound of Dayi's voice. Bits of words, none born whole. I wondered if this was her mouth now, if I had tuned in to the frequency of ghost speech. Beneath us there was a pipeline of voices, intersecting where we stood. Calling down into the hole, I told Dayi that I missed her, that sometimes I felt her fingers pinning words to my tongue, her breath guitaring the strands of my hair. In the morning, I found two letters flapping loose around the yard, spat out by the 口, and I chased them down, my tail perked for the hunt. Pinning them down with my feet, I took the letters home and soaked them in the bathroom sink. In the water, the words thrashed like fish, stilling only when I said them aloud.

GRANDMOTHER

Letter III: In which a knot is tied

Dear third daughter,

Your birth came easy to me   involuntary as
breath. From birth   knots were your only form of
speech: to say your name   you knotted a string
in three places   you knew all the ways to tangle a
thing   I predicted your life knotting   around
your neck   I kept so many things away from you
jump ropes   sewing thread   purse straps
     Still you came home every day with cinched
wrists   young branches recruited   into bracelets
garter snakes   scars   you could braid your own
hair before you could speak   tied knots into it
one for yes   two for no   three for don't
bother me   when you were hungry you unraveled
a knot   two if you were thirsty   you spoke to me
in undoings   I hear your wife is a Hakka woman

a tour guide in the south   that you two are running
a hotel now   her fingers reading your knots   in
the dark   I hear you buried a pair of scissors
together on the beach   for the wedding   I want to
know what you fight about   if you ever
mention me   the mother   the summer I took
you and your sisters to the far shore   the one
facing the mainland   the ghost-
     bridge   you asked why so many people once
crossed the Strait   there was a war a war a war our
island was captured for   I told you the sea here is
sold to the biggest bidder   the country where my
own mother taught me   before crossing any body
of water   you pay it a coin   a bracelet   your life
     How much do you know about forgetting? When
your wife slips   a finger into you do you   think
of it as a birth? Her mouth mentors the dark
between your legs   she pickles her tongue in you
I am not asking   because I want to know   how
you are loved by a woman   once   I kissed my
girlcousin   my teeth all rotted the next month
flew out of my mouth as flies   once I tried to teach
you speech   pressed your hand to the woodstove
waited for you to say   let me go   your palm
sizzling like pork   the skin grew back   bark
your word for mother is missing   here's a story
you were born cordless   you cut it yourself
leashed*   to no one   born to leave me

---

*   WHAT IF YOUR TAIL IS SOME KIND OF REGROWN UMBILICAL
CORD? WHAT IF YOU'RE BEING FED THROUGH IT? I KNOW CORDS
DON'T USUALLY GROW OUT OF THE ASS, BUT IF I WERE AN UM-
BILICAL CORD, I'D WANT TO COME BACK AND AVENGE BEING CUT.

I raised all my daughters   like the dead:
your dead father the first man I married died   a red spy
born a bastard: the son of a servant &
a landlord he had night-sight   born with
nocturnal eyes   he believed rich men should be
rewritten   without bodies he tied his own father to
a fence   flayed him with reeds   years later your
father arrived   on my island   a boat we didn't
recognize   the soldiers brought guns   a language

Your father   half of a foot gone missing in a
war   when he was a child   on the mainland he
stepped on a Japanese landmine   his shin shot up
speared the sky   flesh fountain   it made him
laugh the pain   the doctor   puzzled his foot back
together. He snuck out every day of bedrest   lugged
his dead foot   he found a cave on the fourth day
the clouds shaped like colons   inside the dark   a
girl & her shadow   eight-limbed   . He assumed
she came to meet a man   or a moon   she taught
him how to make shadow puppets on the wall of the
cave   filtering light through fingers   pasting the
dark   over the night in the morning   he crawled
home   spent days practicing silhouettes   nightly
he climbed to the cave   his shadow-tutor casting
stories onto stone. Most about revenge: stories the
boy who grows his foot back twice   as large &
clawed & your father never made love to the
shadow-girl   tried once but the girl was

WHAT ARE UMBILICAL CORDS FOR, ANYWAY? THEY HYPHENATE
TWO BODIES. DO YOU SPEAK THROUGH IT LIKE A TELEPHONE
CORD? DOES IT CARRY MEMORY FROM THE MOTHER TO THE
BABY? —BEN

cave rock   it hurt to enter her   one week

a rockslide down the mountain   he crawled

toward the cave   saw its mouth   gated by boulders

he tackled each stone   by the time light broke in

morning &   no one inside   when he spoke her

name   what he thought was her name: his echo

never noticed that before. He danced   his shadows

along the walls   she never answered his hands with

her own:

    When your father told me this story   I revised

the ending   one day   the shadow-girl waiting

with an oil lamp. She threw it at the entrance   to

enter the cave   he must walk through   burn the

body that brought him   to me   when your father

met me he shadowed me for days   heeled like a

bitch   broke an umbrella in my fist   I said make me

a new one   he folded it from newspaper   oiled

so the water leapt off it   handle carved from the

body of his warpistol   he kissed me beneath   my

skin   wasn't   even raining   the sun a bullet

through us both

GRANDMOTHER

Letter [ ]: In which I am the driver

Dear [ ] daughter, Jiejie, girl I gave to this country,

Today the crotch of my underwear is a landscape
painting. The landscape is mud for miles   cleft-ass
mountains   cloudturds. The zhongyi says
loose anal sphincter   says it's age but I suspect it's
because   your father liked to do dirty things to me.
He must have knocked loose a beam   in my bowels
I let him put it in wherever   I couldn't grow another
daughter   the zhongyi says I'm beginning to lose
motor skills   I say I never knew how to drive anyway.
He laughs   says the body is the motor   in this
situation   says I am the driver   in this situation I
remember   how you learned to drive from that
ghostboy whose balls you licked   you think I didn't
know   heard you joking to your sister   about
planting his balls in the yard   to grow us a son

but could you   find someone to teach me how
to drive? I may shit the seat but I won't hit
anything   living
      Remember   the time you threw a knife to me
no at me   it perched on your sister   let that
be a lesson about intention.   I eavesdropped on all
your bones   laboring to make blood   your
throat   diameter of a fishbone   nothing could fit
down it   I injected water into your belly
needle stolen from the morphine-addicted widow
the one whose doctor husband   disappeared with the
rest of the men   when the rain was raided   the
police   told her to listen to General [   ] [ ]-[   ]
on the radio   transcribing the night into names
of the missing
      because they owned guns   fists   she didn't
tell them she was illiterate   I transcribed General
[   ] [ ]-[   ] 's speeches for her   when the soldiers
came again they told her eat what you've written
they said *a woman is only loyal   with a man's words
inside her*   I watched from the door   you were
strapped to me   batting milk from my breasts the
woman knelt in the road   the roosters   round her
preening   gungloss   round her mouth   O   O
O   she swallowed each sheet of my handwriting
      I used to think the neighborwoman   weak
her needles sinning   through skin now I pray to
replace my blood   something sweet & buzzed
honey   or bees   my bones a hive of memory
make me foamfooted   porridge-headed as your
father never thought I'd marry another soldier   his
sack of government rice   pregnant with rats

your father with his gold bars   love for American
rock   I watched him hawk his Japanese watch
sell his own shoes outside the bars in Taipei
eavesdropping on jukeboxes   he never knew the
lyrics   made them up in dialect   the province he
was born in   north of a river cleaving
mountains like an ass-cleft   when he sang so off-
pitch even birds   offended   shat all over his
shoulders   now his voice is a gnat I slap off my
cheek   you always thought I hated him   saddling
me with shit-stains   the river I   inherited like
debt   following me to bed   bowl of water where I
swim his dentures   at night I wrap him in lamp-
skin   search for a bulb small enough to fit his
mouth   beneath his eyelids clots of flies   I have
always wanted to be that empty   no need to be
anything but living maybe god   a hole we keep
filling with our dead

    I envy the way he watches   me   TV
the way he believes blinking his eyes changes the
channel. Sometimes he thinks shutting off the TV
means   the weather is off   the war has switched
countries   time to halve his skull into bowls
pour out the oil of last week   he thought the TV
a window   tried opening the country   climb in
this week   gardening   I dug a hole in the ground
beneath my chili bush   a rehearsal   the hole sized
for his skull   my chili bush will keep the dogs away
from his body   I'll home him better than any
country   the army claiming they'd pay him enough
to keep hunger   at home   every hole is a crown
the dead wear   save me from what   my hands

plot* when I let them off   the leash of my arms   I
mine for gods   all of them hiding   here I'll dig
him here   he'll share a grave with his gold

　　They always say: cold feet in bed means   a man
will leave you   I have had cold feet my whole life &
still   no luck

———

My tail ticked side to side while I read the fourth letter, beating out of sync with each syllable. Outside, my mother ap-
proached the holes with a butterfly net in her hand, prodding
dirt-mouths with the rod of it. But my holes were not traps:
They didn't shut around squirrels or stray cats, they weren't
triggered by anything but my voice. When they heard me
coming, they lolled open, begging to be fed, and I could smell
the rust on their breath, the blood. Sometimes, when they
were bored, they inhaled birds out of the sky, sucking in a
whole flock and spitting the bones at the moon. When my
mother walked through the yard, the holes grew snails inside
their mouths like blisters. When she tried to rebury the holes,
they grew back in the morning, camouflaged in hats of moss.

　　I sat on the letter to hide it from her. My tail pinned it
down, flattening all of Ama's words into the same sound.
When my mother came in with the butterfly net, a hole
gouged in it from the time my brother tried catching a raccoon, I asked her why I'd never met my fourth aunt. When-

*　　SHE'S BEEN DIGGING HOLES IN HER YARD TOO? AREN'T YOU WOR-
　　RIED SHE'LL COME UP THROUGH THE ONES YOU'VE DUG? THAT
　　SHE'S LOOKING FOR YOU? SHE'S DIGGING A HOLE FOR YOUR
　　AGONG. I WOULD BE WORRIED. VERY WORRIED. DOES HE HAVE
　　LIFE INSURANCE? AND WHAT DOES SHE MEAN BY "PLOTTING"? I
　　HOPE SHE JUST MEANS SHE'S PICKED UP GARDENING. —BEN

ever my mother called her sister, they spoke only in sentence-shards. My mother looked down, tearing the net off the rod like a wig, crumpling the fabric in her hands and tossing it over my head like a veil. There were dead flies floating in the folds of the netting, wings straining light through their mesh.

You look like a bride, she said, turning me toward my reflection in the window. *I made your fourth aunt's veil out of a mosquito net. When she got married, it rose and flew her away.* I said that protection from malaria was very important in a marriage. She laughed, plucking the net from my head, balling it in her hands. When she released it out the window, it opened into a parachute with no body attached, a ghost we watched go.

MOTHER

Journey to the West (II)

Arkansas 1980

It's summer and the sky is vomiting. It rains in chunks, like that time you were sick and threw up into your pillowcase and I sat all night beside you, emptying it every hour, wringing the sweat from your hair.

I calculate that the road trip from Arkansas to California is four days total if we don't pee. Jie and Ba and Ma and I are going to do it in three. Four is a bad omen to begin on. Our new city is east of LA, where some cousin of a cousin of a cousin has promised Ma a job at a skirt factory. Ba will be a fry cook. When the river here gets thick in the middle, he fries us a pyre of riverfish, blackening the bones till they're strands of our hair.

After three years, we paid off our debts—half in labor, half in gold—to the missionaries who did our papers, who bought our plane tickets and rented us the house that's so

thick with mice we call them the carpet, who convinced the
Sunday school to let Jie stay even after she began taking
money with her mouth. She told me she was blowing boys in
the woods, and for years I imagined she was blowing them
up, shearing open their bellies and burying dynamite inside,
necklaces of boymeat dangling from the trees. The Sunday
school teacher called to tell Ma about Jie's *carnal appetite,* but
Ma misheard *penis* as *peanuts* and said no, Jie doesn't have
allergies.

We pack in the dark, take the moon with us. Leave the frying pan with its bottom scarred like a palm. The doorknobs
we sold for nickels. Take the bucket we used to shower with,
threading water through one another's bones, going to bed
wet as newborns. Ma stewed riverfish in our leftover bathwater. We taste of what has touched us. Ma tells us not to take
everything, as if we own more than these bodies. Ba spends
the rest of the gold on a used car, domestic, painted the purple
of a bruised knee. Jie drives, and the ghostboy who taught her
is standing on our driveway the entire time we load up. He's
the same sand color all over, his hair matching his lips. The
boy tries to kiss her goodbye, just like the pastor did, but Jie
veers her face away and the kiss sprawls dead on her neck.

The morning we leave, the sun sags in the sky like a scro-
tum. The car has a dent in the passenger door that looks
human-shaped. Jie spends a whole minute petting the wheel
like she's taming it. Ma is shotgun. Ba and I sit in the backseat, windows down, suitcases trunked, a Spanish song on
the radio that we all somehow know the chorus to.

Jie and I bring jam jars to pee in. Ba fills them all, and we
stop once a day to leave the jars by the side of the road like
lanterns. Our piss is a gradient, darkening from clear to amber
as we run out of water. At night, we pull over and sleep with

the seats reclined, one back window open, headlights on in case of nocturnal animals. In case Ba wanders off, we paint his name with engine grease on the back of his windbreaker, along with these words written by Jie: DO NOT APPROACH. To keep him from sleepwalking, we knot three seatbelts around his limbs at night.

Ba's breath humidifies the whole car, and in the morning we wake with our windows steamed, our bodies hammocked in heat. Jie drives in a spine shape, swerving between lanes, uncontained. We pass Texas and unzip its border with New Mexico, which looks like the same state but thirstier, the cacti more nipplelike, asking for our mouths around them. The desert floor breeds rows of button cacti, and I'm tempted to wander out one night and undress them of their spines. Jie leans her head while she drives, half of her face frying against the window, the left half browning more than the right. I tell her she looks like two women splitting one mouth. *Go deep-throat a cactus,* she says. Go back to sleep. I dream it: my throat perforated with needle-holes, my throat turning into a sprinkler every time I try to drink.

Jie and I buy corn dogs and packaged pies at convenience stores, where the clerks look at us like we're a species of upright armadillo, yellow and armored. They watch through the window as Jie pumps gas, sometimes asking where we're going, sometimes asking where we're from. We say *Taiwan* even though we've never called it that, and the cashier grins big as a window: We see his missing teeth, we smell what he eats. He says he bombed Taiwan back during the war. Says it looked pretty from the air, a severed green finger floating in the sea. Jie tells him that Taiwan's silhouette looks more like a finger flipping you off, then runs out of the store with a stolen lighter up her sleeve. The packaged fruit pies dye our spit different colors, and when Ba sleeps at night with his mouth ajar, I can see his tongue glowing blue-raspberry.

We stop at a seafood restaurant somewhere left of Texas, though the closest sea is the one we dream. There's a live fish tank two feet from our table, and when the waiter hears us speak his dialect he bags us a fish for the road even though we've got no fire to cook it. Finally, we fry it on the hood of our car, the sun seething through flesh. The fish tastes metallic, too much memory of the sea in its bones.

On our maps, we pencil the line from Arkansas to LA: It's straight all the way across, no excuse to get lost. Still, we get lost. In Arizona, we drive in circles around the same three cities until Ma lets us stop at a motel to ask directions. The heat mirages our morning: the sun a severed head, the sky bleeding out from it. By the time we park at another motel, we've hallucinated a vulture plucking at a baby's rib cage (Ma), a Tayal spear wearing a pink wig (Jie), a military of small men dressed in furry purple vests (Ba), and a shark with toddler legs (me). At the motel, we fall asleep side by side by side by side on the queen bed with camouflage sheets.

—

Thirst thorns my throat. When I cough myself awake, I leave the bed and walk alone to the ice machine in the hall, shoveling jewels of it into my mouth with my bare hands, choking on the cold. I feel an urge to find the car and pet its muzzle, to confirm we've got a way to leave. The parking lot looks like an iced-over lake and I'm afraid to step onto it.

Our eggplant car is still there, still hot to the touch like a fever. The car parked beside it—too close—is also bruise-purple, but unlike ours there's no dent in the side, no piss-jars on the dashboard, no pigeon pancaked on the windshield. The bumper's been brushed like teeth and the moon reads me the license plate. TEXAS.

I should say: My sister doesn't star in this part of the story, but I need you to know I can see her always, see her face in the reflection of the window like it's the moon she's become. But I don't listen when the moon shakes its head, tells me to turn back. I go closer to the car.

At first I think I hear the engine revving, but there's no one in the front seat. Then I look to the backseat and there's a boy on his back, mouth open, brandishing his tongue and snoring so loud, I think it's the sky making that sound. I step back from the car when I see him wake up. He's Chinese. The car and his beardlessness and his eyes halving open like seeds.

He swings out of the backseat. Asks my name. Asks in guoyu: _____? I tell it. I speak with Ma's accent, wince at how millet-whipped and field-born it sounds next to his, how full of oxshit my mouth is. He asks if I'm alone. He slides his hand into his pocket and I duck, but he takes out a cigarette. I say my name. I say no. He asks if I am Chinese. I say we're speaking Chinese. He laughs and his teeth are bastard stars, brighter than anything the night owns, no lineage to their light.

I sit in his lap in the backseat. He kisses me a collar of bruises, a shadow to clasp around my neck. He pulls my hair back like reins, calls me by another animal's name. When he falls asleep, the moon peels off its skin, squeezed to pulp in my hands. I walk back to our room and sit in the bathroom till morning, watch a creek of red ants cross my legs five times. In the morning, Ma asks if I'd dreamed of getting pregnant with a flock of flies that tries to leave through my throat.

She told me it happens sometimes, that dream, and you always wake up with your own hands around your neck. Jie traces my neck with her thumb and doesn't ask. We drive the rest of the way in less than a day. Ma complains that Ba's bowels are like a waterslide. So we stop at a reservoir and Ba squats on the shore, the knobs of his hips brassy with sweat. His shit floats on the surface, still as a body. We drive far from the crime.

By the time we reach LA, it's night and we thirst. Our lips crumble off like cake. The car has three more dents, but none of us remember what we hit. Outside the passenger window, I see metal birds the size of trees pecking at the hills, and Jie says they're derricks, blackening their beaks in oil that comes from the soil.

We share a one-bedroom with a shower curtain down the center of it, our cousin and his cousin and his wife and his mistress and his mistress's son in one room, us in the other. Our cousin has a tattoo of a snake that begins on the back of his head and ends somewhere below the waist.

Want to guess where the snake ends? he says to Jie, and she says, *Don't forget I used to kill snakes for a living.* But he doesn't know what we did at the chicken farms, doesn't believe us. He takes our cash and promises us jobs in a few days. He makes us bowls of rice porridge thinner than piss, and we sleep on a mattress with an exposed spring, a hole in the center that we curve our bodies around. We take turns drinking from the faucet, swallowing mouthfuls until our bellies billow out, bigger than anything we could ever birth.

Back in Arkansas we had no faucet, just a hose dangling from the side of the house. Not the kind of hose you know: bigger, bitten by field mice, holes too small for us to see. At night, Jie and I hosed each other down in the dark. Chased each other around the yard even though Ma said someone would see us naked and turn us to salt. But we ran anyway, circling each other until the sky turned over like a bowl and cupped us to the ground. The stars were dandruff and we brushed them off our shoulders.

This is what Jie taught me, but please don't ever learn it: It's a trick where you hug the hose nozzle in your throat and shotgun the water straight into your belly without swallowing. She said that's how the people here drink, without needing a mouth, without a way to stop.

———

Deeper into my life, I meet a man who says he drove from Texas to LA by himself, back when he'd been in the country for a year and stole a car from outside a Cracker Barrel. He later drove back for his mother, but he couldn't remember the route he first took, the one where he passed a casino with two stone dragons by the door. He'd won two hands of blackjack and spent it on his first room in the city: a floor above the butcher's, a building between a church and the restaurant where Ba fried every genre of meat.

When the man says he undressed me in the parking lot of a motel, I try to recall myself, the girl I prayed inside, the boy I mistook for an engine. I have no alibi for that night, no other body I could have been in.

You know the man. I'm sorry for not saying he's your father: I wanted you to meet him as I did. I knew his touch before his name. He marries me, but it's Jie who's been in my bed the longest: When we shared the mattress, I heard her saddle her wrists every night. Her breath belonging to the back of my neck. She moaned a moat around us both.

On our honeymoon in the suburb south of our city, I see my husband's face in the dark and remember. Jie and I once learned to sound the same. In Arkansas, we used to test Ma by walking to her bedside in the dark, asking, *Who am I?* Ma always guessed wrong, always named the absent one. We laughed and said she'd never learn to floss apart our voices, tell her daughters apart.

One night, when I/Jie went to her bedside and asked who I/she was, Ma took out her fist from under the pillow and punched me/her in the throat, that tender cage where our thirsts perch. She said, *You sound different in pain.* It's true: Jie wails like some wounded animal. I go silent, as if the wound is an ear that will eavesdrop on me.

In the dark, I pretend it is Jie's voice saying my husband's name. It's her salt in the sweat we make. I am the mattress, the moon, below and above myself. It's only at the moment of pain that my sister and I individuate. That I'm brought back to my body, reminded it is mine.

—

During the week, Ma sews wholesale skirts in the downtown garment district, which I once imagined was an actual city made of garments. Giant scarves for crosswalks, sweaters on all the trees. But no trees here. In Arkansas, I saw rows of cows rigged to machines, their milk pumped like gasoline. We miss the fields fizzing with our piss, the taro we raised behind the church, the rain fucking our mouths full of a sky's salt. Ma says the factories are worse than farms, where at least a cow could shit whenever it wanted. No bathroom breaks for the ladies.

One time Ma pissed herself and got yelled at, so she

started bringing jars to keep under the table. It's hard to aim and run the needle at the same time, but Ma's always been coordinated. She can drum my sister and me at the same time, each hand keeping a different beat.

Ma says we have to learn quick in this city. Jie got robbed at gunpoint her first week here, working the cashier at the electronics store. It was a Chinese boy with half a beard, the left side. The boy spoke a dialect we'd heard only in movies. We wondered what part he was playing. Jie thought about playing dead, splaying on the vinyl floor until he left. Kept wondering why the boy only had the left side of his beard.

When the bullet spent itself into the wall behind her, it burrowed there like some nest bird. Ma says, *God took a big breath and blew the bullet around your head.* Jie says the boy was so stupid, he wouldn't have been able to shoot the sky. Still, I saw Jie pray that night. She got off the bed and onto her knees, her hair curtaining the bright theater of her teeth. I asked if she was crying. She wiped her nose on my arm and punched me off the bed.

On weekends, Ma cleans houses. You've never even cleaned your own room. You blame your brother for the stains on the mattress, but I see you pissing in your sleep too, both of you born with so many leaks, a lineage of them.

I was washing Ma's pants in the sink and found notes in the pockets, notes she must have stolen from the houses. Some were written on receipts, on napkins, on pink perfumed cards, on orange peels. I wondered why she took what was worth nothing to us, notes we couldn't read, addressed to anyone but us. If I asked, I knew she'd strike me into silence. Say I shouldn't go through other people's pockets. Never put your hands where they aren't getting paid.

When the notes dried, I balled them together into a paper onion and put it back in her pocket. Imagined her taking the bus out to another house in the hills, hands in her pockets the whole ride west, the noteball hot and pulsing in her palm, pumping like an organ that keeps her alive until she's home.

—

At the mannequin factory, Jie is part of the arm team: She's the one who counts the number of fingers on each arm before passing it on to the surgical team. The day after a heat wave, Jie and the other girls walk into the factory and see that all the mannequins have melted together into one body, some linked at the hips, others glued elbow-to-elbow. The girls have to spend three days with handsaws to divide the mannequins from one another, and even after that, most are unidentifiable by the standards of their manual. Jie drags them to the dumpster one by one. One of the mannequins has a belly like it's pregnant: The head of another mannequin has fused to its stomach. When Jie saws the belly open, she finds a single bullet in its center.

We have nothing to shoot it from, so we decide to bury it beneath Ma's chili shrubs. I am supposed to be watering them and haven't, so all the chilies are pale as finger-bones. After we bury the bullet, the chilies grow fat as udders. I pick them for Ma, but she says they've gone bad. I say they can't be bad, I just picked them. I pluck the fattest of the chilies and de-stem it with my teeth: She's right. They taste like rust, like menstrual blood, ripe with shed death.

—

I do yard work for an Armenian woman two streets over. Her hose is patched with kiddie Band-Aids, and she only has one tree that requires constant pruning. The tree bears some kind of fruit I have no language for, and when I try to bite into one, the woman slaps it from my hand. She points at her mouth, then mimes gagging. I think she's telling me they're poisonous, which only makes me wonder why I'm pruning this tree in the first place. The tree's branches grow in an upward curve, the shape of a bowl offered up to the sky. The dead branches are black and wax-soft. I climb into the lower branches and amputate the rotten ones, counting each as it drops. The tree one-ups me, rotting two shades blacker when I blink.

Jie says to be careful: The Armenian woman's husband is a soldier like Ba and shies easily, sometimes even eating the mirror when it shows him his face. The husband doesn't like people watching him, so I always look at his left ear when he pays me in cash. When I mow their lawn, the husband hides under the sofa and says I'll never find him. One weekend, the Armenian woman tells me not to come back. She says her husband is afraid of the monkey in the tree. He told her about it. He's seen it many times.

I say I've never seen any monkey. Describe it to me. Her husband says the monkey had a bald red face and a flat nose, hair thick as needles, a tail made of scissor blades. The monkey could climb high, all the way up to the ceiling of the sky, and sometimes it tried to thieve from the tree, pinching the leaves and pocketing the fruit in its cheek. The monkey had beady eyes and looked to be about breeding age. Her husband says the monkey is frightening him. I say I'm not afraid of any monkey, I'll come anyway. I'll help kill it. The Armenian lady says no, the monkey might bring fleas or babies, and that's when I realize the monkey is me.

—

Ma leaves the house early. Sunup: the sky bleeding where it's given birth. The floor is dappled with blood from the earlier fight, when Jie had thrown a knife. It was aimed at Ma but found its destiny in me. The knife landed in the delta of my inner elbow. My blood was dynamic, leaping out in two directions, avoiding the walls.

Earlier we'd been watching a TV broadcast about a serial killer back on the island. The man claimed to be a former emperor reincarnated into a mailman. He'd beheaded two girls with an axe, claiming they were his concubines from another life and were destined to join him in his death-palace. We reached the place in the footage where the bodies had to be blurred out. There was a head on the sidewalk, an adjacent stain or shadow, and a forensic scientist prodding the head with something like a long fork. Ma said that long ago, our tribe had been headhunters, and that maybe this man was mistaken: In his past life he was not an emperor but a man of our tribe, a hunter in the wrong time. Ma said her grandfather once showed her the head he'd stolen off another tribe's boy, how it was bloodless like a radish. How one eye still blinked, even days after death, and she waved at it in case it was lonely. For weeks, the whole family fed the head, offered it wine. If the skull learned to love the family, the fields would grow.

Jie said, *Enough, I'm trying to listen,* and we watched the beheaded girl's mother get interviewed. The mother said she'd tried walking onto a highway that morning, but god would not let her die, god chose her to outlive grief. Ma said the woman wasn't chosen, just stupid as a melon: She should have just tried in the evening, when there was more traffic and less visibility. Jie turned off the TV. Ba was asleep on the sofa in his cook uniform, a hairnet that's mostly holes, bare feet obscene with blue veins.

One time when Ma needed antidiarrheal medicine, Ba spent the money on a beach umbrella he said was wide enough to eat the wind and digest it into flight. He said if we waited for a storm and got under the umbrella and held the handle together, our feet would quit the floor. Ma said she'd beat his ass like a tambourine, but when she saw he'd fallen asleep on the toilet again, she spread a quilt over his body, covering his face like a corpse's.

—

After two hours of the TV broadcast, Jie said she'd started seeing severed heads everywhere. In the bathroom mirror, she thought her head was attached to nothing, rising off her shoulders like steam. When she saw a birthday balloon in the sky, she assumed someone had let go of their head. Ma said, *Enough about heads.* We ate leftovers from Ba's restaurant, lemon chicken that tasted like soap, broccoli with sauce-sagged heads. Ba dragged his sleeves through the oyster sauce, a slug-slick trail from plate to lap. Ma pinched him hard on the wrists until he noticed.

At the dinner table, Ma asked Ba if he'd remembered to put on his underwear. Ba's hands shook too much, so Jie and I sat on either side of him and took turns feeding him. Ma asked again if he'd remembered to wear underwear. Ba looked up, eyes unfixed, teeth typing on his lower lip. Jie blew on the spoon. She lifted it to Ba's lips. *Make a mouth,* she said. But his tongue was smoke and didn't know shape.

Did you remember to put on your underwear, Ma said again. Ba looked. He'd put his hands down but couldn't remember where. He stood up from the table and unbuttoned his pants, penis lolling out. It looked like a plucked neck, a bird stunned for slaughter. Ma set down her bowl. She reached across the table and clamped Ba's penis between her chopsticks, squeezed. *Don't check when you're at the table,* she said. *I will cut you off and boil the bone out.* Ba trembled, his pants thin from years of scrubbing the stains from his lap, the fabric almost see-through at his crotch. We watched Ma choke his penis with her chopsticks until its tip purpled. Ba's eyes like the fish's, lidless.

That's when Jie went into the kitchen for the knife. The wooden handle was sweat-softened, fingerprinted. Ma used it to sliver guavas in the summer, telling us not to swallow the seeds when we're fertile. *How do we know when we're fertile?* I said. *When you want most to be touched,* Ma said. We never saw her touch Ba unless she was knocking on his head with a spoon or dressing him in the morning, calling him a ____ who couldn't even thread his neck through a hole.

I was standing on Ma's side of the table, opposite of Ba, twisting the skin of her wrist so she'd let go of the chopsticks. Then there was a knife in the soft hinge of my elbow. Coins of blood on the table, the same color as the tablecloth, so at least I wasn't staining anything. Ma dropped Ba's penis, let it bounce off the lip of the table.

Jie stared at my elbow, then at her own palms, not knowing which to apologize for. I felt no ache, just a presence beneath the skin like a splinter. I reached down to withdraw the knife, but Ma said: *Don't.* Ma tied her quilting squares into a tourniquet, yanked it out an hour later. By then, I'd gotten used to its permanence inside me, a new bone. When she drew it out, I felt the absence more than anything, a hole where something once homed.

Ma left the morning after. She'd said nothing about the penis, my sister, my arm. Dinner still on the table from the night before, flies redacting the fish from its bones. She's gone three days before Ba notices, and even then he only asks why we've been eating porridge for every meal. Jie and I walk him to the bus, adjusting his hairnet before he boards, telling him to get off the bus when the road runs out of trees.

On the fourth day, Jie and I forget to wash the spoons and bowls. Collars of mold strangle everything. Ba and Jie and I eat in front of the TV, scooping cold rice porridge with our hands. We look like a litter of pigs, suckling on our fingers like this. We watch Monkey King cartoons on the Chinese channel, translating the Mandarin into Ba's first dialect, watching his mouth mime ours. Ba laughs at the sound effects, what we don't have to translate: In this episode, the Monkey King gets buried alive under a landslide, and the little rocks rivering down the mountain sound like gunfire. *Pa pa pa pa pa pa,* Ba says. Then the Monkey King gets rescued by a monk who asks for a debt paid in bones, so the Monkey King castrates himself and hands the monk his penis and says, *Enough? Ha ha ha ha ha ha,* Ba says.

When Ba is asleep, there's only the news. That's when we see Ma's factory on fire. We recognize the blacked-out windows. The whole factory haloed in flame, smoke we can't smell. There's a close-up of ten hoses spraying the flame at different angles, each one leashed to a different little man. Jie says the hoses look like alien penises. While she laughs, I watch the stretchers, scuttling in and out of the building like beetles.

I wait for Jie to tell me. To tell me Ma must be inside there. To say Ma is ash. Or she can't be, she is in our old house stroking a picture of our three sisters, she is on her knees in the next room praying, she is in the kitchen scraping away the mold that is our fault, she is undressing Ba in the bath and oiling his back.

The reporter on-scene speaks too fast to understand. We scan the screen for a body count, but there is only the day's temperature in the left corner. Jie shuts off the TV and we watch the last ghost-strand of static wriggle in the center of the black screen, then flatline.

Jie tells me to go to bed. She thumbs the broken seam in our sofa, tugs at the thread. *Go to bed,* she says. I ask if Ma is inside there. She says, *Sleep.* I ask if she's sure it's the right factory. I mean the wrong factory. Jie shuts off the light, and we sleep together on the sofa, her chest pressed so deep into my back I feel her heart punching my shoulder blades, harder than anything I've ever been hit with, louder than what we know how to say.

Have you ever wished me dead? I forgive you for that, just as I want you to forgive me for what's next. Ma comes home after six days, two days after the fire is put out. She hadn't been at work. She hadn't even left our block. She slept in the bathroom of the dollar store, locking it from the inside. All day she walked up and down the aisles, fingering pots of plastic putty and flipping the glazed pages of magazines, pretending she could read them. Finally, the employee told her to purchase or leave. Ma says yuanfen kept the fire caged from her, kept her corralled in the dollar store until the fire was done.

When Jie and I first hear Ma knocking, we think it's a debt collector and hide behind the couch. We know it isn't the police: Ma has no ID that can confirm her identity. She has no face in this country, only a fire's record of her body. Then we hear Ma calling our names, Ba's. Her fist flying into the door like a dumb bird. We let her shout. We let her keep knocking with no one answering. It's an entire minute before Jie climbs up from behind the couch, unlatches the door, presses her lips to our mother's knees.

It was easier to want her living when she was dead. We wanted one more day of missing her. We wanted it back, our grief—we wanted it real—but grief was just another thing we lost, another thing she took from us.

—

Sometimes I thank shangdi you won't ever leave home for a man. You can leave me for anyone but a man. Jie gets married two weeks after her graduation. The boy is nineteen and Cantonese and works as an auto mechanic at his father's garage, which is where they first meet. Jie is a serial roadkiller, collecting smashed pigeons on her windshield, daily scraping the dogs and raccoons and squirrels off the fender. When I'm riding with her, that's how I calculate our speed: in miles per dead thing. Jie finally decides that something must be wrong with the car. Maybe it's some kind of animal magnet. Maybe she needs new brakes. So she drives it down to the garage, and the boy is there with a wrench, looking at her in the reflection of his greased hands.

Jie gets married on a Saturday. She stole a bolt of sateen from her second factory job and I sewed her dress from it: It was sheer as rain, the kind of blue that looked green in indoor light, a border color. The morning of her wedding, Ma and Ba and I walk to the Baptist church and sit on the ass-dented pews and wait for the priest to speak. It's morning and the boy's family is also there, his three little sisters identically dressed in red sweaters and jean skirts. The sisters all stole a different part of their mother's face: The youngest one took the flat eyebrows, the middle one got the mouth, the third one's hair is already silver. The father is there too, in his mechanic uniform with a wrench in one hand, like he's waiting for something to use it on. Ma refuses to meet them, so we sit on opposite sides of the church and don't look for too long. Ma says, *Don't marry a man with more oil in his hands than blood.* Ba's hands are so greasy from the restaurant, he can't work open our doorknob. Jie says that engine oil is different from food oil, and it doesn't matter anyway because the boy is smart and going to college, and his oldest brother is a surgeon who once saved a girl with a hook-shaped heart.

Jie gets married in a month without rain. From the kitchen, Ma says it's an omen, says something about no children, but Jie says she doesn't want kids anyway. At night, kneeling in the bathroom, she once tried to insert rat poison into herself, but she got it up the wrong hole. *Now your ass is rat-free,* I said, and she laughed. Another time she drank insecticide and got diarrhea for so many days that our sewage must have dyed the sea brown and bloody. For years I thought babies began as insects, and that's why you drank insecticide to get rid of them. They began as gnats flying in your belly, and then they matured into flies and then into moths, flying out of the dark of your body and into the light that would incinerate its wings.

Jie gets married and the boy hasn't hit her yet. He'll do it only once, when he's home from work and doesn't like the way she's asleep on their couch, curled like some kind of animal in his house. She wakes but hasn't recognized him yet. There's a palm print on her cheek that will turn autumnal and then shed.

When the priest asks if there are any objections to the marriage, I stand up. Ma reaches up for my skirt, tugs me down to the pew. I don't know why I'm standing, only that I've spoken something. It sounds like *no* or *go*.

Before her wedding, we sit together on the mattress we share for the last time and I ask her why she has to get married so soon, why can't she wait till I make some money and we can live together, find a place with a room for Ba. *We can take him,* I say. *We can take care of him all day and work at night in a cemetery or something. We'll buy bars of gold and bury them together.* I tell her this with my hands in her hair, braiding it so it'll wave on its own tomorrow. If I do it wrong it'll frizz like bad wiring, but I always do it right, oiling my hands beforehand.

Jie says, *I don't want him. I don't want either of them,* and she turns around so fast I pull a handful of her hair out. I'm braiding it to the air. That's how I know she really wants to leave, when she turns around to me: her eyes bright from the pain of my braiding. She smells like my hands. She smells like the vinegar we use to clean Ba's piss from the floor.

At the front of the church, Jie kisses the boy and I make a fist around Ma's hands. While she walks back down the aisle with the boy who hasn't smiled yet, Ma pets my knucklebones in her lap, the two of us still here, still sitting as everyone else stands up to cheer.

—

Jie gets a job painting advertisements onto vans. The latest is
a two-day project, a giant crab that needs to span the whole
side of the minivan. It's for a seafood supply chain that recently got sued for polluted fish. Jie hires me to help her paint
the giant crab, which needs to smile and wear a tuxedo and
look like it is completely not poisonous.

We use a mix of house paint and spray paint, wear masks
to avoid inhaling fumes. We learn from Ma, whose lungs on
the X-ray look like nibbled cheese, like some rodent is burrowing a home inside her. Ba has bad lungs too, but that's
from the war, the piece of shrapnel that's still nested in his
chest and once set off the metal detector Jie and I made. It
comforts me, that if he was ever buried I could locate him
with a radio and some wire, no gravestone necessary. No need
for aboveground grief.

Jie traces the shape of the crab with permanent marker
and I fill it in. Orange first, then black for the shadowing. For
practice, Jie and I spray-paint orange crabs all over the street,
some of them lopsided or missing legs, some of them looking
like stains. Sometime in the afternoon, while the sun is pearl-
ing the sweat on our skin, the spray-painted crabs stand up.
They walk up and down the street on their half-assed legs,
limping in circles and mincing the gravel. Jie and I run after
them, flip them onto their backs so they're clawing at air, cutting the clouds. There are two dozen in total, two dozen crabs
we've drawn on the street and traced into meat. I say we
should sell the crabs, but they're too strange-limbed to be
eaten, too botched to breed. Jie decides they'd make good
pets, so we fill a garbage bag with hose-water and toss each of
the crabs inside, knotting it at the neck.

When the van's painted, she drives away inside it, leaves
me with the cans and brushes and stencils. The crabs awake

in her passenger seat, pincers snipping holes in the plastic bag. When we boil them that night, their meat dissolves into salt-foam, and inside their bellies are baby teeth, all the teeth we lost and swallowed in the dark, afraid that Ma would see our parts coming loose and send us back to the factory.

—

At home, Ma is asleep on a stool in the kitchen, her hands in the sink, her palms a litany of calluses. Alone on my mattress for the first time, I told the ceiling I'd leave Ma soon, find a man I can steer out of this city, a man who can snuff the sun out with his thumb.

In the kitchen, I can hear Ma struggling to tug the thread of her breath up her throat. After breathing all the cleaning chemicals and the factory air, Ma's lungs cringed to fists and beat at her ribs. When she needs someone to unsnag her breath, I fill a bowl with hot water and push her head an inch from the surface. The steam speaks for us. Her head bucks against my palm, but I press harder. Sometimes I want to sink her head into the water, remind her of the river, but I'm too afraid she'll become a fish and wriggle out of my fingers. It's more a punishment to keep her in this body, ache-lunged and coughing, skin worn thin as a lampshade.

It's not night yet, but Ma prefers the kitchen dark, says her eyes have never been native to light. When she wakes, her mouth opens before her eyes. She says, *Jie,* and I don't correct her. She gets up from the stool and finishes the dishes. I do the drying. Ba's not home yet, but he's already on the bus, counting the stops with his shirt buttons. At every stop, he unbuttons one. When the shirt's all the way open, the sweat of his chest beaconing through, he knows it's time to get off.

When Ma plunges her hand into the sink, groping for the bowl, she grabs the blade-end of a knife instead, releasing her blood into the water. Taking her hands out of the sink, I dry them on my shirt. I don't know why I'm rescuing her hands from the water when they once tried to d___ me in the r__. In a year I'll leave. I'll marry your father, any man I can ride away from here. The irony: We're the same as Ma. That's what Ma did, marry out of her country, marry out of her body.

—

You only know her as disappeared, but your fourth aunt was the first one to hold me when I was born: I practiced latching on her thumb, crying when I couldn't suck anything out but blood. Her absence now is the size of the sky. The only thing that fills it is night. At night, I watch your yard-holes gaping for the moon to descend into their mouths like a nipple, fill them with milklight.

Two nights after her wedding, she came back to pack the last of her things. Jie said they were driving to Reno for the honeymoon soon, and I told her not to gamble anything she wasn't willing to lose. Folding the denim skirts she'd sewn on Ma's Singer, Jie kept her eyes down on the seams and said she never intended to lose anything.

I told her she could leave most of her things here—her fake jade bangles that were just glass painted with green nail polish, the mannequin hand she stole from the factory and French-manicured, and that Ma almost threw away because she thought we were using it to masturbate. The soda can tabs she liked to pick up off the sidewalk and pocket, the coins she stole from public fountains and didn't spend out of respect for what had been wished on them, the shards of a tortoiseshell headband she once broke during a fistfight with another factory girl, though she couldn't remember what they were fighting over, only that she tore out the girl's ponytail, flapping open her scalp to the bone. A sun-scoured book stolen from the Montebello Library, a book she couldn't even read but that had a cover she liked: two blonde girls painted from behind, almost identical except for the angle of their heads, standing in a field full of some ugly species of flesh-colored flower with petals that looked like foreskin.

One of the girl's heads was half-turned, painted in profile, as if she was going to say something, something to make the other girl stay and watch morning make it here alive. Jie never said why she stole it, except once when she said the field reminded her of the island, reminded her of the time we thought we were being chased by a feral mountain dog but it had only been our own two-headed shadow, and when we finally stopped, we were in some other city where we had no Ma or Ba, where we were only sisters. When she asked if the cover reminded me of the island too, I knew she was asking me something else. But I only answered that there hadn't been any blonde people on the island.

Jie packed everything, which meant she wasn't coming back from the honeymoon, and that night we slept facing each other like we used to, the dark a third body between us, our daughter. From the window came the moon, a buoy we both held on to. I could smell the horse-oil in her hair, the boy on her breath: Her husband was picking her up in the morning, and then they would be in Nevada, the state we had crossed to get here, where the sun looked like a half-peeled orange and the dry air knifed out your lungs.

While she slept that night, I stole something from her suitcase, which was just the same twined-up shepi bag she'd

brought from the island. I took the book. I told myself it
wasn't stealing if the thing had already been stolen once. Two
acts of thievery canceled out, became something more like
salvaging. I still have it, that book. You should read it to me
sometime, skipping all the words you think I don't know. I
won't know them, but I'll pretend to, shame you for thinking
me stupid, and then you'll be so sorry you'll read the whole
book to me all over again, redacting nothing. Maybe you can
tell me what those two girls are doing in that field, what
they're watching for. If they're waiting for something to arrive or to leave. Don't tell me how it ends yet. Tell me that it
doesn't. The cover keeps changing every time I look at it, and
now the field is frazzled with animals, mountain dogs and
mice and a tiger tilling the field with its tail. Under the sofa,
in that dark rind of space where the mice shit and breed and
eat their babies, I slide out the book I stole from her, consider
feeding it page by page to your holes, erasing those two girls
from the field that's waiting to be sown with their bones. But
always, I keep it, something I know she misses, an absence
like a field, growing until it surrounds you. Something I know
she'll return for.

DAUGHTER

Back to Ben

The holes behaved like newborns, mouths open wide enough to swallow our hips, crying all night until the neighbors asked if we were running some kind of illegal orphanage, trafficking sound from the ground. My mother came out with a BB gun and shot them each in the mouth, but they spat the bullets back out and vacuumed the gun right out of her hands, inhaling her arms up to the elbows. My tail, too, was colicky, its stripes steel-bright with sweat. It flicked out in the night, upright between my knees. It was honing itself, rubbing against the whetstone of my bedroom wall. Only stilled when I promised to steer it like a spear, tell it who to stitch through.

Your ama is baiting us, Ben said. *She's getting ready to bury someone.* I said that the holes would tell me what to do, that they were already sirening, an orchestra of mouths warning me. The only time the holes were coherent was when Ben and I touched. When we kissed in front of them, they cinched their lips and listened, opening only to say *yes, yes.* While

night erected itself around us like a tent, we sat cross-legged
on the soil and its tapestry of worms. Ben laced her legs
around my waist. Her mouth so close I could see the serra-
tions of her teeth, sawing every sound in half so that I heard
it twice: my name, my name. I leaned forward, flicked her
upper lip with my bottom one. We met inside our mouths. I
found the seam under her tongue and undid it. With my
hands around her, I felt her spine through her shirt, a ladder
to thirst. All around us, the holes were full of a bright sound,
jingling like a handful of nickels.

My tongue slipped into her nostril and a pebble of dried
mucus dissolved on my tongue. I knew everything she'd
smelled that day: sweat, the soil, me. Ben knelt and kissed my
knees. She pulled my pants down as I lay back, soil gathering
between the halves of my ass. My hip-bone fit in the bowl of
her palm and shone. I sat up and worked her jeans down to
her ankles, the waistband of her underwear biting my finger
blue. When I bent my head to kiss where the elastic striped
her skin, she reached down and nested her fingers in my hair.
I wondered if it was possible for a tongue to turn into a fish
and swim into the dark of someone, disappearing forever
into that ecology of need. Ben gripped my hair, tugged me
closer until my face was not my face but a place where she
beached, where salt scoured my mouth of its name. I was
dew-hungry. I was the sound she made grinding against my
chin-bone, the holes rioting beside us, brimming with spit.
The moon newly minted in the heat and pressure of our
pressed-together bodies.

Later, when both of us stood in front of the bathroom mirror, we looked like we were wearing our graves, dazzling with
dirt, musky with the soil we'd turned on its back. Overnight,
the holes contracted into nostril-holes, breathing out a fog

that was thick as whisked egg, a fog that would fly far north-west to squat on top of the Bay Bridge. The fog smelled like fucking, like us, like our sweat fermented into sweet pudding, and when it began to rise, we found the last letter sprouting out of the ⬚'s lips. It parted the fog, flapping like a sail in trouble, no destination visible, and through the curdled milk of the air I could only see Ben bending down to save it.

GRANDMOTHER

Letter V: In which I name you

Dear final daughter,

   You married a man the opposite of your father
but I need to say   all men are synonyms   none
the word you're looking for   when your husband
went to the mainland you asked if you should have
followed him   I followed your father   to this
country & now I wear a diaper   once I brought a
piglet into my wedding bed   tucked it between my
legs & let your Ba fuck that instead   I wanted to be
the only one   inside my body   the piglet gave
birth later   to a litter of grenades   each with a
girl face   I pulled their pins   threw them into the
river one by one   rending the water   into rain
   I see the zhongyi once a month & I pay him   in
memories   my only currency once when you were
little I said you could love   your father or your

mother but you had to pick one   the one you love
is your leash   the other is a house you burn down
you never told me what you chose but I know
myself   to fend off ash   I tied the river in my
hair like a ribbon   I told you a lie   there is no
choice   you have no father

but me*   the one you call Ba   is not yours   I
conceived you with the river† I   mothered &
fathered you both   the Ba you love better than me
never sired you   I milked you   from the
mountain Papakwaka   I never named   you
answered to a whistle the same sound   summoning
dogs   every neighborhood bitch   born stray
when you were born I was dry   nursed you on a
bitch's teat   you slept   knotting your arms so
tight they never learned how to be straight. I stood
you against a wall   for posture   but you can't
train a spine to disobey itself   I am sending all
these letters separately   but know   I wrote this one
first. To my last   my not-son   my knot daughter.
You   born with your legs tied together   trussed
like a pig   in the tissue of me   birds circled your
cry   your namelessness: there are certain gods
nameless   true I didn't name you   isn't that a
form   of divinity? To be known to the world by
body   alone? Wake

your father sleeping beside me   you may think
you'll steal him someday   but I let him be taken
from his body   I lent him this life & now he owes

---

*   MISTRANSLATION? —BEN

†   ?????????????????????????????? —BEN

me   a country where I'm alive   today I wanted to
sever his tongue   skin it for the fish inside   in
this country you always spoke for   me when the
cashiers told me how much was owed   you counted
the money over   I want to know how much   you
will forgive me for   if I sewed his tongue to the
back of his skull   if I told you the truth about who
fathered you   when I say   come take him   I
mean take me   out of this sentence   I'm running
out of hands to hurt with   words to make you
return to me   I mean I mean the river
      today   on the Taiwanese radio channel
reports of two murders in one day   big news for a
shit-small island   one   happened on the train
older woman stabbing a stranger's child no motive
second about a mother sneaking onto the elevator of
a hotel throwing her baby off the rooftop garden
      dozens of witnesses stuck   evening traffic
straddling electric scooters   smoking out taxi
windows   that's when they saw the falling thing
a blue hospital blanket   same sky shade   some
described it   a stunned bird   a baguette   a
piece of meteor a plastic bag even after the clean-up
interviews   arrest   on-scene vigils   candles
no one would name what it was   the hotel renamed
itself & the mother   later a prisoner in Taoyuan
sentenced to labor in a candy factory   photo in the
papers   wearing a striped uniform hairnet   I
turned off the broadcast before her live interview
before she could say why she did it   I have always
known
      your favorite story: Hu Gu Po   you drew stripes

on your skin with ink   you the tiger-woman
never the child commissioned to kill it   pouring
oil into its mouth until   boiled from the inside-out
some of us   born to play predator   I know you
sometimes move your sleeping daughter from her
mattress to yours   replacing your husband's heat
with hers   you put her back before morning. You
just like to hear her breathing   at night a daughter
is a source of light   among others: fireflies   you
used to catch in your teeth bite open   drink their
assfuel   beast undressed of its stripes   the river
licking its stones like teeth   in my dreams   my
shits are soldiers   I bury them in my yard   my
bed   I mourn my bones that believe   they're
home   the moon a sound & your sisters   the
stripes I wear. This light I lair. Now my holes are
many   . Gods   blame me   though
memory. I taste torn   ,   .   brine   I. I have
many names

        hiring a home   from water,   . A history of
the hole   still family.   Forgive me
because   & I watched you   with my
mouth.   threw you   I loved
                          drown
                                    you
            to life.

                        —

I read the last letter aloud in my yard. Ben sat in front of me
with her legs forked open in the soil, her hand petting the ⏹.

Reading aloud to the holes, I mispronounced all the silences, rewrote them with my own prayer.

She's getting ready to bury him, Ben said. *She's baiting us.* My tail curled in on itself, fit in my hand like a stone. I wanted a window. I wanted to see something shatter because of me. I said I wasn't going to let her bury anything. The bone in my tail was wincing down to a wick, preparing for me to light it. Its marrow was memory.

When my mother came home from the foot spa that night, I said I was volunteering to be her weapon. She softened the knots of her hands in a bowl of hot water, said she was tired. But I said it anyway: *Ama is going to hurt Agong.*

She turned away from the window, her face wiped of light. The sink behind her was full, the water silver with knives.

You think I don't know? she said, and I knew she was mocking me, her voice stretched out of shape over the words. Everything in my mouth sounded already wrong, gone sour. I looked down at the bruised tile floor, at her shadow grazing on mine, eating it whole.

I know about the river, I said, looking up. *I think it's time to dam her.* My mother's knees must have come unscrewed: She knelt down, her back against the wall, her hands snagging in her hair when she tried to shift it out of her face. I moved forward through the dim of the kitchen, tugged down on her left ear like she always did for me when I was having a bad dream. When she jerked her head away from me, I told her she didn't have to be afraid of Ama. While I untangled the hair from around her fingers, I imagined loosing my tail like an arrow, shortcutting it through Ama's body, her ribs making a fist around her heart.

Do you remember that story I told you? my mother said. I asked her which one, and she told me about the women who hanged themselves with their own hair when the mountains were mowed over. Once, we lived inside the ground. The sun swung like a bucket of our blood. When I asked her why they hanged themselves, she said the only way to own your body is to die inside it. I said that wasn't true anymore.

She stood up and tugged her own ear, checking to see if we were dream-speaking. Steaming her hands over the bowl of water, she said, *You're not listening.* The steam opened her fists like flowers. The story about the women, she said, was a story about choice. How we had one. How we chose to be dead in our own bodies than alive without our language.

I chose you, my mother said, but it was like a channel had changed too quickly, one image unable to fade while the other overlapped it, contaminating all the colors, one story told as two. I was still thinking of the women who harnessed gravity with their hair, braids knotted to branches. The braids must still be there, still growing after the bodies were cut down. Braids vining down to the ground, growing so long they became some species of snake that strangles its prey.

When I asked what she meant by choosing, my mother said, *This family. I started it to save me.* I asked her why she couldn't go back for Agong. *Just for him,* I said. *No one else.* She still called daily to ask if Agong was wearing pants, even when Ama didn't pick up. I knew she wanted to dress him herself, to fill her clothes with his body.

I got out, my mother said, as if a family were a fire. *I chose your father over my father.* My father, who was not here. My father, who once bought me a popsicle at a zoo while I watched a monkey try to eat a broken bottle someone had hurtled into the enclosure. I wanted to say she'd made the wrong choice, but that would mean reversing my own body, returning to water inside her.

My mother opened the window above the sink. She was trying not to look at me, but her shadow acted as her opposite, circling me on the floor. *Do you know what it means to leave something?* she said. The air outside was too bright to breathe, dyed by with moon. *To give birth to yourself again and again? To lock yourself out of your life?*

I said we could knock. We could knock on Ama's door, and ask her to give up Agong. I'd keep my hand over my tail as we walked in, ready to draw it like a hilt.

Reaching up, I touched my fingers to her cheek, but she shook them off like flies. I walked around her and shut the window above the sink, relieving the window of its duty to breathe.

Ma, I said, and she shook her head, said that was what she called her mother and I should never let that sound out of my mouth. *Let's go now,* I said, whispering as if Ama could hear us from another city. *Let's bring him home and you'll be happy again. You'll be a daughter again.*

My mother laughed. *A daughter again? You're the same daughter until you die,* she said. Once, I asked her what happened to a body when it died. She said it became a story, and death was just another translation of it. Another time, I asked if gegu was true, if daughters really used to stir-fry their own flesh to feed their sick fathers. My mother said, *It's as true as you.* She'd laughed and said I was conceived in her mouth, born between her teeth and tongue.

If she kills Agong, I said. *Will you take him home then? Will you bury him in the holes I've made? Will he become a story?* My mother stopped laughing. She sat down on the bruised tiles and folded, perching her chin on her knees.

A story? she said, looking above my head at the leak in our ceiling. *I'm running out of them.*

One last one, I said. *A story to make Agong safe.* I got down on my knees and took her feet in my hands, remembering the time my brother and I had scissored through the socks. She let me hold them, her ankle-bones smooth inside my palm, stones shaped by my worrying thumbs. With her feet cradled to my chest, my mother said she'd never told me about her toes, the lineage of their loss. What she chose. I told her I thought Hu Gu Po ate them, that Ama had weeded them from her feet. She said no, the toes were casualties. When I asked her which war, she said I wouldn't know it by name.

If this story is supposed to sheathe me, I said, *it's too late. I'm already drawn. I'm already your best weapon.* My mother said I wasn't any kind of weapon if I didn't know what I was forged from, what I was shaped around.

The river, I said, trying to give her a beginning. But my mother said the river was nothing like either of us: It couldn't hold a hole. When hit with a stone or a fist or a baby, the river opened to swallow the body but sewed itself shut around it. *The river is revision,* my mother said, *but you're no river, so what I say is what you need to remember. Don't delete anything from me.*

MOTHER

Rabbit moon (I)

Three stories, then you can live. The first: We are born stone.
Papakwaka is our mountain, the nipple-peak we are weaned
from. A rock cracks itself against the side of the mountain
and spills two yolks, one brother and one sister. They are the
only animals on the island, and the girl gets lonely. She asks
her brother to marry her so she can birth a family. She in-
vents trees to be her bridesmaids. The brother refuses to
marry his own sister, so the sister solicits him as a stranger,
her face foreign with smeared ash. We owe our bodies to that
betrayal. We are conceived from deceit.

The second: Back on the island, Ba told me the moon was
pregnant with a rabbit. You and your brother are obsessed
with animal births. On the Animal Planet channel, you watch
shows about animals that fuck outside of their species and
give birth to babies that look like neither parent, that look
more like unassembled pieces, bloodied and without a blue-
print. Before you were born, I had dreams of giving birth to

your head before the rest of your body. I thought I'd have to sew you together with floss, puzzle your bones back together. I understand animals that eat their runts. Better to swallow them back into your body than let them be taken, buried outside of you.

You spend hours frying your eyes on a screen, sucking on suanmei and spitting the pits, impressed by 2-D animals that are 3-D where I'm born. *The forest is lit by eyes,* you say to the TV, which would be poetic if you weren't wrong. That's not a forest. It's a jungle. You wouldn't know the difference: A forest is a kind of growth. A jungle is hunger, a desire to dethrone light. Its only lineage is rain. Forests grow upward, fingers to the sun. Jungles grow sideways, outward, downward, whatever direction is the opposite of death. I used to think our island floated on the sea like leaves, but nothing named a country is light enough. I say *our island* even though you were never with me: You're here, watching bald-assed monkeys masturbate on TV.

After the program on big cats, you and your brother decide to live nocturnally. Your brother's learned at school that the sun is due to burn out someday, so we might as well live the darkness fully. *We're just pregaming the apocalypse,* your brother says, lidding our windows with butcher paper. I've always wanted you to dodge the sun. Your brother is the light one, coin-bright, and you're the rust clung to his side.

I call every week and tell Ma to put Ba on the phone. I pretend to take out the trash so you won't hear my voice, though the city is landfill anyway, and taking out the trash mostly means flinging it out the window. When you hear me speak to Ba, you look at me like you're watching TV in a language you don't speak. You move your mouth in sync with mine, trying to match the words to a preexisting key, but there are certain sorrows I've severed from you. This is all of them: When Ba calls me by my Jie's name, or my mother's name, even though Ma is right beside him, waiting for him to misspeak so she can whip him with the phone cord. When I was still a girlsapling, Ba made whips for the oxen he steered through the fields in summer, drying the cowhide on our laundry line. The whips were made of the same skin they scarred. That's when I learned: The best thing for breaking skin is skin.

Ma says she's started taking Ba to some doctor. The kind that asks you to swallow a bead and measures how long it takes for it to come out the other end, diagnosing you based on the speed of your shit. *I'm a better doctor,* I tell Ma. I tell her to send him to me, or I'll drive down myself and take him home—you're not the only one who has thought of this. Ma says no, she won't let him go, and I say, *That's exactly how you're killing him.* Ma says, *Killing him?* and you wouldn't know, you aren't listening, but that question is what tethers us. It's not that she's ashamed of having tried to kill us. It's that she failed, changed her mind, which means she wanted us despite what we made her: a mother.

You've moved on from jungles. Now you're all about domesticated animals. Dog-grooming shows, cats caught on home video, rodents that require complex surgery on their raisin brains. You think I don't know about your tail, but from the day it was born I watched it outgrow you. I saw it that first day when you walked into the kitchen and there was a shadow on the floor, a shadow too slim to match any of your limbs. Even when the tail's hidden, I can see where the light bends its head to groom it.

I tell you the moon is a rabbit. That's a myth from the mainlander side of you, my ba's side. Your father's side, too. I thought I'd married someone the opposite of Ba, a man who drives himself like a plow, a man I could steer anywhere. Now I wake in my bed alone and the sun hits my body like a closed fist.

What do you feel with Ben? Is she someone so literate in need, she makes your body a language for it?

You don't remember, but he cried sometimes, cried when he belted the breath out of us, and later I found him asleep with his head in the toilet bowl. *Be Papakwaka,* I told him. *Be harder. Be my rock-brother and I'll be your stone-wife.*

Remember that gumball machine outside the Ranch 99 where he skinned fish? Remember how you only wanted the green ones, the ones you said would taste like our planet, and when you got the red one, you cried? Your father fed it more quarters, but the next one was white, then yellow, then pink, then white again. The gumballs stained your palms like a crime scene, and still you asked for green. He went inside the store and exchanged half a day's wage for more quarters, kept feeding the machine until you got your green, your planet to suck soft, to embalm in spit. This is the man I want you to remember, the one who committed himself to your hunger: his hands cradling quarters, your green mouth glowing *go* like a stoplight. Don't tell me when to stop. Here's the third story, the one you need to believe. There was a god sent to earth, looking for disciples. He walked the forest—not jungle—and told all the animals that he was starving. The snakes volunteered to steal him an egg. The birds left to hunt him a mouse. The fox skulked off to rob a neighboring chicken farm in Arkansas. Only the rabbit offered itself. It leapt straight into the starving man's cooking fire, inviting teeth to its meat. To commemorate the rabbit, the god hung the rabbit's bones in the sky. And that is the moon. That's how we know all sources of light begin as sacrifice.

Your father, born year of the rabbit, hated that story. He thought no god was owed flesh or fidelity. But he still expected both of me. The year we were married I asked him to get baptized. Ma says our tribe used to have as many deities as trees, and that having many gods only multiplies your losses, diversifies your debts. The moon was our priest that night. I filled a kiddie pool with water from a park fountain. He said he wanted to be baptized in his own spit. I said no man can fit inside his own mouth. Get in.

On the third day, your brother removes the paper from the windows. You decide that being nocturnal is lonely, and when you check the mirror, your eyes aren't glowing. When your brother rips away the paper, I see you in the light for the first time in days, and your skin is no closer to being bone. When you go outside to feed your yard-holes, I drag you home by your calf. You bite my hand but I stay holding you. You'll need more than teeth to be free of me.

—

The last time I talked to Ba in person was after my wedding. My belly was filling with your brother, but I wouldn't know for another month. I wanted Ba to live with me, in a new city with my new husband. Ma said: Either leave him or take us both. I said I'd take them both: I'd let Ma beat your brother out of me if it meant Ba would get to witness the birth, bring the baby its first breath. That's what I said, but I should have known that when I speak something, it's no longer mine. It's the air now, breathed in by everybody, exhaled as nothing.

The week I moved out, Ma was in the kitchen rinsing Ba's pants in the sink. She said if he shit himself again she'd feed him his own stain. I toweled between his butt cheeks. He hadn't showered in months since Ma stopped helping him. I stood him over the sink, washed him everywhere below the waist. His penis looked like a boiled prawn.

Ma took my hands off him. She said, *If he can't do it himself, he doesn't deserve to be clean,* and then she scrubbed my hands so raw they hurt to hold air and your brother inside me asked to leave. Your brother was the one who kicked my skin into a sky, a constellation of bruises on my belly; you were the one who didn't move, who wanted to stay inside me, who kept your eyes closed for days, not yet committed to your body or this world, still waiting to see if you could be returned. And look now: You want me to go back.

Ma said, *Take us both or no one,* and I chose no one, which means I chose myself. Daily, I see myself like I'm on TV: I leave LA in your father's car. A rabbit jumps into the starving man's fire and saves him and becomes the moon. But everyone always forgets the rabbit's sacrifice means nothing. The starving man was not starving at all: He was not even a man. He was a god. Hunger was the weather he invented. The rabbit died for a fraudulent want. When I left, Ba was still standing over the sink. So still he might have been praying. Or waiting.

In another life, another story, a daughter who is not me says: *Both. I'll take you both.* She takes her Ma and Ba, replants them in another city, becomes a truce between trees. Memories ago, when you and your brother were asleep and your father was newly home from the mainland, I took the car and drove halfway down to LA before pulling into a motel. I thought I'd finally take Ba home, but then I remembered

that my house is not mine, that your father's money paid the
bills and I didn't even know what my ba could eat anymore,
if I still knew how to make sugar-hearted dates the way he
liked them, with so much syrup it sealed his jaw. The sign
outside the motel said NO VACANCIES, but I asked for a room
anyway. The woman at the counter thought I was a whore
and I let her think it. Inside, the TV's already on: war, war,
weather, news at eleven. Outside, the sun pregnant with the
moon. When my mother gave birth to me, she barely had to
squat. I stole myself out. The year I married and left Ma, I
scoured my room clean. I took my toothbrush out of the bathroom, the one I'd used for so many years that the bristles
were balding. Most nights I scrubbed my teeth with a finger:
I like to feel what's sharp in myself.

I threw the toothbrush away, and that's when I saw it in
the trash, half-wrapped in toilet paper: a hair dye box with an
Asian model on it, the darkest shade available. Ba's hair had
been white since I was born, and Ma said it meant his brains
were made of cloud. I thought of Ma dying her hair in secret,
tarring each strand until it was her shadow, refusing the soft-
ness of silver.

I sat on the bathroom floor. I walked into the kitchen
where Ma was rinsing bone-colored gaolicai. Her hair in pink
curlers, pinned up and tumorous. She said, *Eat this cabbage
on your wedding night. It will fill your belly with water and
leave no room for a baby.* Her hands shucked the leaves,
cracked the cabbage-heads like skulls. She'd saved me all the
fresh leaves. The leaves that surrendered at the edges were
the ones she'd feed Ba. *What if I want a baby?* I said, not
knowing your brother was the size of a bird. She slit a leaf
along its veins.

Every year your child grows is another that's subtracted

from you, she said. *The older your children grow,* she said, *the more jealous a god will become. The god will look for reasons to steal the child back: a name that's too long, skin with no moles or scars.* Maybe that's why Ma threw me into that river: to save me from being stolen.

My last night living in that house, I took the bag of cabbage out of the refrigerator and slept with my body cleaved to it, cradling its cold. I slipped it under the belly of my nightgown and kissed it, imagined it was growing inside me into you, my not-yet daughter, my slaughter.

—

This isn't the story I promised you. I know. My toes were a toll I paid for this body. You think they were thieved by Hu Gu Po, the tiger who inhabits us like our own bones. Sometimes I want to pluck the rest of my toes like grapes, suck the sweet from their skins. Jie once said I'd better keep my toes and be buried whole or I won't be allowed into the afterlife, but I don't believe bodies are born as wholes. We aren't born anything but holes, throats and anuses and pores: ways of being entered and left.

Here's a lesson about light. In your language, they say life is *extinguished.* But that assumes our bodies are made of light, and light is always limited. We are sacks of dark, and the dark resists direction, resists capture: When I open the tin where I keep my toes, the dark doesn't leave in a beam. Light can be measured and spent, a number printed on the backs of lightbulb boxes, but the dark has no quantity. I measure it in memories, in myths. You and I beneath the sheets, your feet feathering in my mouth, flocking out by morning.

—

I'm fifteen, a daughter, all knees. First summer in Arkansas and a storm steals leaves off the trees. Arkansas looks like our island, same rain, air so thick we can spoon it into our mouths. We need names here. We try to find them in other things, in the trees, in electric fences, in cow patties coined by our feet.

The summer we arrive to the farms, the chickens lay eggs the size of pearls. Everyone needs something new to blame: The rain like diarrhea, brown and sizzling. The unspiced sky, the river too arthritic to bend, the paved roads cracking like lips. The new chinks in town with their bowlegged daughters.

What you know: We work first at the chicken farm, scraping shit off the walls with a pallet knife, beheading snakes with rakes. The soil's made of snakes, so many snakes we eat snake meat for months before the church folk find out and bring us cans of luncheon loaf, boneless bricks of pink. Ma doesn't trust meat without bones, without organs. All meat in America comes from some species of animal that doesn't shit or speak or eat. *Must be people-meat,* Jie says.

The snakes are smart: They wake up before the sky and tunnel down through the soil and into the coops. We spend mornings wading through shit-crusted hens, whacking off snake heads with rakes. When they strike at us, we shove the rake-pole down their throats. Their mouths are our windows and we look inside for the weather: wet. Ma says that snakes become women at night, especially if they're white, so I fling the white ones into the trees, where they dangle like nooses. We pray to all the names multiplying inside the trees like rings, the names of everyone hanged here, everyone who paid their lives to this land so that we never have to.

Sometimes I believe the snakes and I share a breed, feeding off foreign sources of heat. At night I park my stomach against Ma's spine. Without her, my blood depletes its own heat. I whisper against her shoulders, speak mouth to marrow: *I killed three snakes today. I opened their dead mouths and touched their fangs. My hands are numb up to the wrists. I'm telling no one but you. You're the only one who knows I've been dying all day.*

I like slaughtering snakes. They die clean. We fling them into piles. No need to grieve what doesn't bleed. My only competitors are the red-tailed hawks that snip the hens' heads off their necks. There's a gun leaning against the long wall of the coop for the purpose of shooting them down. In the heat, the barrel goes limp as silk, roves the house on its snakebelly.

—

Ba beheaded a snake in the city where I was born. By then, he'd changed his name to a tree's. In another country, he'd strung his mother in a tree by her thumbs. The soldiers asked him to do it. He double-tied the knot, tested the branch with his own weight. He beat her and tried to imagine the rain removing her face. Tried to imagine the body as water, able to take any shape and survive it. But all he saw was the time his mother told him to close his eyes as she walked him around the fields and placed his hands on everything he'd someday need the name of, a goat's beard, a well, a tree with leaves like keys, the sky a door that swung open to the sun.

Years later, when he was beating a woman in the street for having broken curfew, and the woman asked him why he was doing this, why there were so many men in her city, why they had shot her dog and leashed her father, Ba had said nothing. There were nights he misplaced his hands, couldn't tell what he was beating, if it was a dog or a woman or a sack of flour mixed with sand to make it last, if what buttered the road was blood or the pulp of fruit orphaned by a tree.

He began to give away his memories to the morning, bleaching them with light so that later in another country, he would remember only the color white. The White Terror: When I tell you its name, you think I mean *white* as in the American kind. It's true, the Americans gave the bullets, but these are the men that spent them: your agong your agong your agong.

Not even the stars were spared a curfew. Someone once told me if the moon stayed out too long, the soldiers would shoot it down by morning. Ba ran away from his post for months at a time, selling coconuts on a mountain road. He emptied the coconut of water and meat, placed two bars of gold inside, hid it at the bottom of his stack. One day, there was a snake slung across the road. He cleaved its head off, slung the body around his neck. By the time you were born, Ba could only tell one piece of the story at a time before he forgot it was about him. The first day, he would say, *I was a soldier.* On the second day, he would say, *I was a snake.*

Once, you stole the phone from my hands. You spoke into it, to him: *Agong, tell me the story about the snake.* And he said,   *I slung a mother   my neck. They strung up my snake in the branches. They beat it   sticks. I killed a mother in the middle of the road. I took her head   home. The mother was so long   it died.   wanted to go back home but I was afraid   it still dying.   I sent letters to the snake   the sea shut off*

            and I   never arrived

—

The toes, my toes, I know. You're still waiting for me to explain my feet. You're asking what this has to do with saving Agong. This story was meant to show you: The ones we should save are already dead. Before he was your agong, he was my ba. Before he was my ba, he was a soldier. When you're a soldier, nothing comes before or after. Don't think I forgive him. Forgiveness is surgery, and I don't have the hand or the eye. I can't see him as Ma must have seen him: his gun first, then his hands. I hear only the way his hands shake when he holds the phone, when he has to prop it against a wall and speak to me like I'm standing there, like I never left, like his shadow is mine.

Second summer in Arkansas, we try renewing our papers. We go all the way to Little Rock, where the governor lives in a house so big it doesn't fit in our bus window when we pass it. At the immigration office they ask for name, birthdate, country of origin. Ma doesn't know her birthdate or ours. She only knows the weather on the days we were born. Jie and I are rain. Ma answers rain, rain, rain to all three questions. She doesn't know when the day was, so she describes it: *The day I was born it was raining red snakes. The day I was born three other people were born.* Ma explains that there is only one day and it lives like a body, getting up before us and falling asleep when we do, putting on the sky like a skirt. There aren't many, or if there are, it's the same day dressed as different countries.

The paper people say no, no. Ask how we got here. There's a man in the corner wearing a uniform, handcuffs hanging from his hip. The cuffs bared like teeth. Silver mouths that circle into smiles. Ma herds us out of the office and we take the bus out of the city, back to the chicken farm, and I still don't know what day I'm born. Later, the missionaries as-

signed a birthday to me and Jie, the day we were baptized, the
only time we wore white when nobody had died.

In the summer we sleep in different corners of the house
to keep cool. Ma in the bedroom alone. The shotgun's shadow
stalking the walls. I sleep on the porch outside, bury myself in
tarps to keep mosquitos out. Jie is a dog curled behind the
front door.

Near morning when I hear the gun go off. Light limping
down from the sky. My spit purifies to glass in my throat. I
wake and think the gunshot flew out from my dreams, but
I can't remember what I've been aiming at, if I have hands.
I check for a gun and find my fist.

Jie runs barefoot onto the porch, takes me by the armpits.
Ba's got the gun, she says. We thread out of the house. A second gunshot guts the clouds. We run to the backyard and he's
there, panting and pantsless, bleeding sweat everywhere, bullets bucking the air. Backfire makes him stumble, knees grieving to the ground. Ama's there too, her hands reining in his
shoulders. *Give it back,* she says. Agong lowers it to the trees.
I haven't seen him stand straight in months. He lifts his left
hand to the sky, pointing or saluting.

We try to see what he's pointing at, but the sky speaks
nothing, not a bird. Clouds cockroaching across the sky. I an-
ticipate holes in the blue, but there's no wound. Ba shakes the
sweat off his upper lip and says, *They're coming, they're coming.*

In his hands, the shotgun is boneless. Ma bites the ball of
his shoulder, tells him the war, both, are behind him. Ba looks
behind him, at her. His eyes are seedless, white. He says,
Where are the planes? I spot a wounded bird in the corner of
the sky, shedding blood, flying in circles with one wing

wrenched out. Ma says, *You got them all, you got them.* But Ba's eyes are years behind, stalled on the same sky: back when warplanes had anuses that dilated open and shat dung-bombs, spraying a diarrhea that scarred your skin.

Ba ba ba ba ba, I say. He turns and sees Jie and me, shoulder-to-shoulder like soldiers. Hems of our nightgowns baptized in mud. He raises the gun at me. He has no daughters. He's a boy counting Japanese bombs from the roof of his house, so many they outnumber rain. He's the boy who hid in a well for three days, the sky as big as the hole he came down. *No,* Ma says, and grabs the gun-barrel. Tugs it down toward the ground. Ba fires once and sees a soldier in front of him burst into birds.

Jie shouts. I eat my spit. The light scatters to salt. Don't move in this part of the story. Watch. I'm waiting for the bullet to birth its hole in me. I want to know what it feels like, to be a soldier like Ba, to die like one. Did you see that? He smiled when he fired, all his teeth. Have you ever seen him smile like that? Don't answer me. You aren't even born yet and you already know he never has. I wait for the bullet to reach into me and flip me inside-out. But the bullet's gone slant into the soil, the shotgun knocked diagonal by Ma's hands.

Look down now at this choreography of shadows: The bullets nose-diving into my toes. Ma pulling me back into the house by my armpits. Ba crouching in the dirt with his hands leafed over his head. See my left foot before Ma wraps it in newspaper, the same way a butcher wraps her best cut.

There are days between the wound and the fever in my spine, but I don't know how many. I rip the sheets to sleep. I smell rot in my foot, sour and sizzling. My brain spit-roasting in my skull, a hand reaching in to spin it. One night I wake believing my hands are torches, lit to the wrist. I limp into the backyard to run them under the hose. Ba's been put to sleep on the kitchen floor.

In a week my skin's still a stove, so Ma says, *We have to amputate before it spreads.* Jie boils the knives. You choose the night. The night before the amputation, I dream that Ma fills a bucket with hose-water and carries me outside like a bride. Ma washes my infected foot in the water, praying over it. Kissing the bark of my heel. You say it's not a dream, but it has to be: When I wake, it's back to blades. Ma's knife is guiding the light into me.

Ma's hand hot on my ankle, pinning my foot to the cutting board. The infection in two of my neighboring toes, three rotten in total. My blood on the board looks fake, a staged slaughter. Dousing my foot in rice wine, she wraps it in a cotton shirt. Fills a jam jar with a brine of salt and rice vinegar, seals my three toes inside. They float for the first few days, then shrink to the size of bullets and sink.

Ba sees my toes swimming in the jar on our windowsill and says, *Those fish are dead.* You're listening hard now. You ask if this is why I tread lightly on my left foot, rely on the right. I hid the jar from Ba, grateful there's one memory I can keep him from cannibalizing.

While I'm frying in a fever, I sheathe a cleaver in a sock. Sleep with it between my breasts, arm myself for a war that happened before I was born. Still waiting for Ba to return. You remind me we used to share a bed, and you never saw me sleep with a blade.

It's time to bring him back, you say. I don't recognize that voice in you. We're in the kitchen. The holes you've dug in my yard are mouths again, spitting at our window.

Your ama once taught me, I say, *there are two categories for everything. Yours and not yours. Everything that's mine is already here.*

Ama's wrong, you say, and I laugh at the way your mouth can shape any sound certain as stone. You forget she's been my mother longer than your grandmother. You forget I've had her blood longer.

He's not yours or Ama's or mine. He just needs to be shown home. You tell me you know how to end things now. You say all this with a tail tucked in your pants, a tail that tapers into a blade.

You take my car keys out of my best knock-off purse on the counter. You give them to me. You say Ben has a key around her neck. She's an emergency exit. You are clutching my wrists, moving me out the door. Since when have you been tall enough to unlock it? How long have you been my height? You are telling me to unlock the car and I do. You buckle your brother into the backseat. I grip the wheel so hard you ask if I'm strangling it. I remember the hens we killed at the chicken farm, their necks in our hands, quick wrist, their bodies reliving their deaths, pecking the mud without their heads.

When I turn the key like a blade inside a body, when I thread the car onto the highway and head south, I remember what you said: *Ba isn't hers. Isn't mine. He's shaped like my love for him, a river with many tributaries, digressions, points of departure.*

In the backseat, you lean forward and put your hands on my shoulders, steering me. I tell you all houses are made of skin: Once you've left one, it stitches shut again. You say if it's skin, it is always open. It's made of holes, hairs, pores. It's my own body I'm returning to.

An hour in, your brother says he needs to pee. I say, *Do it out the window. I'm not stopping.* Your brother hunches, holds his bladder like it's a bomb. I hear the door rattle open, the air outside climbing onto our laps. Your brother peeing through the crack in the door, ribbons of piss fluttering around us. Framing our flight in gold.

His piss hits a windshield behind us and the man honks, swerves. You tell me to accelerate, press the pedal to mud, take us to the woman who birthed me who birthed you. The car shrinks to the size of your mouth. The radio has your voice in it and I remember the Dolly Parton song that was playing the time Jie and I ditched work to drive downtown. I asked Jie to translate the lyrics and she sang about sewing a coat of tongues, when all I wanted was to never know a needle again, to never be the girl at the factory who falls asleep and runs her thumb through the machine, stitching herself to what will be sold.

You try to sing along to the radio, but there's only static on. Your brother once convinced you that static is an alien language spoken by the moonborn, so you listen as if it means something. You bob up and down in the backseat like a buoy. A warning: The water ahead will wreck me. Keep away. The only thing that keeps my hands on the wheel: If I don't look at the city ahead, if I watch your face in the rearview mirror instead, I can pretend I'm driving toward you, you: the only home that owns me. *Look-look,* you say, you sing sweet as toothache: Here's the city, the honeydew moon above it, waiting for us to bash it open and begin.

DAUGHTER

Rabbit moon (II)

When my brother propped his penis in his palm and peed out the door, wetting a mile of highway with rain, my mother said he must have the bladder of a horse. I asked how she knew about the anatomies of horses and she said she knew what it is to be ridden. We rode up the highway to a city of factories: concrete buildings converted into showrooms, the upper windows blacked out, headless mannequins haunting the sidewalks. We circled twice around Ama's block. Hers was a house sitting on its haunches, afraid to stand all the way up. Its pelt of paint was perpetually wet, and all kinds of creatures got stuck to the sides of the house: squirrels, pigeons, a collage of flies.

Our mother drove with her elbows while she smoked out the window, spitting into the cup holder. When she spoke of her father now, he was no longer our agong, just her ba, which meant he belonged to her and not to us. Our blood was borrowed.

When we reached Ama's driveway, the moon was not yet nailed in the sky. Ama always said the moon was the corpse of the sun, meaning every night is a funeral. During our week as nocturnal animals, my brother and I had trained our eyes to adjust to any density of dark, and now neither of us tripped on Ama's root-risen driveway. Our mother didn't ring the doorbell, which had been taped over. She pounded on the door. When no one answered, she told my brother to get the flashlight from the glove box.

She went up to the front window, the flashlight flaccid-looking in her hands. Her arm coiled back. My brother grabbed her wrist, but the flashlight was already through the glass. We waited for the alarm, waited to run like she wasn't our mother and the night didn't know us, but there was no sound except for a neighbor's dog, barking like we'd come just to kill it.

I could see my mother squinting back and forth between me and the window, calculating if she could toss me in too, but then all the lights in the house opened their eyes. The hole in the window filled with Ama's face. She stood looking out at us, our faces reflected next to hers in the glass. Barefoot and bathrobed, hair in pink curlers, her face was narrower than my mother's, cheekbones hanging their shadows. She looked at us through the hole in the window as if we were the weather forecast, expected. The air had tattled on us, and now she darted her tongue in and out of her mouth, licking at our evaporated sweat, tasting the hard kernels of rain inside our veins. The knife in her left fist was upright, like some flower she had just picked for us.

My brother walked back to the car and started it, a sound we thought was far away in someone else's night. *Let's go home,* he said, and my mother didn't turn her head. Ama opened the door, beckoned us in with her blade. The night beat us inside, stars sprinkling themselves like salt all over her carpet.

I'd slit a hole in my skirt for the tail to slide out, a knife to draw on her throat before she could use her own. Tapping at the root of my tail, I told it to get ready.

My mother shouldered past Ama. We followed her to the left, my brother running back to join us, the car still running. We went down the hall so narrow we walked sideways, comical as crabs. There was a smell like singed hair, Ama's curlers filling with smoke. All the walls were exposed brick, rough and dark as scabs. My mother told me that one summer, Ama had asked Agong to paint the interior a color closer to the sky, any color but white. Agong went to the store for paint and came back with a hammer instead. Ama threw the hammer at him, its silver head gouging the brick wall behind him. Now, as we walked toward Agong, my mother petted each wall as we passed it, trying to find that old injury, that hole in the brick where she used to hide cigarettes, coins, a highway map. She'd planted pieces of her past inside the wall, waiting for the house to grow a future worth staying for.

We stopped before the bedroom door, Ama behind my left shoulder, walking so close to my tail that I wanted to turn and bind her wrists together with it. We could smell Agong behind the bedroom door, a mulch of shit and sweat. Our mother opened the door and the smell coiled back, hit like a fist.

The window was barricaded with a dresser, and a chair in the corner kept only three of its limbs. There were no mirrors—fengshuibuhao—but something had shattered, and there were crumbs of glass in the carpet, burrowing into our feet as we neared the bed. What I thought was slicked-back hair was a bruise spanning his scalp. The liverspots on his hands were the size of quarters and I wanted to pluck them off one by one, spend them on new skin for him. Agong's mouth was all movement. His tongue worming through the skin of his cheek.

My mother got on her knees beside the bed, pressing her forehead to the mattress, and when she lifted her forehead it was bright with blood. The mattress was ripe with it. I squinted at his chest to see if something still lived in it. My brother's hand was damp inside mine, though I couldn't re-member when I'd reached out for it. *Hold your breath,* my brother said. He once told me it was important to hold your breath around dying people. That way, the sick person had more air for themselves. But I didn't think Agong had lungs anymore: His chest was bowled, carrying a soup of sweat. My tail clenched around my thigh when I saw his neck, mottled with moles, so thin I wanted to pluck it with my fingers, make music of this silence.

When my mother stood up, her eyes arrowed through ev-erything again: the dresser in front of the window, Ama in the doorway with her hands sprouting a knife, the chair's bruised knees, my brother and I holding hands. She lifted Agong off the bed, bridal-style, his bones propped in her arms. The skin below his chin was so loose it flapped when he swallowed, and I wanted to iron it down, pleat him smooth. Ama said, *Don't touch him.* My mother cradled Agong closer.

In a dialect I'd never heard before, Ama spat a word at the walls, making the paint shine the same as her teeth. I stepped forward between my mother and Ama, palm pressed to my sheathed tail, legs apart. Ama didn't look at me, but I knew how to hinge her, how to latch my tail around her leg and bring her to her knees.

Kneeling with Agong in her arms, my mother arranged his limbs on the carpet beside the bed. *Careful, there's glass,* I said, though no one was listening. Ama said, *I had to do it,* flitting her hand through the air, touching the curlers at her forehead. *There is something inside of him, eating him.*

Ama's hands were canyoned with calluses, carved out by some river she'd reined in her hands. Turning to me, she kneeled as if to pray. The deeper the lines in your palm, she told me, the farther from home you'll die. She said my hands are antonyms. My right hand is inherited from my mother and my left one is descended from Ama. Neither was mine. But Ama didn't know my third hand, my tail, honed for this night.

Parting the dark, Ama leaned closer and said, *There's something inside him. I hear it in his body at night, running around in his veins, impersonating his blood.* Ama showed us the sound with her wrists, circling them so that I could hear her bones graveling.

My brother crawled forward to pillow his fingers against Agong's pulse. In the dark I couldn't see my hands move, couldn't tell what was a shadow and what was a body. My brother said, *Agong's blood is still inside him.* My mother said, *Find the light, the light.* I walked my hands along the walls until I found a switch. Light trickled from the bare bulb and down the walls, thick as nosebleed, but it was only enough for us to see the outline of him.

Agong's legs forked apart. He moaned and Ama said, *You see, he doesn't want you to see him like this.* My mother said, *Find where he's bleeding,* but all we could find was blood fos-

silized into stains on his unbuttoned shirt. His pajamas were
white cotton, translucent at the knees. My mother opened his
shirt farther and tapped on the base of his throat in some
kind of Morse code, trying to pick up a signal from his body.
Agong answered by shifting his legs into a broader *V* and
bending them, bracing to give birth.

Cupping Agong's skull in her palms, my mother bent her
head to kiss it, to tongue his eyelids open. Ama pointed down
at his legs, her other hand worrying her hair curlers. *Look,
look.* The crotch of Agong's pajamas tore open. A white flicker
between his legs, a light turned on and off inside him. Agong
widened his legs again, mouth ripening around a shout.

My brother thought Agong was shitting himself, but no
shit was bone-white. The torn cloth at his crotch widened into
a coin-slot, then a mouth. From between his legs, he pushed
out a fist of light, punching through the seams of the dark. It
was a rabbit, robed in mucus. So thin-skinned we could see
the grape of its heart. None of us dared to touch its eyelids,
beating like moths in the dark of his blood. The rabbit was
tongue-slack in my mother's hand, hind legs gummed to its
torso, no mouth, not breathing. I thought it must be a prema-
ture moon, stillborn. There was no sky small enough to use it.
Agong shivered, blood tendriling out of his anus. He moved
his wrist to his mouth and sucked the skin silver, watching us
as if we were abstract patterns of light on the wall, no meaning to our shapes. No difference between a daughter and her
shadow.

My mother stood up, pinned her back to the wall. Her
hands were short-circuiting, closing around something in the
air that wasn't there. My brother backed toward the doorway
where the dark ruptured, bled out into the hall. I came closer,

wanting to see the rabbit's knotted-up face, wanting to name its resemblance to something. But Ama moved before me, kneeling beside Agong and holding the knife upright again, bringing the blade up to his face, magnifying it. My fur slicked back, sleeking my tail into a fletched arrow, my whole body tensed like a bow.

We have to open him, Ama said. *There could be more inside him.* She posed the blade over his belly. Curling my fingers and toes into claws, I leapt toward the light of it. Agong turned his head side to side, the way my brother did in his sleep, saying no to something I couldn't see. All I could see was the knife lowering to swim into his belly. My night vision brightened Ama's silhouette, tracing her shape in salt. I stood over her, my tail whipping forward between my knees to knock the knife from her hands.

Her hands streaked silver against the dark as she moved them away, dodging me without looking. I tried to recoil my tail, rescind it from the air, but it only knew to move forward, lashing Agong in the chest. He made a sound that soured all my spit, a cry like an infant's, his ribs flinching beneath the skin. Where my tail had raked him, a stripe of skin reared up on his chest, a dark jelly of blood beneath it. He arched his back, pressing the burn on his chest to the dark. My mother kneeled in front of me, caging her body over his, blocking him from me.

My tail had mistranslated everything I'd told it. I'd wanted Ama's wrists, wanted to break all the bones inside them. I tried to tell this to my mother, but she was bowed over Agong. She kneeled over him and spat on his chest, slicking the burn, trying to put out the pain. My tail was curdled stiff, lagging behind me while I tried to move closer, apologize. *You hurt him,* my mother said, speaking to the burn on his chest, ruby with her spit.

I crawled forward to them, towing my tail behind me in the dark. It felt heavier, a moon tethered to the end of it.

Ama took my tail in her hands, tugged on it like a leash. I tried to keep crawling, to reach my mother huddling with her back to me, but Ama jerked me back. She could steer me with it, drag me out to the yard and bury me anywhere. When I told her to let go, she yanked back again, ripping out wisps of my fur. She sneezed, batting at the strands like dust. Pulling once on my tail, she brought me to my feet.

See, Ama said. *We're the same beast.* Ama stroked my tail-tip with her thumb. Bent her head and sniffed it. She asked if I knew the story of Hu Gu Po, a story about the cost of having a body. The cost was butchery. She said there were no tigers on her island and there had never been. The story had been born somewhere else, brought over by men and stuffed into the bellies of women who didn't want it. The women gave birth anyway, to daughters that did not resemble them.

When I gave birth to my first daughter, Ama said, *I saw her face and it was a soldier's.* No one in her tribe had ever seen a tiger, and when Ama first heard the story, she imagined that it walked upright. She imagined its skin was made of two textures: The orange stripes were fire and the black stripes were river, canceling out into smoke. My tail twitched out of her hands, singed by the heat of her palms. I was the beast she'd imagined: tail stubbly as a beard, my shadow big as a soldier's.

You have the blood of soldiers and slaughterers. You think you're a different story from me? she said. I stood hunched, my tail so heavy I forgot how I'd ever been able to stand against gravity. I was tied to the stone of it. If she had thrown me in the river the way she had my mother, I would have sunk. The tail's marrow solid as gold. I'd beach at the river bottom, live in the mud of all I'd done, eat what was thrown down to me.

My mother was watching us, pinching the dead rabbit off the carpet and lifting it in her palms, a vestigial heart, a light source. She looked between Ama and me, trying to decide who to protect Agong from. Ama spun my tail in her hand, and when I looked down at our shadow, its shape was a bridge that hyphenated us, an umbilical cord that had grown without our knowing. I wanted to sever it, to separate us, differentiate our shadows, our hungers. Slit the cord and sun-dry it, soften it into something that couldn't solicit blood, couldn't strike skin without hurting itself. There would be nothing for her to hold of me.

Let go, I said, but she didn't. My bladder pricked open, leaked down my legs. Ama walked to the doorway, tugging me by the tail down the hallway and out into the backyard where the grass was rusted brown as a bloodstain.

She told me to piss here. Like the beast I was, I squatted. Her fist cinched tighter around my tail, but I no longer felt it. I could see only Ama's face, the way she looked at me like I was a soldier she'd seen before, a soldier she'd married before, gripping my tail not because she was afraid I'd run, but because she knew I'd turn and spear it through the unlit spaces between her ribs.

It was only after I pissed that I noticed: All the soil in Ama's yard was white. The ground looked like bone-sand, but beneath my feet it moved as dirt, wet with sweat and shadow.

Ama let go of me, told me to find what she'd buried. I eyed her hands, then the soil, squinting at its bleached skin. In the corner where the chili bushes grew, I saw a row of holes like bone sockets. I walked to the holes, my tail a swinging weight. The holes were deeper than mine, dull inside, lined with gray like the sky before rain.

I sleeved my arms into the hole nearest the door and snagged my fingers on something sharp at the bottom. Ama watched behind me, silent, her shadow shawled over me. I knew she was waiting for me to find something. My fingers found an earring rolled in dirt, its clasp come loose. I felt around the bottom again and withdrew a bracelet with bone beads, then a plastic spoon, then a penny. I raked the soil with my fingers until I was slit by something: a page. Tugging it loose from the soil, I slid it out and held it with the tips of my fingers. On both sides it was blank, white as the soil.

For you to write back to me, Ama said. I dropped it back into the hole. I said I would never. She smiled, half her teeth missing, places for morning to pour into her mouth. She said the letters were meant for anyone listening, and I was the one who had been translating. I was the one who wanted to witness. I thought of everything I'd fed to the holes: Dayi's goose, Ben's birdcage, my tail. While Ama watched me, I thought of kidnapping the rest of her teeth, holding them hostage in my mouth. She'd have to beg me to return them to her, give her back the ability to speak.

You'll write back. I know you will. I said no, I didn't have the history to forgive her, and Ama said, *I never wanted you to forgive me. Weren't you reading?*

Behind her, the garden hose spewed into the soil. She kneeled in the white, held out her palms. She said she must have dreamt of growing a tail just like this when she was a girl, but sometimes a wound skips a generation or two, appearing again in the body that is most ready to wield it. I said I never wanted to wield anything ever again, that I had seen Agong's chest branded by me.

You'll write back, Ama said. *Not because you've forgiven me, but because I will never hate you for what you've done. Because I'm the only one who knows what you're capable of.* She bowed her head like a knight in a fairy tale, all parody, and at the nape of her neck, there was a cowlick the same size and shape of my mother's. It was like seeing again a species of bird you thought went extinct: I couldn't stop myself from cooing down at it, petting it.

With the tip of my soiled thumb, I touched the spot where her hair grew circular like my mother's, the tip of the strand chasing its own root. I stirred the cowlick with my thumb and told her this was what my mother did before I fell asleep: She traversed my hairline with her finger, renaming my widow's peak Papakwaka, every part of me a creation story. Ama didn't raise her head, but I knew she was listening, the soil turning bright-wet as the whites of her eyes.

From the front doorway, my mother's voice threaded through the house and into the yard. She called to me in a voice so like Ama's, I thought for a moment that Ama was speaking from outside her own body. But only my mother could call to me like that, a sound worn fist-smooth, a sound I could saddle and ride, relieved for a second of my own weight while she carried me in her mouth.

—

According to Ama, the moon is the corpse of the sun. There were once two sons, double yolks that had been hard-boiled in the sea. A warrior shot down one of the sons, inventing dusk. The dead sun ascended to the bone-throne of night. The first sun grieved their separation, and we have morning, where the dead son and the living son kiss once. But one of them always sets while the other rises. Grief is their gravity.

—

My mother carried Agong to the car, his legs clacking together, glass-veined. Above us, the moon was marinating in its own silver sweat. I wondered if Agong knew what he'd given birth to. We folded him into the backseat and drove away, the dark chasing us home like a stray. If my mother was still afraid of me, she no longer looked it: She nudged me into the car with her knee. It was hot inside and my armpits were jungled with sweat. On the way home, Agong gurgled in his sleep, his tongue frothing. When we realized he was choking, we took turns holding his mouth open, scooping out the spit with two fingers. Flinging strands of it out the window. They stuck like stars to the night.

Ama didn't speak when we carried him out. She'd walked to the kitchen and removed her curlers one by one, her hair already singed. The strands glowed orange, faded black. The colors of my tail. She bundled the little rabbit in newspaper and said she'd get rid of it. We saw her go through her drawers for a box of matches to burn it with.

I knew it was inside him, Ama said about the rabbit. We didn't know if it had been born inside him or if it was planted in him. We didn't know how it'd been able to breathe inside his body. *I knew there was something in his body I had to save him from,* Ama said again. I wanted to say that she was the one inside of him, that she didn't know the differ-

ence between who he was and what she had done to him.
Ama's hands shook when she tried to strike the match. She
dropped each one, singeing hole after hole into the carpet,
charring her heels to stamp out the flames. Smoke ghouling
up from the ground. Finally, my mother reached forward
and took the match from Ama's hand, striking it alive on her
own callused palm. She lit the rabbit's newspaper-shroud
and I lowered its body into the sink, basketing the light in
my hands. Even after we were gone, the rabbit-fetus burned.
We searched for its bones in the sky, mourning that our
agong was now moonless.

———

In the car, I asked my mother if Agong was really her father.
In Ama's last letter, she'd written that my mother was conceived with the river, and Agong didn't look like a river to me,
except when he wet himself, his piss souring the seat, drib-
bling out of his bladder like the juice of a squeezed fruit. Instead of answering, my mother lowered the window and
tossed out her cigarette butts. They dotted the street like acne.
She laughed and asked me to define a father. I said it was
someone who didn't have the strength to carry his own name
and had to employ others to do it. She laughed again, but this
laughter sounded like a recording of the last, too repetitive to
be real.

    I wedged Agong's head between my knees, stroked the
blank spot on his forehead where his eyebrows drifted in opposite directions, where he most resembled my mother:
When she slept, the skin between her eyes pleated in two
places, and she always told me to stay up by her bedside and
iron it down with my fingers so she wouldn't wake in the

morning with wrinkles. But I always fell asleep beside her, and in the morning she asked if she'd aged. *Yes,* I said, *you're as wrinkled-up as an asshole,* and then she'd laugh and roll me off the bed, saying that one day I'd have this face too.

When my mother asked if I was begging for another story, I breathed steam onto the backseat window, wrote the word *yes* on the forehead of night. Turning onto the highway, steering with one hand only, she said the problem with memory was that I turned all of hers into currency, bought my future with forgetting. *Keep your memories, then,* I said. *Give me someone else's.*

—

An Abbreviated History of the River and Her Lesbian Lover (My Great-Grandmother Nawi)

A NOTE OF CAUTION: All references to water may be slightly exaggerated, but when your agong is pissing all over the backseat, every river feels literal.

A SECOND, AND MUCH BROADER, NOTE OF CAUTION: My mother always says that the story you believe depends on the body you're in. What you believe will depend on the color of your hair, your word for god, how many times you've been born, your zip code, whether you have health insurance, what your first language is, and how many snakes you have known personally.

Ama's mother was birthed from the belly of a crab. Her head rolled out in a helmet of orange shellac and her hands were toothed pinchers, capable of splitting rocks to sand. Her father—Old Guang the pirate—sucked her out of the crab's disked stomach and spat her across the table, where she landed on clawed feet. Named Nawi, she walked sideways like a crab and ate shelled meat: beetles sucked clean, shrimp from the sea. When she turned fourteen, Nawi married a boy who had been born a beaver—he had four teeth like hinged doors—and bore thirteen children. The last one was born with a snake for a penis. Nawi stroked it, letting it learn the diameter of her wrist. Its voice filled her skull with its silk: *I am your daughter and born to break you. I am your son and spine.*

Nawi believed the snake would eventually loosen like milk teeth or grow into another limb, vestigial and shriveled. The snake threaded its head into the baby's diaper, forked tongue slurring the same song, like steam escaping, like a rock striking a river and then sinking. Whenever Nawi tried to nurse the baby, the snake nibbled her breasts and nipples, seeding her skin with poison. Her milk came out burnt and bitter silver. The snake stretched out, whipping the air with its tongue.

Nawi decided to slaughter it. The snake was a bloodless white, rooted to the baby's crotch like a radish. She brought the knife down and it cut as if through light. The snake never woke. In place of blood, smoke spiraled out of its body. It looked smaller not attached to anything, blue head tucked, tongue flickering, hungering. No scarring, no evidence of severance. The baby's crotch was smooth as a tree stump. She tossed the snake's body into the fire, slept with the milk-bulged baby in her arms.

The next morning, the baby was awake and batting at Nawi's braids, yanking her scalp awake. Where the stump had been, there was now a clutch of eggs, clinging clear as rain. She tried to dab them away. By evening, a dozen more were dewed to the baby's crotch. Only three eggs bore snakes, braiding and unbraiding. They spoke at once, a knot of song, a tangle of telling. *We are your daughters. We are your sons. Stroke us and we will save you. Feed us and we will not forget you.* The snakes' mouths outnumbered her own, so she obeyed them. She fed the snakes better than any of her children, even slaughtered the pigs and split the meat among the three heads, the hooves too. The snakes' jaws opened wide as doorways. Hunger amplified them, sweeping up their songs like seeds, planting each note deep in her ears. She woke sobbing some nights, praying to be swallowed soon.

The next month, the river receded like a hairline. At night the stars flaked off the sky as dandruff, salting the soil white. The snake-child grew up to be my Ama. Her snakes vined up the length of her legs and whisked around her waist when she walked. Ama and her snakes were saints: Shamans and priests asked to see what they'd grown from, flipping up Ama's skirt, but the snakes bit their wrists blue.

She whistled to wake them. Ama tapped each one on the head, their eyes milk-lit. She fed them mice from the fields and rats from the gutters on both sides of the road and turtles swept out of the river by typhoons and minnows the size of her pinkies. The farmers who once wanted to dam the river, the ones who never dared to visit the indigenous township for anything other than cheap millet wine, now came in pairs to pet the snakes under her skirts.

The year Ama turned fourteen, the river railed against the fields. Typhoons tore up the fences and the hens that weren't tied down in baskets were swallowed into the sky. Ama straddled the narrowest part of the river to piss into it. When she pissed, the snakes lunged open their mouths. The farmers said she was the one poisoning the water, turning it rancid, handcuffing the crops to the soil so they wouldn't grow. But they wouldn't hurt the girl who hissed piss out of a snake's mouth.

When the river stood up again in the banks, Ama ran outside. Ama's snakes were bobbing out the bottom of her skirt, leashing her to the river. She walked toward the water that begged to be beaten, its surface a skin, and waded in to her knees. Her leftmost snake extended itself like an arm and then doubled back, its head pointing between her legs. It entered her body and nosed its way up her asshole. The right snake looped around itself too, turning toward her body and hooking its head into her vagina. The middle snake, the one thick as her wrist, lifted itself to Ama's lips. Opened its eyes in the dark of her mouth. Her teeth were pried apart. The snake shimmied down her throat and she couldn't breathe until it entered her belly. All three snakes snapped off at the crotch-root, two convening in her stomach, one in her womb.

Ama pissed and shat and birthed at the same time, baby snakes streaming out of her. The river hooded over her head and she opened her mouth underwater, exhaling snakes. They poured out from her mouth and anus and vagina by the dozens, writhing away from the radius of her belly. It was a new breed no one had seen before, rain-red. When the rain ended, the river returned to its socket, the shape of a spine misaligned. The mud returned to its color, but the snakes inside remained red. They browsed the water for meat. The army*

---

*   **Fact:** The Nationalists confiscated my grandmother's land a second time. *Watakushi,* she said again and again. *It is mine. It is mine.* She claims her land in a language that's not hers. She lines up her *I*s like a fence: IIIIIIIIIIIIIIIIIIIII. The *I* doesn't indicate a presence but an absence, the place where a body has been redacted from the sentence.
       Story: Ama married a soldier, the only type of man who keeps his job

discarded its prisoners here, holing the boys' wrists to thread
a wire through. When the first boy was shot, the rest fell in
with him. The army saved bullets this way. Polishing their
names on its tongue, the river strung through their skulls and
necklaced them. Snakes erased the boys' bodies, entering
through eye sockets to eat the rubymeat of their brains.

At night, the river cleaved from its bed and heaved itself
onto land, roaming as a snake. The red rain receded to a
rumor, but some said the day the river was impregnated with
snakes, there was a woman seen on the banks. Some said this
woman had no spine, snakes for arms, teeth for eyes, adding
details until she was nothing they could name.

One night when she was almost nineteen and married to
Agong, her second soldierfuck, Ama went down to the banks
in the dark to see if it was true, if her snakes were women at
night, if the river walked itself. Ama waded in and the river
didn't budge, thick as jelly.

Ama waited for the snakes to circle her ankles, the snakes

---

forever. In return, she received a daily ration of rice. Her fields regrew as
fingers and made a fist around the U.S. military base. The American soldiers taught her how to hunt communists, how to shoot a winter melon
the size of a commie skull. The [   ], led by General [   ] [ ]-[   ], banned
all languages but [   ]. This alphabet was banned too, meaning that this
text does not exist in history. The soldiers broke glass bottles on the beach,
cementing the shards along the shore to gouge the feet of invading com-
mies. The radio said to prepare for an invasion at night, prepare for soldiers who come to eat your feet, and Ama said: *What about the soldiers*
already here? What about the ones in my bed, the ones who fuck me into five
daughters, the first one who sees only shadows, the second one I beat into
bone, into something that floats?
Myth: If you said anything about General [   ] [ ]-[   ], the river tattled on
you. The river was made of ears and started a rumor of snakes. The snakes
slithered into the bodies of dumped prisoners, feasting on the brains and
swallowing their memories. Now the snakes are the only ones who tell
stories.

she'd birthed on her own. The moon pimpled the skin of the river. She walked back to the bank and sat in the mud, wondering where the snakes had gone, if they still loved her, if they still missed the color inside her. She closed her eyes and lay on her back, imagining all her ribs were the rungs of a raft. How bright a boat she would be.

When she opened her eyes, three moons in the sky. One was whole and the others were halves. She sat up and saw a snake hanging on to her calf by its fangs. Ama wrenched it off. Before she could lie back down, the water tore in two. A body nosed onto the banks, gutting the mud. It was a woman with scales the color of blood, wearing her skin inside-out. She tucked her arms and legs into her body before oaring them out, shoving away the mud with each winging. Ama undressed and curled beside the riverwoman in the mud, soaking in the palm-sweat of night. She lowered her head to the riverwoman's skin, tilting her tongue into the belly button, lapping out its sour lake of sweat.

Ama remembered the river was conceived not by the sea but by a body: It had been pissed down the mountain Papakwaka, cleaving streams into the stone. Ama propped herself above the riverwoman's ribs. The mud slapped against itself, a sound like farting, and they both laughed. Ama kneeled between the riverwoman's knees and touched with her tongue the black hair there, gummy with mud and moonmilk. Ama's tongue was its own language, a language that didn't need to be taught to it. When the riverwoman came in her mouth, Ama didn't rinse it for days, kept tonguing the salt between her teeth.

The riverwoman flipped onto her stomach and the mud opened around her, her limbs waning back into her body. Red scales rushed up her belly like a flame and she slid forward through silt, belly-flopping back into the river.

Back home, Ama undressed and scrubbed the mud from her dress, but it had ground itself too deep into the weave and become inseparable from the fabric. She shook it out, went outside to dry it anyway, and saw something clinging to its hem. A scale the size of her toenail. Ama placed the scale on her tongue and sucked on it all day until it blurred away. When her belly rose as rapidly as bread, she knew this would be her last daughter.

Ama thought of the riverwoman whose belly never left the ground, the way her hips gave into honey. The scale Ama swallowed: It must have doubled itself inside her, daughtering. This daughter was only hers. Hers and the river's. Hers and the dead's. This daughter—my mother—was the one Ama would see as her second body, a liability. Months later, when Ama tossed all her daughters off the bridge and into the river red, she would watch the snakes warring over their meat. She was waiting for the riverwoman to bring her daughters out of the water, her tongue hooking their mouths, dragging them back to the surface.

While Ama was dropping her daughters into the river, trying to skip the last baby like a stone, she thought of water as the best of all mothers. Water had none of its own wants: It served only the thirst of others. Ama knew being needed was a kind of divinity, and she was tired of being that good, that god. When she dropped my mother into the river last, Ama thought: I am returning her to the river that will raise her better, raise her like a flood I will run from.

—

In her house there was only her. When we'd pulled away, I'd looked through the back windshield, holding Agong's head in my lap like a fruit I couldn't figure out how to fit in my mouth. Ama watched me from the dark of her doorway, her knees blurring into each other. Her mouth was pitted from her face, a hole where she once had a name. She welded her left hand to the doorframe, held the dark open for us to exit through. The night was the same throat-dark as the inside of her house, and leaving felt like being swallowed, like symmetry: The farther we drove, the lower down we lived in her throat.

We didn't know if she was waiting for us to leave or to come back, only that she stood there longer than I looked, that the road startled like skin when we backed onto it. Even after we left, I found her face in a palm tree, a run-over dog, cows scabbing over a field, the dark bracketing our car, my mother in the rearview mirror, teething on her tongue to keep herself awake, one hand hooking out the window. Her fingers undoing the button of the moon. With my sleeve, I dabbed at the window like a wound, tried to wipe away Ama's resemblance to the night. She let us go because years ago she'd tried to sever herself from her daughters, and not even the river could cut through them. She let us go, knowing she was with us in the car and in our yard, a fishline threaded through our spines.

When I was home, I walked between my yard-holes, knowing Ama was on the other end of them. I fed my hands to the □, imagined that Ama was doing the same on her end, our hands touching halfway between her city and mine, knotting at the wrist-root. This was the only way we could see each other, with our hands alone: without our full bodies to hurt each other, without words to want from each other. In the holes, a reforested dark. In a month, a tree would grow from the □, a subterranean sapling just beginning to breach ground, touch night. The tree would have bark thick as buckles, a hollow trunk. It would grow to her height, dress in her shadow, a tree narrating her absence. In a month, when the tree braided out of the hole, born from no seed but my hands, I would water it.

DAUGHTER

Birdbirth

When we arrived home, my mother unfolded Agong on the sofa while I visited my yard-holes and made sure Ama hadn't emerged from one of them, hadn't followed us back by swimming beneath the highway, bobbing her head out of the ☐ to breathe. I walked through the yard, parting the darkness of the night like a pair of thighs. From the ☐, something white poked out of the soil, bone-bright. When I plucked it out and held it up to the window, it was blank. It was the sheet of paper Ama had buried for me, saying I'd write back someday. I considered folding the sheet into a minnow and feeding it back to the ☐, but instead I kept it, sliding it into my waistband. The paper molded to my belly, metal-hot. I had no words to write yet, but it didn't feel right to bury something blank. Inside the house, my mother tucked Agong into our sofa, its cushions still smelling of Dayi's sweat. She'd tried embroidering Bible verses onto them with silver thread but gave up halfway, each sentence left open like a body midsurgery. The word *righteous* was unraveling to its root.

My mother and I kneeled together beside Agong, turning his head to the side and opening his mouth to irrigate his drool, redirecting it into an ashtray. I wanted to say I never meant to hurt him. She cut a hole in his shirt so that it wouldn't chafe against his burn wound, a steak-raw stripe the length of my hand. Dabbing the wound with spit and mud from the yard, my mother told me not to touch it. It glowed like plum meat, stripped of its skin, pus drying into sap. I wanted to say that my tail had outgrown me, grown crooked like the roots of Duck Uncle's tree that time our sidewalk split open and scabbed. Its reach was beyond this body, this city.

When I tried to speak, my mouth felt full of bees. I didn't know how to own what I'd done. My mother touched her knuckle to the back of my neck, told me to go away and sleep. She'd stay awake all night to watch him, to pad the sweat off his cheeks with her sleeves, to reel him in from dreams too deep. He reminded me of the neighborhood stray with a spotted face. It was incontinent, dragging a river of piss up the driveway.

That night I dreamed of Ama in the yard, feeding chicks out of her left hand. With her right hand, she practiced the width of the hens' necks. She dug into the soil, tore out white carrots that glowed like rib bones. She sat all night in front of the TV the way my mother did, face scabbed in blue light, watching soap operas about women who married their husbands' ghosts when they didn't return from war. In one of the scenes, the wife doesn't want to sleep with her ghost husband, so she tricks him by dressing a dead goat in her clothes, tucking the goat into her side of the bed. But the ghost husband isn't tricked. He gets revenge by cleaving the goat open and sewing his wife into its body. When the wife-goat is slaughtered and spit-roasted for a feast, no one ever finds out who they are eating. I woke, wanting to know the ending, but there was no one in the room to tell it.

—

The verb *cleave* has two meanings: to split from and stick to. Another doubling: When my mother says *mother* she means the body that gave birth to her and the one that tried to kill her.

In the kitchen, my mother's cleaver was pinned above the sink like an earring, its shadow spanning the whole floor. I took it down, holding the wooden handle that still wore her hands' heat. My mother said Americans waste money on sets of many knives, but we only needed one. *A cleaver,* she said, *does the job of memory. It only knows how to multiply a thing.* I asked if the cleaver felt sorry for what it hurt, and she said, *There's no use feeling guilt for what it was built to do.*

—

My brother farted close to Agong's face, pulling down his pants and posing his butt cheeks next to Agong's dreaming mouth. Sometimes Agong woke, skin shimmering in sores. Sometimes his nostrils trumpeted open, breathing it all in. I imagined that his body was full of my brother's farts, and that one day he'd rise from the bed like a balloon we let go of, a balloon butting the moon aside to replace it.

We jarred Agong's shit and brought it to our zhongyi, who looked at it under light and in the dark, who poked it with a straw and smelled it through one nostril and then the other, reading the odor out loud to us. The zhongyi combed it with a salad fork. We weren't sure what he was looking for. Maybe death could be unburied from his body like a seed and be replanted in someone else. My brother and I spent hours killing him in our mind, rehearsing our grief early. We invented so many ways to kill him before he died of his own body. We knew he would be proud of us. *With a plastic bag. With a deep fryer. With a blow dryer. With a tree branch. With a tire swing. With a rope and a pantry.* We didn't know how old he was, but we figured that was another way we could kill him: cutting him down like a tree to count his rings.

At the Chinese pharmacy in Milpitas, my mother asked for a powder that would remarry Agong's mind to his memories. Instead, they gave her aicao and told her to bathe him in blackened water, summoning the soul back into his body. *His soul is inside him,* my mother said. *It's just that he doesn't recognize it.* At the back of the store, Agong was grinding a dried ginger root against his teeth, swatting away the sunlight. We paid for the ginger and left, and when Agong saw our reflections in the window, he spat at it. I flinched even though I knew it wasn't really my face in the window, just the image it widowed. Twice a day, we spoon-fed Agong a mash of bananas and rice. He straddled the armrest of our sofa like a pony, simulating hoof-noises with his boots and neighing through his nose. A strand of spit was yo-yoing from his mouth, descending before he slurped it up again.

Instead of helping him remember, the aicao bath gave him diarrhea. We reached into the toilet with a pair of barbecue tongs, picking out fragments of bullets from his shit so that they wouldn't bruise our pipes. My mother gave him vitamins that made his nipples shrivel and slough their black velvet. Sometimes the vitamins gave him earaches too, and for relief my mother plugged his ears with ice cubes. *He's crying out of his ears,* I said, drying the sides of his neck.

In the morning before school, I heard my mother in the kitchen, grinding pills with her wooden bowl and pestle. I looked into the bowl and the powder inside was dust-fine, the air choking on chalk. She was sweating, arms flexing as she crushed the shards to sand. I asked her if she'd found a new vitamin to try, and my mother answered by grinding harder, the bowl buzzing in her hands.

While she bobbed the pestle up and down, I told Agong the story of the Monkey King, plucking out a strand of his ash-colored hair to demonstrate how the monkey had multiplied himself, each strand growing into a soldier. My mother overheard me and said I shouldn't give him ideas. So I told him the other monkey myth, the one about my mother's cousin. The cousin's boyfriend gave her a monkey when she turned nineteen. He brought it to her in a bamboo cage with a rope bow-tied around it. My mother's cousin said, *I fuck this boy and he gives me a monkey? I'd rather he'd given me syphilis.*

She gave the monkey away to a neighbor, who tied it in his tree and put a little bell around its neck. The neighborhood boys liked to come around and throw stones at it, pull it down out of the tree and kick it down the street. The monkey turned mean, peeing on your head or ejaculating onto your shoulders, yanking on your hair like a leash when you walked under its tree. It got so mean it jumped down on my mother one time, tried to skin her skull like a tangerine. Parting her hair with her fingers, my mother showed me a bald spot the size of a quarter where the monkey had hooked its claw.

Then one month, the monkey disappeared and Ama grew

wounds all down her arms and cheeks, her chin skinned so
bad that the flute of her jawbone was exposed. *Ama freed the
monkey?* I asked, and my mother said, *That's not the end of
the story.* The monkey turned up drowned in the river, all battered up, its bones crushed into ellipses. *Once an animal gets
mean,* Ama liked to say, *there's no way to make it good again.
You kill what can't be saved.* All of her murders began as mer-
cies.

 I get it, I said to my mother. *The moral is you can't really
save anything.* My mother laughed and said listen, little anus,
the story's still singeing: The neighbor's tree, the one that had
once carried the monkey, burned down in a night. No one had
seen anything or smelled any smoke, but one morning the
tree had no torso. There wasn't even a stump, just a socket in
the ground that bled for a month. *The same woman who did
that,* my mother said, *threw us into the river.* I said, *Maybe she
thought you were a fire.* But I thought of what Ama had said:
Maybe it was true that a mean thing could not be made good
again. Maybe my tail had been corrupted into something that
couldn't be saved. I'd whipped it against Agong. Ama had
walked me with it like a leash. I no longer knew how to hold
it, and at night when it tried to cuddle against my leg, I swat-
ted it away, orphaning it to the other side of the bed.

 After grinding the powder, my mother squatted next to
the sofa. She propped up Agong's head with a pillow and
tried opening and closing his mouth with her hands. *He won't
swallow,* she said. She said she'd tried everything: pinching
his nose shut, sugaring the spoon, tickling his throat. *Agong,*
I said. *If you don't swallow, your stomach will get so light it'll
float out of your body. You need to anchor it with something
solid.* He was listening. He swallowed.

 I remembered the story of gegu: to cure your father by

cutting your own flesh and feeding it to him. I glanced at my mother's thighs, but they were the same size I remembered. That night I stayed awake to the soundtrack of my father's voice saying *thigh,* saying *knife,* saying *father.*

When I was tired of counting the leaks in our ceiling, I slipped off of the mattress and walked to the pantry, where my mother kept her toes in the cookie tin. The lid popped from its socket soundlessly and I looked inside, knowing already what had been taken. The tin was empty, rinsed clean, my mouth mirrored back at me. I thought of my mother in the kitchen, grinding out powder for hours. The pestle multiplying her toe-bones. *To give something a new shape,* she'd said. *You have to break it.*

In the morning, Agong seemed familiar with himself, passing the mirror without spitting at his own face inside it. My mother gave him her hand mirror, introducing himself to himself, and Agong nodded. My mother pointed to herself: *your daughter.* Then at me: *your daughter's daughter.* Agong agreed. He ate a frozen waffle with his fingers, the edges laced with ice. He asked if it was snowing outside and we explained it was ash from the wildfires up north. He wanted to go outside and catch ash in his mouth, but we said the ash was made of corpses, the air carrying bones on its tongue. Inside the house, he watched TV with the sound off, substituting the dialogue with his own memories: *Once, I fished with my father. He taught me which ones to throw back: He said if it's bigger than your dick, butcher it. If it's not, give it back to the river.*

But when the week ended and looped back, Agong repeated the stories with words in a dialect I'd never heard before. I tried to rearrange his words back into a narrative, but Agong spoke in a rhythm like swimming, dipping down and out of his own stories until I understood nothing. *Once in a river I fished my father raw. He taught me butcher me.* He tried to bite off his tongue until my mother held his jaw open and told him to stop, reciting a list of everything inside his body that was still his. *Tongue. Bones. Blood. Throat. Mouth. Eyes. Ears. Anus. Neck. Intestines.* When we ran out of things inside him, we repeated them all again in different dialects: *This is your tongue. These are your teeth. They are not enemies.*

Agong untied all the leaves from our white birch tree and ate them, copying the squirrels. He didn't know his own species. I'd read online that memories can be startled back into a person, then pulled out of the mouth like a magician's scarf. My brother and I tried to scare Agong into remembering us by mimicking the sounds of war. We filled pots with pebbles, popped balloons to impersonate gunfire. Sometimes it worked, and he leapt from the bed as if boiled, fondling the imaginary gun in his waistband, calling us guizi, guizi, guizi. My mother told us to stop—she thought we could trigger another heart attack, which in Agong's dialect sounded like heart war. Back then I thought a heart attack was when your heart grew legs like a soldier, walked out of your chest, and invaded the nearest body. I thought bowels were a breed of bird, and bowel movements were how they migrated.

Agong claimed he once ate sparrows for an entire year, back when fullness was foreign to his body, and some of the sparrows were all bone. We took him to a monk in the neighborhood to be blessed, a former soldier who told us that the only cure for forgetting was to approach your own future like a fort. Say: Surrender.

That night, I walked to the kitchen and touched the cleaver hanging above the sink, my face foreign in its reflection. My mother said gegu hadn't worked for Agong because the toes she'd fed him were only marrow: The meat had quit their bones long ago, and only meat could cure a father of his forgetfulness. But my tail was as much meat and tendon as bone. If I severed it, if I fed it to Agong, maybe I could give it a purpose that wasn't hurt. My tail behaved like a flipper, frantic between my legs, knowing what I wanted of it.

I called Ben in the morning, told her: *I have something that needs to be cleaved.* In the morning the sky was milk, already mourning me. Ben met me in the yard, the □ breathing at our feet, exhaling moths that flew toward the light inside the house, clattering against the windows, attracted to ache. Turning to me, Ben stroked the skin behind my ears where no light lived. *Cleave it from me,* I said, sliding the tail out of my waistband. It hummed in my hand, thinner, reshaped by Ama's fist. I told her how Ama had used it as a leash, how I'd lost the ability to steer it. Ben said there were two definitions of *cleave.* I said she knew which one I meant. My brother had been right to say my tail was a liability.

Having a body is a liability, Ben said. *And I like your body.* My tail went still. I used to think stillness would save me, the way some animals choose stillness so they won't be seen as moving prey. I turned around to show her the way it dangled, almost to the floor now, its weight like an anchor. Soon it would drown me and I'd have to evacuate from my body. Standing behind me, Ben pressed her belly against my back. She combed my hair with her fingers, pulled it back from my shoulders. I pretended I was a tree and her hands in my hair were perching birds. I tried to be a place she could stay.

What would you be without this tail, she said, reaching down to grasp it. *Free,* I said, but I knew it wasn't true. It was my umbilical cord, and I'd never been freer than inside my

mother's belly, Ama's blood braiding into me. My body multiplied by theirs. Ben nudged her nose into my neck. The ☐
squinted at our feet, watching us through hyphen-shaped
eyes.

You should see what my tail did, I told her. But it wasn't
the tail I blamed for hurting him. It was me, and Ben knew,
and when she stepped back from me, tugging me by the tail
so that I walked backward into the house, it was tenderness
that tethered me to her, a desire to be crowned by her teeth,
queened by them. She pulled me into the doorway, nipped
my chin. Held me by the hips so tight I'd find the forensic
outline of her fingers there later. I'd place my fingers in the
same place and replay the ache that was my name. She kissed
me and my bladder almost unzipped itself, eager to empty, to
be filled with what she could give me. I reeled the tail up from
between my legs and held it between our bellies, both of us
grinding hard against it. It hurt, but it was a hurt that harmonized with my hunger, with the hum of my backmost teeth. I
could feel her through my tail, the fur frizzing with our friction, and I knew I couldn't be undaughtered from it.

Behind us, on the sofa, Agong was breathing loud as a
beehive, though we still didn't know how to smoke the sickness out of him. Maybe he would never remember our names,
never fish our faces out of whatever water he'd dropped us
into, but it was safer that way, safer that I couldn't save him:
He was preserved in the brine of his boyhood, before bullets,
before he knew what he was capable of killing.

When his hands have forgotten how to hold things, to
make a fist, to clean a gun or wipe his own ass, we draw faces
on all his fingers and say: *These are your family, the ones
killed in the war, your mother on your thumb and your father*

on your forefinger, and now they are with you every time you
lift your hand, now they are walking on wind, now they can
never be taken from you.

———

My mother said that when Agong was a boy—I imagined it
was so long ago that knees didn't have the technology to
bend—Agong helped the men drill wells into the wetlands
and drag the saltwater out in buckets. Dogs and oxen ran into
the bog and buckled, their bones broken into song. The deer
sank so deep only their antlers jutted out of the ground like
velvet saplings.

Agong scoured our walls for salt, shucking away the plas-
ter with his nails. When he found my mother's salt bowl in a
cabinet next to the sink, he pickled his palms in it. One night
when he was asleep on the sofa, I spooned salt onto his face,
his neck, his belly button. He shrilled with pain when I sprin-
kled his bed sores, each one as big and pink as a slice of balo-
ney. In the morning, when my mother saw what I'd done, she
propped him up in the yard and rinsed him off with the hose.
I said salt would preserve him like jerky, drying his flesh to
threads. But my mother said if I ever did that again she'd
pickle my feet and feed them back to me.

When he was my size, Agong sanded salt into blocks and
shipped them down the river. He dreamed of tossing the
blocks overboard, salting the river into a bloodstream. Agong
was told not to taste the salt, but he licked every block when
the crew was asleep, unable to resist their glow. As punishment for stealing, the merchants lashed both his hands until
his skin ribboned off. This evening, I saw Agong crawling in
the yard, hounding the soil for salt he'd buried, but the holes

gave nothing back. The sofa cushions grew crowns of crystals. Salt icicles clung to the ceiling above his sleep. My mother shattered them with a broom and collected the saltcicles in buckets. We cooked with pinches of his powdered sweat. Sucking on saltshards, we preserved our mouths in the shape of his name.

———

I tell Ben to bring me the letters. I live their translations, but she owns the originals. When she gets to my door, I pull her in and she licks me everywhere like a dog. My name is whatever she calls me.

In the yard, I feed the letters one by one back into the □, all the holes scabbing over before picking themselves open again, empty. Ben asks what I'm doing. I say I'm sending them back to Ama. I unfold a sixth sheet from my pocket, the letter creased so many times it's tender with lines. A lace of holes where I've written the words and then erased them, inventing a language from friction:

Dear Ama,

You define a daughter   as something   done
to you   at night   without your permission   I
dream Agong in the window   a face I forage for
resemblance   the only thing we share is   sorry
you say   there's no such thing as death   only
debt   only deferring   the next life   I once
thought you'd given birth to me directly   skipped
my mother entirely   you conceived me by

screaming   into a peach   eating around its seed
planting it inside your shit   watering it into me
a story like all stories   treeing out of you   all
stories are about ownership   I'm mistaken: you
aren't the tiger spirit   you're the woman   it wears
you tell me choices   are made by men   militaries
     language is not what's said but what's silenced
Agong told me today   I could become anything by
mimicking it   he lay down in the middle of every
road   said   *now I'm every way home*   I pen his
mouth here by punching   the page   Agong
kneels in the yard   digs a birdbath   where I
rinse my hands   you say a mouth   is all I wanted
for you my name goes nude   maiden name
meaning   what survives   is what I choose to
remember

—

After I feed the letters back, Ben and I stand over the holes as
they breathe. The moon a bared tooth. We ask our mothers if
we can sleep out in the yard tonight, and when they both say
no, we do it anyway, build a tent out of blankets and brooms.

My mother watches us out the window for an hour, then
comes out with a quilt to use as our roof, the one with Ama's
denim river sutured down its center. She brings the border to
her nose and breathes all the blue out of the fabric. Then she
hooks the blanket over our broomsticks, hanging it above us,
and the river is resurrected as our sky. Ben and I fall asleep
paired like quotation marks, my mother between us, my
mother the thing we speak. I couch my head on my mother's
belly and listen to her bowels fill with wing-beats. She perches

her fingers in my hair and names each strand with her hands, singing a song that Agong learned from the crows, a song about camphor trees that grow to be girls.

My mother rolls my head off her belly, reaches down for my feet and says they're ripe enough to eat. *Imagine this: I eat your foot like a fruit. I shit out its seed in some city far from here. The seed grows into a tree. You walk by the tree and know I've been there. You cut down the tree, count its rings, add it to how old I am. Wherever you're going, I'm already there, a tree waiting.* Massaging my mother's feet until she sleeps, I slot my knuckles between her toes, trying to tell when they'll be tender. At the back of her heels and calves, I know each of her tendons by note. Pluck them into music, play away their pain. She once told me that a tree's leaves are its ears: A leaf listens to the light. I want many ears growing from my skin, a whole field to listen with. When my mother farts in her sleep, I shape the steam with my hands and release it outside as fog. I remember the story she once told me about how all mountains were once hammered out of mist, and that's how they move, how they rise and dissolve, returning to the genealogy of the sky.

At night, Ben climbs over my mother's body and nestles her head in my armpit. We kiss until our tongues can't tell themselves apart. I dream of biting off her nipple, spitting the coin of it back into her palm. *Make a wish,* I say, while she flings the nipple-coin into her mouth, swallows. We wake together at the same time, our names in each other's mouths, our heat making glue of the moon, and it means we've come true.

Halfway through the night, we hear chirping. At first I think it's the sky raining teeth. Ben crawls out of our tent, one hand extended like the sound is a string she can pull on, lure in. I crawl out after her, my arm slipping down the sleeve of a hole. We are beaded with mosquitos, slapping them off each other's thighs, our hands bright with the blood we've stolen back from their bellies. A laced wing is cleaved to the corner of her mouth and I lean forward, lick it off. We scan the sky and the top of the fence, but both are empty. Ben says, *Listen,* kneeling to the soil. *It's coming from under.* The sound comes from beneath our feet, a symphony of the buried. Needling my toes into the soil, I can almost feel the fester of wings. The key around Ben's neck is the nearest light and I reach for it. A moon docking in the dark of my throat. Reaching up, Ben plucks a strand of sound from the air, follows it back to the ground where it was planted. I hold the hem of her shirt and she steers me toward the ☐ where the chirping is clearest, where the sound is ambering inside our mouths.

In the center of the yard, I look up and see where our wet roof is angled just right for the moon to catch it and turn it into a mirror, deflecting dawn for as long as we want. Ben kneels and says this is where the ☐ begins, where the soil is soft as snot and darker than the night around us. *We need to dig them out,* Ben says, sharpening her wrists against each other. She places my hand on the ground and I almost feel a pulse, a place to part the soil.

We work our hands into the seam-lipped ☐, squatting the way we once did when we dug shitholes in her father's lot, imagining that if we dug deep enough we'd hit water and our shits would float up as islands we'd founded together. Our hands struggle into the soil, grabbing and emptying, adding to the mound at our backs that will soon outgrow us. It's Ben who meets metal first, three feet below: the silver scalp of a cage-top. It's her birdcage, the one we fed to the ☐, the one she claimed not to mourn. But her hands accelerate, and I know she wants it home in her hands again, rust coating her palms like sugar.

We work downward with our fingers, revealing the spine of each bar, the locked door. It's dented but undigested, with only a few bars missing. We stand now, grinding our heels into the soil to uproot the cage. Ben is panting out a pearled fog. I'm dressed in my sweat. I hunt for my own hands in the dark, find them grasped around hers.

When we lift it together, the cage disrobes its dirt. It's full of birds. The perch in the center is crowded with some winged species, each body no bigger than a thumb, feathers moving fluent as tongues. They're the color of the dark, a dark only our mouths can make. Ben sets down the cage and we kneel in front of it. She sockets the key into the lock and hooks the door open with her pinky. When the birds flock out, they multiply in the dark, mating with the night to become many. They fly toward the trees, branches parting like legs to let them in. They land on the roof of the shack and along the fence redheaded with rust. The birds call to one another in our voices. Ben and I agree that in the spring, we'll cut off our hair and scatter it here so the birds can collect the strands in their beaks and build their nests out of us. We'll let them breed in the black of our hair.

Pursing its lips, our hole spits a flock of black sparrows. They flee the □'s throat, threading in and out of clouds, sewing the dark whole. There are so many birds in the sky that by morning, it is still night. Ben shouts, points at a bird with a meloning belly, so big it butts out the sun. Behind us, in front of the house, the road is rearing and bucking into a river, asphalt dissolving to ink, a flood reaching our feet. We wear the river around our ankles. It rises between our legs, splitting open in birth. A tail breaches the surface, legs wading after it. Out of the riverroad   the tiger runs to us   brightwet   mouth wider than night   calling   *Mother   mothermothermother*

ACKNOWLEDGMENTS

Thank you to my family (my Sega World team!). To my mother: You're the best and most inventive storyteller I know, and thank you for all the laughter and the gossip.

Thank you to my agent Julia Kardon for being my first supporter. You told me during our first phone call that we'd be team Year of the Tiger, and I'm so grateful to have you rooting for me.

Thank you to my editors, Victory Matsui and Nicole Counts. Victory: Thank you for leading me to the tail and the holes, and for being the best reader I could possibly imagine. You asked me what my characters desired, and in writing those desires, I learned what I wanted, too.

Nicole: Thank you for midwifing this story into the world, and for being the most incredible advocate. Your enthusiasm, generosity, and support mean everything to me. Whenever I doubt myself, I think about your comments in the margins of my manuscript.

Thank you to everyone on the One World team for their support and brilliance: Chris Jackson, Cecil Flores, and so many others. Thank you to Dennis Ambrose for his copyediting expertise. And my deepest gratitude to Andrea Lau for designing the inside of the book, and to Michael Morris for giving me the cover of my dreams.

Thank you to Rachel Rokicki, Claire Strickland, Jess Bonet, and the entire publicity and marketing team—your enthusiasm and creativity are an inspiration to me.

Thank you to Mikaela Pedlow for your passion and support—I'm so grateful to the Harvill Secker team for their warm reception.

Thank you to Deborah Sun De La Cruz and the Hamish Hamilton team—your enthusiasm for this book has buoyed me.

My deep gratitude to Mei Lum and the entire W.O.W. family for welcoming me and for showing me the power of storytelling and intergenerational community.

Thank you to Rattawut Lapcharoensap for your advice, support, and for all of our conversations, literary and otherwise—you saw things in my work that I didn't even know were there.

Thank you to Jennifer Tseng for reading a very messy early draft and seeing so much in it. Many, many thanks to Rachel Eliza Griffiths for reading my very first essay and telling me to write a whole book. I did, and it's all because you believed I could.

Thank you to Marilyn Chin, whose book made this one possible. And to Maxine Hong Kingston, Jessica Hagedorn, Toni Morrison, Dorothy Allison, Larissa Lai, Helen Oyeyemi, and so many more.

Thank you to my Agong. You deserve everything. Thank you for your smile and the way you held your hands behind your back. I miss the paper pinwheels and the garden with the tree and the chili bushes. Wherever you are, I hope your pigeons are with you and that they've finally made it home.

ABOUT THE AUTHOR

K-MING CHANG was born in the Year of the Tiger. She is a Kundiman Fellow. Her poems have been anthologized in *Ink Knows No Borders, Best New Poets 2018, Bettering American Poetry Vol. 3*, the 2019 Pushcart Prize Anthology, and elsewhere. Raised in California, she now lives in New York. *Bestiary* is her first novel.

kmingchang.com
Twitter: @k_mingchang